BETRAYED BY EVIL

A Bridget Bishop FBI Mystery Thriller,
Book Eight

Melinda Woodhall

Melinda Woodhall
Visit my website at www.melindawoodhall.com
Printed in the United States of America
First Printing: October 2023
Creative Magnolia

CHAPTER ONE

The waxing moon hung in the starless sky, its silvery surface half hidden by celestial shadow as Nicole Webster drove down Shackleton Highway. Slowing as she passed the exit for Moonstone Cavern, she continued down the dark road, looking for the historical marker that would let her know she'd arrived at her destination.

Glancing at the clock on the old Bronco's dashboard, Nicole saw that it was just past midnight and cursed silently under her breath. She was late.

April had ended and it was now officially the first of May, which meant that the Circle's celebration of spring's end and summer's arrival would soon begin.

Just then the Bronco's headlights illuminated a silver metal sign with black lettering.

Die Hexenbaum
(The Witch's Tree)
1769

Nicole released the breath she'd been holding and pulled onto the shoulder of the road. She bumped along uneven ground before coming to a stop in the grass and turning off the engine along with the headlights.

Climbing out of the SUV, she stood still and looked around into the inky darkness, keenly aware that there were no other people or cars nearby.

"Hello?"

Her voice carried on the cool spring wind but elicited no reply. Could this silent greeting be part of the initiation?

Or am I in the wrong place?

Wishing the Beltane festival had fallen during a full moon, she activated the flashlight on her phone, then reached into her pocket, feeling around for the printout of the private message she'd received just that morning.

The message had been sent by a user named Raven who had been first to respond to Nicole's initial post on the Circle's main message board.

The friendly reception she'd received from the coven members in the last few months had been unexpected. Their eagerness to welcome her into the Wicca group almost made her feel guilty for her pretended interest in joining.

But as she pulled out the creased piece of printer paper, she reminded herself that she'd come home to Tempest Grove to find out what had happened to Natasha. Too many years had already passed.

Now that she was finally starting to remember, there was a chance she could get to the truth. She couldn't allow a guilty conscience or anything else to get in her way.

With a resolute sigh, Nicole lifted her phone, using its light to re-read Raven's message.

Meet me under the Witch's Tree tonight at midnight to join the Circle and take part in the Beltane festival. The initiation ceremony is open only to true seekers, so come alone and don't be late.

Looking over her shoulder toward the historic marker as if to make sure she hadn't imagined it, Nicole assured herself she was definitely in the right place.

She just needed to find her way through the thick forest to the giant, gnarled sycamore tree recorded in history books as *die Hexenbaum*.

When she'd been a freshman at the local high school, Nicole had learned how German settlers passing through the area on their way west centuries earlier had accused an old woman of witchcraft.

With no government or legal system in place to hold a trial, they'd simply left her hanging on one of the big tree's sprawling branches and continued on their journey.

Now known simply as the Witch's Tree to those who'd grown up in the area, the sycamore was thought to be more than two-hundred-fifty years old and stood eighty feet tall.

But in the darkness, Nicole could make out little of the tree's massive frame and could see nothing of the group that was supposed to be there to welcome her into their fold.

Disappointment washed over her as she realized Raven's message must have been some sort of prank.

She wouldn't be initiated into the Circle, and she wouldn't discover what had happened the night Natasha disappeared.

Slipping a hand back into her pocket, Nicole carefully extracted a tattered newspaper clipping she'd found tucked away in her mother's dresser drawer.

She scanned the front page of the Tempest Grove Gazette.

Local Teen Attacked, Twin Sister Reported Missing.

Her heart squeezed as she studied the grainy photo of two teenage girls that accompanied the article.

It had been taken on their fourteenth birthday, and it was the last photo she'd ever taken with her sister.

Only months later Natasha had vanished without a trace and Nicole's life had changed forever.

In the decades since, she had struggled to move on, traumatized by a past she couldn't see, haunted by questions that had never been answered.

She'd even been institutionalized for a period of time, although it was hard for her to remember those dark days now. As soon as she'd been released, she'd run away, ending up at her grandparents' house in Florida never to go home.

At least, not until the past winter. Not until after she had started to see a therapist specializing in trauma, and after her divorce.

That's when the bad dreams that had invaded her sleep for years began to show up during waking hours as flashbacks and unwanted memories.

After decades of running and hiding, Nicole had finally decided to go home. It was time to face the truth, and the only way to find it was to return to Tempest Grove.

Moving the light from her phone closer to the photo in the newspaper, she tried to remember the day it had been taken.

Was Natasha angry with me? Was that why we were standing slightly apart? Was that why she wasn't smiling?

They had been so close when they were little, always holding hands and playing secret games to which only they knew the rules.

But time and teenage angst had strained their bond, sparking conflict and lodging a wedge between them as they had started classes at Tempest Grove High School.

Natasha had been known as the smart, pretty, popular twin, while Nicole had gotten a reputation as the plain, awkward twin who sulked in her sister's shadow.

And while Natasha had shown interest in their mother's unconventional spiritual practices, Nicole had wanted nothing to do with the Circle of Eternal Light or its members.

Then in 1996, just past midnight on the first of May, Nicole had watched Natasha climb through the back bedroom window of their childhood home.

She could remember slipping out after her sister and following her into the woods.

The next thing Nicole knew, it was daylight, and she was wandering down the side of the road, her head and hands covered in blood. She had been rescued, but Natasha was never seen again.

The faint smell of smoke now drew Nicole's eyes away from the paper in her hand, bringing her back to the present.

Taking a step forward, she could see a soft flicker of flames through the bushes and branches ahead.

As she made her way further into the woods, she came to a clearing. A massive sycamore tree stood before her, its gnarled branches reaching out in all directions.

A small fire had been lit before it, the flames flickering and dancing in the night, casting moving shadows over the roots and earth at Nicole's feet.

"Hello?" she called, stepping closer to the fire. "I'm here for the Beltane festival. Raven invited me."

Pushing back a lock of red hair, she looked down at the flames, then around at the dark forest in frustration.

She'd read on the Circle's message board that they usually celebrated Beltane with a special bonfire, which they believed had protective powers.

While Nicole had no faith in the magical powers of smoke, ashes, and flame, she had nothing against the coven lighting a cozy campfire. But where was everyone?

Wasn't this supposed to be a celebration of spring? Shouldn't there be singing or chanting or something?

A sliver of unease worked its way down her spine as she stood in silence, listening to the crackle of burning wood at her feet. She may not be familiar with Wicca practices, but she knew something wasn't right.

Whatever prank Raven is trying to play has gone far enough.

Spinning around, Nicole took a step in the direction of the Bronco, then stopped as she saw movement ahead.

A hooded figure stepped out of the flickering shadows.

Nicole jumped at the sudden sound of a man's voice.

"So, you're finally here."

The speaker's face was hidden by the hood he wore, but his voice sounded familiar.

As he moved forward, Nicole saw something in his hand. It appeared to be a strip of black cloth.

"Are you the one who sent me this message?" Nicole asked, taking a step backward as she held up the crumpled printout. "Are you Raven?"

"That's my craft name, although, when you were a child, you knew me by a different name. And I knew you as *Nikki*."

His words lit an inexplicable spark of fear in her belly.

"It's as if I've heard your voice before somewhere," she said. "Although maybe it was..."

Her words trailed away as the man moved behind her, lifting the black strip of cloth to cover her eyes.

"The initiation is a secret ritual revealed only to true seekers of the light," he said as he tied the blindfold around her head. "Your eyes have been closed to the truth. Now, thanks to the wisdom of the Old Ones, you will see again."

A hand reached out and grasped hers, leading her forward, closer to the Witch's Tree.

Fighting the impulse to turn and run, she sucked in a breath of air, inhaling a lungful of smoke in the process.

Choking on the smoke, Nicole coughed and backed away.

"I don't want to do this," she said, reaching for the blindfold. "I just want to go-"

Cold fingers gripped her wrist, wrenching her arm behind her back, forcing it upward with a painful thrust.

As the printout was plucked from her other hand, a fevered whisper sounded in her ear.

"Here we are again, *Nikki*," the man hissed. "Die Hexenbaum is waiting for you, just as it waited for your sister all those years ago."

Suddenly, time fell away, and Nicole recognized the voice beside her. It was a voice she had tried so hard to forget.

Her legs buckled beneath her at the memory of her sister's terrified scream, which had preceded her own.

"You came to find the devil," Raven hissed. "Here I am."

He forced a coarse loop of rope over her head and pulled it tight around her throat with a vicious grunt of satisfaction.

Lifting her free hand, Nicole clawed at the rope, desperate for air. With her strength fading, she groped for the blindfold, tearing it from her eyes.

She looked up at the twisted, gnarled branches of the sycamore tree, which appeared to be moving in the flickering light of the flames.

Raven released her arm to grab the length of rope he'd left dangling from a low-hanging branch, and wrenched on it with both hands, jerking Nicole up and off the ground.

Pain encircled her neck as she dangled from the rope, twisting and straining to reach solid ground. But her feet found only empty air.

With one last burst of strength, she grabbed out at Raven.

Her fingers gripped the soft fabric of his hood, ripping it from his head to reveal a flushed face and wide, fanatical

8

eyes filled with terrifying glee.

The face had aged, but the eyes hadn't changed. She'd seen those same eyes the night her twin sister had gone missing. She could remember turning away in a blind panic, desperate to escape her sister's killer.

That night she had run. In her fear and haste, she had fallen. She'd hit her head and then everything had gone dark.

But now, after all this time, she could finally remember what had happened. Only it was too late to tell anyone what she knew. Too late to warn them. Too late to scream.

CHAPTER TWO

Bridget Bishop frowned as she pulled into the little parking lot adjacent to Bishop & Company Investigations. Her father's silver sedan was missing from the lot, which meant he had either failed to show up for work that morning or was already out investigating a case.

Bringing her white Ford Explorer to a stop, she stepped out onto the pavement and inhaled deeply, taking in a deep lungful of fresh spring air. She jumped as an impatient bark interrupted the peaceful moment.

"Hold your horses, Hank," she admonished, borrowing one of her friend Daphne's favorite expressions.

The Irish setter stuck his furry red head out the open back window and barked again, eager to get inside where Paloma was sure to be waiting with his morning treat.

Bridget's stepmother was the office manager at the private investigation agency, as well as the de facto dogsitter for Hank on the days Bridget drove over to Quantico for her role as a profiler and analyst with the FBI's Behavioral Analysis Unit.

"Morning!" Bridget called as Hank scurried through the

door in front of her. "Where's Dad? Don't tell me he's taken on another big case already?"

She stopped in front of her stepmother's desk, noticing that the morning light coming in from the window gave the ·older woman's strawberry blonde hair a soft pink glow.

Paloma was already reaching into her desk drawer. Holding out a pumpkin doggie biscuit, she waited for Hank to take it from her hand before turning to Bridget.

"Your father left the house first thing this morning. Couldn't get out of there fast enough when he heard a body had been found hanging from the Witch's Tree out by Moonstone Cavern."

"A body was hanging from *which tree?*" Bridget asked.

"Yes, *the Witch's Tree,*" her stepmother repeated as if Bridget was hard of hearing. "You know the one. It's that creepy-looking sycamore off Shackleton Highway, just before the West Virginia border."

She stood and crossed to the coffee pot.

"It's been all over the news," she added. "Apparently, a hiker stumbled onto the body first thing this morning."

Refilling her mug with steaming coffee, Paloma added a large spoonful of sugar and a splash of cream.

"I'm surprised you aren't up there, too," she said as she returned to her desk. "Sounds like your type of case."

Bridget couldn't really argue with her stepmother's logic. After all, she had made a career out of investigating serial murders and profiling psychopathic killers.

Before she could ask another question, the phone on Paloma's desk began to ring.

"Good morning, you've reached Bishop & Company Investigations," Paloma trilled into the handset. "How can I help you today?"

As her stepmother began to grill a potential new client for information, Bridget took the opportunity to bid Hank goodbye and slip quietly out the door.

After backing the Explorer out of the lot, she impulsively headed north on Ashburn Avenue, heading toward Shackleton Highway. Her drive out to Quantico would have to wait.

First, she wanted to make a stop out by Moonstone Cavern.

She hadn't been out to the area since a victim of the Second Strangler serial killer had been found during a particularly gruesome homicide investigation.

Bridget gripped the Explorer's steering wheel tighter as she pictured the young woman's body discarded in the rocks and weeds outside the cavern.

Images of the past crime scene and surrounding area were fresh in her mind, although she couldn't remember seeing or hearing anything about a creepy sycamore tree.

Entering the destination as *Witch's Tree* into her GPS, Bridget was surprised to see driving directions to a historical landmark by that name appear on the screen.

So, there really is such a thing as the Witch's Tree. Paloma didn't get the name wrong after all.

As she switched on the radio and settled in for the thirty-minute drive, Bridget's phone buzzed on the dashboard.

Terrance Gage's number appeared on the display and for

a minute Bridget wondered if he somehow knew what she was doing, and that she would likely be late for work.

But her boss quickly dispelled the notion.

"I need to cancel all my meetings today," he said, sounding tense. "I'm on my way to see my lawyer now."

"What's happened?" Bridget asked, instantly concerned. "Why do you need a lawyer?"

She heard a muttered curse and then a long, loud honk.

"These foolish tourists don't know how to drive," he griped. "They come to the city and-"

Another blast of the horn cut off the end of his sentence.

"Gage, take it easy," Bridget urged. "Try to calm-"

"Don't tell me to *calm down*," he snapped. "I may lose custody of Russell if I don't figure out what to do."

His words stunned Bridget into silence.

"I just received notice that a parole hearing has been approved for Estelle Malone. She could get out within weeks, which means Russell could be taken from me soon after."

Exhaling loud enough for Bridget to hear it through the phone, Gage lowered his voice.

"How is it that someone who has only served two years of a five-year involuntary manslaughter sentence is up for parole anyway?" he fumed.

Bridget had been wondering the same thing but decided voicing her opinion would only feed Gage's anger.

"Just because Estelle has a hearing, doesn't mean she'll be granted parole," Bridget said. "And it's unlikely she'll be granted immediate custody of Russell even if she does, considering the situation."

"I hope you're right," Gage said. "I've got to go."

As she ended the call, Bridget felt a pang of worry for Gage's fourteen-year-old foster son.

Russell Malone had been traumatized after his father's sudden death in an accident that had been caused by his mother's addiction.

Bridget hated to think that the stable life Gage had built for the teenager was at risk yet again.

Promising herself she'd follow up with her boss later to see how he'd gotten on at the lawyer's office, Bridget saw the upcoming exit for Moonstone Cavern and changed lanes.

She followed the GPS past the exit, slowing down as she neared the spot where the historical marker had been erected by the side of the road.

Two black and white Wisteria Falls PD cruisers flanked the Witch's Tree marker as Bridget drove past, their light bars on top of the vehicles flashing red and blue.

Pulling onto the shoulder of the road, she wedged the Explorer between Bob Bishop's silver sedan and a Ford Bronco, then stepped out onto the grassy shoulder.

"Bridget!"

Looking around, she saw Cecil Fitzgerald waving to her from the tree line. The Wisteria Falls police chief looked past her as she approached, a frown creasing his weathered face.

"Where's the evidence response team I requested?" he asked, running a hand through his close-cropped gray hair.

"You aren't the only agent they sent, are you?"

"I'm afraid no one sent me," Bridget admitted. "I heard that my father had come out here and I thought I'd stop by to see if I could help."

Cecil's frown deepened.

"But I'm sure the ERT is on the way," she quickly assured him. "You can fill me in on the scene while we're waiting."

Hitching up his belt, the police chief sighed.

"I'm sure you've already heard it on the news," he said. "A hiker found a woman hanging from a tree in the woods this morning. She called 911 and then proceeded to tell everybody she knew what she'd seen."

"Is it true that the victim was found in the Witch's Tree?" Bridget asked. "That's what the reporters are saying."

Cecil rolled his eyes.

"The reporters wouldn't know a lick about that tree if it wasn't for the historical marker by the road," he said. "It doesn't get much attention anymore. Now my grandparents used to call it by its proper name, *die Hexenbaum*."

He pronounced the words with a mock German accent.

"They also said that *their grandparents* had told them stories about a woman named Brunhilde Kistler who was accused of witchcraft. She was hung from the old tree," he said. "And when I was a kid, the old folks used to think Brunhilde still haunted the area seeking revenge."

The idea seemed to amuse him.

"It sounds crazy, I know. But according to that marker

over there, there's truth behind the stories," he said. "At least, the part about the woman being hung, not the haunting part."

Bridget cocked her head and frowned.

"I knew there'd been a few witch trials in Virginia," she said. "But I never knew they'd actually hung anyone."

"They didn't," Cecil replied. "Not officially. The folks who strung up poor Brunhilde were German settlers passing through the area. They acted on their own. Today, they'd be tried for murder. Back then, they just rode off into the sunset. Of course, that was long before Wisteria Falls was founded."

Motioning for Bridget to follow him, he walked toward the tree line, passing the medical examiner's van where his wife, Opal Fitzgerald, and her forensic technician, Greg Alcott, were unloading a gurney.

"Opal and Greg were over at the scene of a fatal crash when the call came in, so they haven't been here long," Cecil said. "Once they get all the pictures they need, we'll cut the poor girl down."

He shook his head dolefully.

"But then, Nikki's not a girl anymore. She's grown now."

Bridget raised an eyebrow.

"Nikki?" she asked. "Is that the victim? You sound as if you knew her."

Cecil shrugged.

"No, I didn't know the girl personally, but I knew *of* her," he conceded. "When we found a West Virginia driver's license for Nicole Webster, the name didn't ring a bell. Not until we found this in her pocket."

He held up a clear evidence bag. Inside was a faded newspaper clipping from the Tempest Grove Gazette. It was dated May 1, 1996.

Local Teen Attacked, Twin Sister Reported Missing.

Scanning the article, Bridget saw that it covered a random attack on a local teenager named Nicole Prescott and the disappearance of her twin sister, Natasha.

A black and white photo of two teenage girls accompanied the article. One teen was grinning widely at the camera, while the other looked away in sullen disinterest.

"I remember the case as if it were yesterday. The missing girl was never found," Cecil admitted, pointing to the grinning girl in the photo. "That's Natasha there."

He tapped his thick finger on the other girl.

"That's her twin sister, Nicole. Everyone called her Nikki back then," he said. "She's the one hanging in the tree."

Bridget stared down at the grainy image, studying the twin sisters. She could see that while they shared many features, they weren't identical.

"You can't tell from the photo," Cecil said. "But they were both redheads, as was their mother from what I remember."

Bridget frowned as she read the article and scanned the newspaper mast at the top of the page.

"Tempest Grove?" she murmured. "Why does that name sound so familiar?"

"It's a little town just over the West Virginia state line,"

Cecil said. "Not more than a thirty- or forty-minute drive from here on a clear day."

He hooked a thumb in a northerly direction.

"I've already notified the Tempest Grove PD about the situation here," he added. "If Nicole was abducted from her home across the state line and brought here, Chief Aquinas will want his department to be involved from the get-go."

Bridget nodded, her eyes still on the newspaper clipping.

Lifting her head, she saw Cecil waving to a thin, dark-haired woman with a sour expression.

"Kirby, over here!"

Bridget recognized the woman as she approached. She'd been a junior detective on the Wisteria Falls police force when her father had retired.

"Bridget, you remember Yvonne Kirby, don't you?"

He didn't wait for an answer before plowing on.

"Yvonne will be leading the investigation from our end," he said. "Now that both your father and Harry Kemp have retired, she's been promoted to senior detective."

"Call me Kirby," the detective said sharply. "Only my mother still calls me Yvonne."

Glancing at Bridget, she nodded curtly.

"I've heard a lot about you, Dr. Bishop."

The detective's accusatory tone suggested that perhaps she'd heard a little too much. It was a reaction Bridget had encountered before, and she tried not to let it bother her.

After all, the press had been relentless in their coverage of Bridget's career as an FBI profiler and analyst with the BAU.

Over the last few years, her role in identifying and capturing a succession of high-profile serial killers had been both glorified and vilified, depending on who was doing the reporting. As a result, not everyone was a fan.

"Bridget, what are you doing here?"

Turning at the familiar voice, she saw Bob Bishop.

"Paloma told me you were here when I dropped off Hank," Bridget admitted. "I came to see what you were up to. Then Cecil started telling me about the Witch's Tree and about Tempest Grove."

She pointed toward the evidence bag in Cecil's hand. The one that held the old newspaper clipping from the Tempest Grove Gazette.

"Were you on the force when Natasha Prescott went missing?" she asked. "Did you hear about the case, Dad?"

Bob's eyes dropped to the headline.

"Yes, but that was a long time ago," he said. "You were just a little girl, so you won't remember, but it was big news around here, even though Natasha lived in Tempest Grove."

"Tempest Grove," Bridget repeated softly. "Why does that name sound so familiar?"

Bob hesitated.

"After her sister went missing, Nikki's family brought her to Wisteria Falls for specialized therapy."

He cleared his throat.

"She was your mother's patient," he said. "At first Edith counselled her privately but eventually Nikki was admitted to a psychiatric hospital."

A pained expression passed over his face.

"Your mother would drive over to Tempest Grove to visit her in the hospital several times a week," he said. "One night she was driving back late. It had been a long day and she must have been exhausted. That was..."

Bob's voice faltered. He swallowed hard, then forced himself to continue.

"That was the night your mother had her accident."

Their eyes met and held.

"That's probably why the name of the town sounds familiar," Bob said softly. "It's on your mother's death certificate. She died in Tempest Grove."

CHAPTER THREE

Bob saw the flash of surprise in Bridget's eyes. They were a bright shade of blue she'd inherited from his late wife. Of course, his daughter's resemblance to her mother went much further than blue eyes and chestnut-brown hair. She had also inherited Edith's keen interest in human behavior and her strong empathetic nature.

Both women had ended up choosing psychology for their careers, and neither one had ever been able to turn away from an unsolved problem or a person in need.

"We'll talk more later," Bob said in a low voice, suspecting a list of unanswered questions was quicky forming in his daughter's mind. "But the reporters are already here, so we won't have much time until the news about Nikki gets out."

He gestured toward a news van that had parked along the road. Its crew was busy unloading cameras and equipment.

He turned back to Cecil.

"Have you notified Faye Thackery?"

Bob's heart sank at the thought of the therapist.

"Why would I notify Faye?" the police chief asked,

clearly confused. "Was Nicole Webster one of her patients?"

Shaking his head, Bob sighed.

"No, not her patient," he said. "Nikki was her niece."

He sighed again even louder as he contemplated breaking the bad news to the therapist, who often counseled victims of trauma referred by the Wisteria Falls PD.

This time, when the call from the police came, Faye would be left to deal with her own trauma.

"You think she'd be willing to make an initial identification and let the rest of the family know what's happened?" Cecil asked.

Bob hesitated, then nodded.

"I think so," he said. "And as far as I know, Nikki's mother and father still live in Tempest Grove, so Faye may be able to break the news to them in person."

Feeling Bridget shifting beside him, he glanced over, remembering that Faye Thackery had been his daughter's therapist for several years. He'd even been the one to recommend Faye after Bridget had handled a particularly grisly serial murder investigation.

He winced inwardly as he saw a familiar gleam in his daughter's eyes as she met his gaze.

He knew what that gleam meant.

It meant she wanted to know more. That she *had* to know more. Past experience had taught him that when she got that look in her eyes, she wouldn't give up until she'd uncovered the whole story.

The only difference was that this time, the subject of the story that had captured her interest wasn't a serial killer or a victim of crime, it was her own mother.

A rush of guilt rolled through Bob as he thought of all the times he'd skirted the subject, avoiding the painful task of telling Bridget about the terrible night her mother had died.

I shouldn't have taken the easy way out. I shouldn't have kept the memories and the pain locked up and hidden away.

Edith's daughter had a right to know everything about her mother's life, as well as her untimely death. But before he could tell her anything, Bridget turned to Cecil.

"I know Faye pretty well," she said, swallowing hard. "I can give her the news about her niece if you want me to."

A loud cough reminded Bob that Detective Kirby was still there, standing behind her boss.

She cleared her throat as if prepared to object to Bridget's suggestion, but Cecil was already nodding in agreement.

"That would be highly appreciated," he said. "You're certainly more than qualified to deliver that sort of news."

Catching sight of Kirby's scowl, he raised a gray eyebrow.

"Besides, my team will be busy here for quite some time."

As the police chief walked away, Bob wondered if it was a good idea for Bridget to go see Faye on her own.

Maybe I should go with her. It'll give us a chance to talk.

He tried to sound casual as he made the suggestion, knowing she didn't like him treating her as if she were a child who needed protection.

"Maybe we can do it together," he offered. "The

notification to Faye, I mean."

Bridget hesitated, then nodded.

"Okay, but first I want to speak to Charlie."

Brushing past him, she moved toward a big black Expedition that had just pulled up.

Bob was relieved to see that Special Agent Charlie Day had arrived. The agent had successfully worked with Bridget on several serial cases in the past and had saved his daughter's life on more than one occasion.

He knew if Charlie was at the scene, the Bureau must be taking the case seriously.

Emerging from the driver's side of the vehicle, Charlie pushed back a wayward strand of golden blonde hair and squinted into the morning sun before slipping on a pair of dark sunglasses.

Bridget called out as the agent approached.

"Where's Hale?" she asked.

Charlie shrugged.

"He was in a meeting with Calloway when I got the call about a body in a tree," she said. "So, I brought Special Agent Bailey Flynn instead."

She looked back to where a young female agent had emerged from the passenger's side of the Expedition.

The woman wore an FBI tactical vest and slim black pants. Dark blonde hair skimmed her shoulders in messy layers as she scanned the area with alert green eyes.

Opening the back door of the Expedition, Bailey waited for a black and tan German Shepherd to jump out, then walked toward them, leading the energetic dog on a leash.

"Agent Flynn, this is Special Agent Bridget Bishop with the BAU," Charlie said. "And this is her father, Bob Bishop, recently retired from the Wisteria Falls PD."

Bob offered a hand, which Bailey shook with enthusiasm.

"Bailey's a recent transfer from our field office in Miami," Charlie said. "She moved up to D.C. to join the special crimes unit. Calloway's *restructuring* again."

"Ludwig's new to the unit, too," Bailey said, glancing at the German Shepherd with obvious affection.

Smiling down at the dog, Bob remained silent as Bridget filled Charlie and Bailey in on what had been found thus far.

"A hiker happened upon the body of a woman this morning. Driver's license tells us she's Nicole Webster from Tempest Grove," Bridget said. "She was hanging from an old sycamore tree. It's a local landmark called the Witch's Tree."

"Okay, who can point me toward the crime scene?" Charlie asked.

She looked past Kirby to where Bridget stood, but before his daughter could answer, Bob jumped in again.

"The Witch's Tree is that way," he said, pointing to a path surrounded by a jumble of bushes and branches. "Opal Fitzgerald is back there now."

"But the requested evidence response team hasn't arrived yet and the scene isn't secure," Kirby protested. "So-"

"So, let's go see what we've got," Charlie said in a tense voice that betrayed her unease, despite her cavalier words.

Bob knew from his own career in law enforcement that

for most people, viewing dead bodies and grisly crime scenes never got easier. Some people were just better at hiding the impact. As he followed Charlie Day down the path, he decided she was one of those people.

"To your left," Bob called out to Charlie as she navigated though the trees. "It's just up ahead."

Pushing her way past a thick fall of leaves, Charlie stepped out into the clearing, then jerked to a sudden stop, causing Baily and Ludwig to narrowly miss running into her.

By the time Bob and Bridget had finally made their way up beside her, Charlie was standing frozen in place, staring up in horror at the dead woman hanging in the shadow of the massive sycamore tree.

Nicole Webster's head slumped slightly forward over the tight twist of rope around her neck, and her hair hung down in dark red strands, partially veiling her slack face, which, in the strange light, appeared to be the palest shade of blue.

Seeing the stricken look on Bridget's face, Bob put a hand on her arm and squeezed.

"Are you okay?" he asked, glad for an excuse to look away from the unnerving sight.

"Isn't it *strange?*" Bridget murmured. "I mean, that she's found on the same day of the year Natasha went missing."

Her words seemed to release Charlie from the horrified trance she'd been in. The agent pulled her eyes away from the tree to look at Bridget.

"What do you mean?" she asked. "Who's Natasha?"

Bridget moved closer to Charlie, navigating through the

maze of roots that jutted out from the ground at all angles.

"Natasha is the victim's twin sister. She went missing on May 1, 1996, and was never seen again," she explained. "And now Nicole is found murdered on the first of May almost three decades later. Can that really be a coincidence?"

"Are you sure this is *murder*?" Bailey asked.

The young agent cocked her head, unwittingly assuming the same posture as Ludwig, who was looking up at his handler with an alert, curious expression.

"What if the anniversary of her sister's disappearance threw the victim into a state of depression?" she proposed. "Could she have taken matters into her own hands?"

Bob turned as a snort sounded behind him. Detective Kirby stood in the shadows shaking her head.

"There's no way this was self-inflicted," she said. "Someone *obviously* put the rope around her neck and used the branch to hoist her up before tying it off."

Not liking Kirby's tone, Bob cleared his throat.

"The fact that it's the anniversary of her sister's death and that she was found with the newspaper clipping in her pocket, makes me think Agent Flynn might be right about Nikki taking matters into her own hands."

He ignored Kirby's scowl.

"Not by taking her own life, but by trying to find out what happened to her sister," he explained. "If she was asking questions about Natasha, maybe she was getting too close. Maybe somebody hung her up in that tree to silence her."

Bridget frowned at her father.

"But why come home after all these years?" she asked. "Why start asking questions now?"

Before Bob could answer, a bark sounded somewhere past the trees. Glancing down, he saw that Ludwig was no longer by Bailey's feet. He looked around the clearing, but the German shepherd was nowhere in sight.

"Is that..."

His question trailed away as another bark sounded and Bailey took off toward the trees.

Bob looked over at Bridget.

"You think he caught a scent?" he asked, then turned to Charlie. "Is he a cadaver dog?"

"He's a search and rescue dog," she said. "One of the best from what I've been told."

Bob raised an eyebrow.

"I thought SAR dogs worked from a scent."

"They usually do," Charlie confirmed as she headed after Bailey. "If you give them a scent, they'll track down a victim, either living or dead."

CHAPTER FOUR

Charlie plunged into the trees at a quick jog, chasing after Bailey and Ludwig, navigating through the thick woods in the direction of the German Shepherd's frantic barks. Calculating that they must be heading toward Moonstone Cavern, she began looking for a path or trail that would lead her to the big cave.

Dodging tree branches and jumping over thick, protruding roots, she wove her way through the forest until she finally caught a glimpse of Bailey's dark blonde hair up ahead.

As Charlie slowed to a walk, she heard another loud bark.

"Why is he barking?" she called out. "What's he found?"

Bailey, who was once again holding Ludwig's leash, looked over her shoulder.

"I don't know," she admitted. "He's signaling like he's found something, but I didn't give him a scent to track."

She pointed to the ground ahead.

"There's some sort of ravine just up there," she said. "It's a sudden drop off, so be careful, it looks pretty steep."

Charlie moved forward to peer down into a deep, jagged trench in the ground. The incline was unnervingly steep, and she instinctively stepped backward, sending a scattering of rocks bouncing down the side, watching as they disappeared under the brambles and bushes covering the slope.

Jumping as Ludwig barked again, she began to inch toward the big dog, who was standing on the edge of the ravine looking back and forth between his handler and the shadowy trench below.

At the approaching sound of heavy footsteps and loud voices, Charlie glanced back to see Cecil emerge from the trees behind her, his face flushed with exertion and his gray hair damp with sweat.

Seconds later Kirby skidded to a stop behind the police chief, closely followed by Bridget and her father.

They all stared expectantly at Ludwig, who was looking down into the ravine, barking intermittently and scratching at the rocky ground with his front paws.

"That's his signal," Bailey told the gathered group. "He's got a scent. Likely human remains."

Her face was tense and somber, the friendly smile she'd worn earlier now replaced by a resolute frown.

Without warning, she called out a firm command.

"Show me, Ludwig," she commanded, releasing his leash.

The German Shepherd scrambled into action, deftly making his way down the incline, maneuvering past the sharp rocks and wild, prickly shrubs blanketing the ground.

Once he'd made it to the bottom, he barked again, then looked back to Bailey, who started down after him.

The agent was nearly as nimble as her dog, and within minutes she, too, was standing at the bottom of the ravine, her green eyes wide and alert.

"We've found something," she called back up to Charlie, who was peering over the edge. "I think you're going to want to see this."

Sucking in a deep breath, Charlie began inching her way down the steep slope, glad she'd decided to wear low-heeled boots that morning instead of her high-heeled pumps as she inadvertently kicked what appeared to be a whitish-gray rock half-buried in the dirt.

A voice sounded at her shoulder, and she realized that Kirby was close behind her, following her into the trench.

"Is that a moonstone?"

The detective stopped to scoop up the displaced rock and examined it, wiping off the dirt on the sleeve of her police-issued jacket.

Before Charlie could answer, Opal Fitzgerald's face appeared above them, peering over the side of the ravine.

"I heard the barks and figured I may be needed," she said.

Her eyes widened as she looked down at Kirby.

"Why are you holding a patella?" she asked.

Kirby blinked.

"What's a patella?"

She held up her hand.

"You mean this rock?"

The medical examiner raised both eyebrows.

"It's not a rock. It's a kneecap. A human bone."

With a yelp of surprise, Kirby dropped the bone at her feet and began to scramble up the side of the ravine as Charlie descended to stand beside Bailey.

As Ludwig barked again, she surveyed the litter of bones scattered in the weeds, then raised her eyes to meet Bailey's.

"Good job, Ludwig," Bailey said in an enthusiastic voice that contrasted with the solemn expression on her face.

Taking a treat from her pocket, she offered it to the German Shepherd, then took hold of his leash.

"Good job," she said again, rubbing his head with affection. "Come on, let's go, boy."

Charlie watched as the handler led the dog up the steep incline. She waited until they'd reached the top, then called to Opal, who was still standing at the edge looking down.

"It's human remains. We have another body down here."

"From the look of that patella, I'd say the body's been there quite a while," Opal called back. "We'll need the evidence response team's help with the excavation of those bones. It's gonna take a while."

* * *

Charlie watched as Bridget's white Ford Explorer pulled out onto Shackleton Highway, heading back toward Wisteria Falls. She and her father were heading to Faye Thackery's house, burdened with the unenviable task of telling the therapist that her niece was dead.

Death notifications were never easy, but they went with

the job. It was the part Charlie always dreaded the most.

As she turned back to the scene, she felt a guilty sense of relief that this time the task had fallen on other shoulders.

Making her way back into the woods, she emerged into the clearing to see Jason Chan talking to a gathering of crime scene investigators, all dressed in protective coveralls and booties.

"Okay, we're going to be splitting up into two groups," Jason told the team. "Group A will focus on the scene by the tree, while Group B will be working in the ravine."

Charlie agreed silently with Jason's strategy.

They couldn't know for sure if the two scenes were connected until they'd had a chance to collect and analyze the evidence. Cross-contamination could skew the results.

As she started to turn away, Charlie heard a shout from the depths of the ravine.

Running to the edge, she looked down to see a figure in protective coveralls pointing down to a faded patch of material that was just visible beneath a pile of brambles.

Straining to watch as the investigators photographed their find, Charlie didn't notice that Cecil had come up beside her until the chief cleared his throat.

"Agent Day? I wanted to introduce you to Detective Matthew Landon with the Tempest Grove PD," Cecil said. "Our victim was living in his town, so I figured we might need his help."

Charlie turned to face the detective, who towered over her by half a foot. He smiled through a thick, unruly beard.

"Good to meet you, Agent Day," he said, sticking out a

big hand. "I'm glad Chief Fitzgerald called in the Bureau. Of course, we'd like to assist with the investigation, as well, seeing that a Tempest Grove citizen has been the victim of foul play here."

Taking his hand in hers, she gave it a firm shake, taking note of his faint mountain accent.

"We'll accept all the help we can get," she assured him. "We believe there may be a link between Nicole Webster's death and the disappearance of her twin sister Natasha back in 1996, so anything you can tell us about the investigation would be a good start."

Landon frowned and crossed his arms over his wide chest.

"Well, that was before my time," he said, rocking back on his heels. "I don't imagine anyone's worked it for years. Maybe decades. It's one of the coldest cases we've got."

After considering his words, Charlie narrowed her eyes.

"One of the coldest cases?" she asked, thinking of the bones in the ravine. "Are there other missing person cases that have gone cold in Tempest Grove?"

"Not really," Landon admitted. "It's a pretty quiet place. Although, we do have the occasional runaway."

A voice called up from the ravine, pulling Charlie back to the edge. She looked down with interest as Opal held up the tattered remains of what appeared to be a jacket.

The red fabric had faded to a sickly pink, and the tiger's face on the back of the jacket had been mostly worn away.

Landon raised thick eyebrows in surprise.

"That's a Tempest Grove High letterman jacket," he said.

"What's it doing down there?"

"We found it with the remains," Charlie explained.

Confusion creased Landon's broad face.

"I thought Nicole Webster was found hanging in a tree?"

"She was," Charlie agreed. "And I believe there's a good chance the bones in that ravine belong to her sister."

CHAPTER FIVE

B ridget drove toward the little bungalow at the edge
of Wisteria Falls that served as Faye Thackery's
home-based office. Her father was in the
passenger's seat riding shotgun, holding onto the grab
handle and nervously pointing out every car and pedestrian
that crossed their path.

"Just relax, Dad," Bridget said with a sideways glance at
his tense face. "I haven't run over anyone in a long time."

But Bob continued to grip the handle as if she hadn't
spoken, his mind obviously far away as they approached
their destination.

Had the memory of the circumstances leading up to her
mother's death unsettled him? Or was he dreading Faye's
reaction to the devastating news they were about to deliver?

Bridget felt her own anxiety rise as they rode side by
side.

"I never told you that your mother and Faye went to
college together, did I?" he asked, finally breaking the
silence. "They even worked together for a short time, too."

He kept his eyes on the road as Bridget shook her head.

"I guess that's why Faye asked Edith to counsel Nikki

after her sister went missing," he said. "The girl was only fourteen years old, but I think Edith said she'd been having problems for a while before that."

Sitting back in his seat, Bob glanced over at Bridget.

"It's hard to remember exactly what she said about the girl. So much happened that year. And it was so long ago."

He furrowed his brow as if trying to think.

"Has it really been twenty-seven years?"

The words were little more than a whisper. A question to himself. Closing his eyes, he dropped his head in his hands.

"It seems like a nightmare now. Like a bad dream. I try not to think about it, but sometimes..."

There it was. That familiar sadness in her father's voice that stopped Bridget from asking the questions that had always filled her mind. The same questions had remained unanswered since she'd been a six-year-old child.

Pushing back a twinge of resentment, she accepted that once again her father's pain would take precedence over her need to know more about her mother.

His discomfort with the subject had long ago prompted Bridget to voice her thoughts and memories of her mother only in her head. Eventually, the memory of her mother started talking back.

"There's the turnoff now," Bob said, sounding relieved as Faye's bungalow came into view. "We'll talk about it later."

During her childhood, Bridget had heard the same phrase too many times to count. Too many times to believe it now.

As she pulled the Explorer onto the driveway, she

remembered the task that lay ahead with a jolt of dread.

Opening the door, she stepped outside, all thoughts of her own pain and loss evaporating into the mild spring air.

"Okay...let's go tell Faye," Bob said, his voice grim. "She deserves to hear it from us, not from some reporter calling up to ask her for a comment."

He set off for the front door, but Bridget called after him.

"She'll be in her office now," she said, pointing to the side entrance. "She may even be in a session."

But Faye was alone when they knocked on the office door.

"Come on in," she said, stepping back to let them inside.

Lifting a small hand, she patted her silvery pixie cut.

"Is everything okay? Has something happened?"

Bridget inhaled deeply, knowing it would be best to tell Faye the truth straight away. Stalling or trying to soften the blow would only make it more painful.

"I'm so sorry," Bridget said, putting a hand on the therapist's arm. "We've got bad news...about your niece."

She forced herself to continue despite the look of alarm that had taken over Faye's face.

"Nicole's body was found this morning in the woods out by Moonstone Cavern," Bridget said gently. "It looks as if she was the victim of a homicide and-"

"No! That's not possible," Faye cried out, shaking her head in denial. "I just saw her over the weekend. She was fine. Everything was...just...*fine!*"

Her words erupted into an anguished wail as she turned away, moving fast toward the session room, trying to escape.

"It had to be done," Bob said, meeting Bridget's worried eyes and patting her arm. "I'll go after her."

Following her father into the session room, she stood quietly beside him as he comforted Faye the best he could.

"Are you sure it's Nikki?" Faye asked, sniffing into the tissue Bob had handed her.

"Yes, Nicole's driver's license was in her pocket when she was found," Bob confirmed. "And Rowan Prescott was listed as her emergency contact. He's your brother, right?"

Faye nodded, then let out an anguished moan.

"Oh God, how am I going to tell Rowan and Joelle?"

After another bout of weeping, the therapist looked up at Bridget with puffy, red-rimmed eyes.

"My brother had just gotten his daughter back, and now *she's gone*," she said in a wavering voice. "You see, Nikki went down to Florida when she was only a teenager. It was after Natasha was gone and, well, she'd had issues..."

She shook her head as if trying to make it all go away.

"She was supposed to visit her grandparents for a few weeks, but she refused to come home. In fact, she didn't come back to Tempest Grove until earlier this year. She'd been gone for more than twenty-five years."

Sensing the therapist's need to tell her niece's story, Bridget sat beside her on the sofa to listen.

"I only managed to see Nikki a few times after she left home," she said in a faint voice. "Whenever I went down to Florida, I gave her no choice. I just showed up at her door carrying a beach bag and towel. But those trips were few and far between."

Her small hands trembled as she dried her eyes.

"So, when she moved back to Tempest Grove earlier this year, I was excited. It's less than an hour away from Wisteria Falls. I thought we'd finally get the chance to spend some real time together. I hoped we'd get to know each other. And we *were* trying."

"Why do you think she stayed away so long?" Bob asked. "Do you think it was because of Natasha?"

Bridget glared at him, worried the question would throw Faye into another crying jag, but she only nodded sadly.

"Yes, I suspect it was," she said. "Nikki had a terrible time after her sister went missing. Although, she was struggling long before that. She always was a sensitive girl."

Plucking another tissue from the box she kept on the coffee table for her patients, Faye dabbed at her eyes.

"I guess the real trouble started during the twins' first year at Tempest Grove High," she said. "Natasha made plenty of new friends, but Nicole had a hard time fitting in."

She shook her head at the memory.

"They weren't identical, you know," she said. "They were actually very different. At least personality-wise. At the end, it felt as if they were always at each other's throats. I think that made it even harder for Nikki to accept what happened."

Exhaling deeply, Faye stood and crossed to the window.

"It was the first day of May when my brother Rowan

woke up to someone pounding on his front door. It was a local farmer. A man named Abner Chumbley. He'd found Nicole wandering down the road. She was dazed and bleeding from the head. He brought her home."

Closing her eyes, Faye leaned her forehead against the glass windowpane.

"Nikki seemed confused and scared. She claimed Natasha had snuck out of the house the night before. She said she'd followed her sister to see where she was going. She said someone must have hit her over the head because she couldn't remember what happened next.

"Rowan ran back to the girls' bedroom to find out what was going on, but the door was locked from the inside. Once he finally got into the room, Natasha's bed was empty, and the window was open.

"He begged Nikki to tell him where her sister had gone...we all did...but she said she couldn't remember."

Lifting her head, Faye turned away from the window.

"Of course, Rowan and Joelle called the police," she continued. "They started the search for Natasha straight away. But they never found her. She never came back."

"And what about Nicole?" Bridget asked, unable to hold back the question. "Did she ever remember anything else about that night?"

Faye sighed.

"Nikki was taken to the hospital, and they treated her head wound. But the injury was deemed superficial. They told my brother the cause of the memory loss was psychological."

She glanced over at Bob, producing a tearful smile.

"That's when I called Edith," she said, before turning her swollen eyes back to Bridget. "Your mother had been my mentor all through graduate school. She helped me get a job at a practice here in Wisteria Falls after I got my doctorate. So, when Nikki needed help, she was the first therapist I thought of."

Bridget leaned forward at the mention of her mother.

"Edith held several sessions with Nikki," Faye continued. "And at first, they made progress. Edith said Nikki was starting to remember bits and pieces of the night. But then she had a setback. She ended up in the psych ward."

"Why, what happened?" Bridget asked.

Faye shrugged.

"I'm not really sure," she admitted. "As time passed and Natasha wasn't found, Nikki had become more withdrawn. The press had been relentless and missing person posters had been hung all over town. There'd even been rumors that Nikki had something to do with her sister's disappearance."

Her face grew hard at the memory.

"Finally, Edith recommended that Nikki be admitted. She said my niece needed help to come to terms with what she'd witnessed."

"Are you saying my mother thought Nikki had witnessed Natasha's abduction?" Bridget asked. "Do you know if she was able to get her to remember any details or provide a description?"

She held her breath, waiting for an answer.

"Your mother called me after that last session," Faye said. "It was late, and she sounded tired but hopeful. She was convinced she was about to make a breakthrough. Only, she never got the chance."

Bridget felt her chest tighten as the events leading up to her mother's death began to take shape in her mind.

Mom was trying to help Nicole recover her memory. But she died before she could find out what happened to Natasha.

Bob had always told her that her mother died in a tragic accident. And that was true. But it wasn't the whole story.

She was trying to find answers. Trying to solve a mystery.

Her mother would never have been on the road that night if it hadn't been for the disappearance of Natasha Prescott.

The thought swirled through Bridget's mind as Faye began to pace back and forth across the room.

"After Edith's accident, the hospital psychologist took over Nikki's care. Eventually, she was released," Faye said.

"Rowan sent her to Florida to visit her grandparents. I think he wanted Nikki to get away from all the memories and the gossip. And he wanted her to be safe. He didn't know then that it would be decades before she'd come back."

Faye stopped in front of Bridget.

"At first, I thought maybe he and Joelle would move, too, but Rowan said he couldn't leave Tempest Grove. Not if there was the slightest chance that Natasha was still alive and that she might come home."

"And Nikki seemed to be doing well in Florida. She went to college and got married down there. She'd gotten her life on track. At least, that's what she told us."

A new sheen of tears appeared in her eyes.

"Then last winter, she just showed up in Tempest Grove. She said she'd gotten a divorce and had started therapy again. She seemed...stronger, and I was happy for her."

Ripping at the tear-damp tissue in her hands, Faye sank onto the sofa beside Bridget.

"As soon as Nikki moved home, she started getting involved in the local community. And when she came to see me over the weekend, she was asking a lot of questions about the past. She'd even gone with Joelle to one of her Circle of Light meetings."

Her eyes dropped to the tissue in her hands.

"Before she left my house, she confirmed what I'd suspected. She told me that she'd come home to find out what had really happened to Natasha. She was angry that the police had never solved the case and angry at herself for not being able to remember what had happened that night."

"Nikki also told me she'd heard rumors at that Circle meeting. People were saying several women had gone missing. She suspected that whatever had happened to Natasha may have happened to them, too. She even said she was thinking about going to the police."

"And did she?" Bob asked. "Did she tell the police?"

Faye shook her head.

"I don't think so," she admitted. "It sounded as if she was scared of stirring up a hornet's nest."

The hard tone had returned.

"Besides, in her opinion, the Tempest Grove PD was

pretty much useless."

As Faye fell silent, Bridget turned to her.

"What's the Circle of Light?" she asked. "You said Nicole had gone to one of their meetings. Is it some kind of sewing circle or a church group?"

Faye hesitated.

"I guess you could say it's something like that," she said. "My sister-in-law Joelle is a member of the Tempest Grove Circle of Eternal Light."

"What kind of church is that?" Bridget asked.

"It isn't exactly a church," Faye admitted. "It's a coven."

* * *

That night, when Bridget and Hank returned to their red brick house on Fern Creek Road, Deputy Marshal Vic Santino was already there waiting with dinner on the table.

"I know I've been promising to make you my mother's famous lasagna for a while," he said as Bridget followed the strong scent of garlic and onions into the dining room. "But I had to stop by my place and pack a suitcase before heading over. It took longer than I'd planned."

He flashed her an apologetic smile as she stared down at a brown cardboard pizza box. An open bottle of cabernet and two wine glasses stood next to it.

"Antonio's again?"

Bridget tried not to sound ungrateful as she dropped her bag on the table and picked up one of the glasses.

"Tell me the truth. Do you own stock in the place?"

"Not yet, but now that you mentioned it, maybe I should."

Picking up the wine bottle, he deftly filled her glass with the deep red cabernet.

"I hear you're working a new case," he said as she took a long sip of the wine. "You want to tell me about it?"

"I could do that," she said dryly. "Or you could just turn on the news and see for yourself. It's on every channel."

She crossed to the living room and picked up the remote, jabbing at the buttons until she saw the historic marker she'd seen earlier in the day.

"The Witch's Tree?" Santino said, raising an eyebrow as he read the news feed scrolling across the bottom of the screen. "Someone was hung from that old sycamore?"

Bridget nodded.

"What you won't see on the news, is that the victim was Faye Thackery's niece. And my father and I went to see her. We were the ones who delivered the notification."

Closing her eyes, she tried to block out the image of Faye's tear-stained face as they'd said goodbye.

Santino took her wine glass and set it on the table.

"That must have been hard," he said. "Notifying next-of-kin is always the worst part of the job."

He pulled her gently against him, letting her rest her head on his strong, solid shoulder.

"I can try to delay my trip to New York if you need me to stay," he offered. "Or maybe ask for a replacement to-"

"No, I'll be fine," she insisted.

She lifted her head, not wanting him to worry.

"It's just a really strange case."

She struggled to keep her voice steady.

"Turns out the victim was one of my mother's patients. At least, she was until my mother had a car accident on the way home from one of their sessions. That's when she...died."

Bridget cleared her throat, surprised that, for a moment, she hadn't been sure she'd be able to finish the sentence.

Her mother had died decades earlier, and normally, she was able to talk about her without getting too emotional.

Of course, she had never discovered a connection to her mother's past at a crime scene before.

"It is a strange coincidence," Santino agreed, unable to hide his surprise. "How long has it been since the accident?"

"Twenty-seven years," Bridget said without hesitation. "I was only six years old at the time, but I remember the day my father told me the news as if it were yesterday."

She shrugged off his hands and motioned to the pizza box.

"We'd better go ahead and eat. You have a flight to catch."

Santino hesitated, then nodded. As he went to get plates from the kitchen, Bridget watched the end of the news.

She was relieved to see that Nicole Webster hadn't yet been named as the victim and that the bones discovered in the ravine hadn't been mentioned.

Of course, it was only a matter of time before the reporters heard about the bones. Only a matter of time before everyone knew that a recent visitor to the local coven had been found hanging from the Witch's Tree.

CHAPTER SIX

Faye set out from Wisteria Falls in her new Mini Cooper, driving northwest on Shackleton Highway toward Tempest Grove. Looking up through the windshield at the waxing moon, she considered putting the trip off until morning, then reluctantly decided it wasn't a good idea.

It was up to her to notify her brother Rowan and his wife Joelle that their only remaining child had been killed. Although she wasn't sure she knew how.

What's the best way to tell someone that their daughter is dead and that her body was left hanging in a tree?

While Faye had worked with traumatized patients for decades, she realized that she had always been called in after the tragic news had already been delivered. She'd never had to be the bearer of such tidings herself.

But I promised Bridget I'd go tell Rowan and Joelle in person. Any delay could mean they'll hear about Nikki from someone else.

As she crossed the state line into West Virginia, she pressed her size five shoe down harder on the gas and tightened her grip on the steering wheel.

Switching on the radio, she tuned it to a local radio

station, then jumped as a familiar voice boomed through the car.

"Good evening, all you listeners out there in radio land. This is your DJ Spike Oswald coming at you from Tempest Grove tonight with a special news bulletin."

Faye steeled herself for what was sure to come next.

"This morning our very own Tempest Grove Police Department responded to a 911 call from a hiker out by Moonstone Cavern. Responding offers found a woman's body hanging from the old Witch's Tree, and our sources in the department tell us that foul play is suspected."

The disc jockey sounded strangely excited.

He spoke rapidly, using the same glib, silky-smooth voice Faye remembered listening to when she'd left Tempest Grove to go off to college almost forty years earlier. Back then, Spike Oswald had been new to WARP 102.5 FM.

The fact that he was still on-air startled Faye.

The guy must be pushing sixty years old, just like me.

Spotting the exit to downtown Tempest Grove ahead, Faye quickly changed lanes and prepared to exit as Spike continued with his special bulletin.

"That's right, you heard me. A woman's body has been recovered from the Witch's Tree out by Moonstone Cavern, also known as *die Hexenbaum* to any of you history buffs or German-speaking listeners out there," he continued. "So far, police have yet to identify the-"

Switching off the radio, Faye navigated through the dimly lit streets of her hometown, turning not toward her brother's house on Forester Way, but instead taking a right onto Fairview Avenue, heading east toward Tempest Grove High.

For the last few weeks, Joelle had been talking nonstop about the school's spring musical. Her theater students would be giving several performances in May, and that evening was to be their opening show.

Although Faye hated the thought of ruining her sister-in-law's big night, she knew she had no choice.

Not after hearing Spike Oswald's eager radio report. It would only be a matter of time before his buddies at the police department leaked more details. No doubt someone at the school was already spreading the news.

I can't let Rowan and Joelle hear about Nicole from Spike Oswald or from school gossip, can I?

Pulling the Mini Cooper into the crowded parking lot, Faye parked in the loading zone and climbed out of the car.

She looked up at the old building, which hadn't changed much in the four decades since she'd been a student, and inhaled deeply, steeling herself for the task ahead.

The sweet scent of bluebells drifted up from the flowerbeds by the auditorium entrance as she walked toward the double doors, above which hung a banner announcing the student production of *Les Misérables*.

Dramatic music swelled from within as she slipped inside and let the door swing shut behind her.

Although she'd never gotten a chance to see the famous musical on stage, Faye had read the Victor Hugo novel on which it was based and had purchased the DVD version of the movie when it had come out.

She knew the story well enough to know she'd walked in on the final act. The act where the main character dies with his adopted daughter by his side.

In the movie version, it was the scene that always made her cry, no matter how many times she saw it.

Moving quietly through the darkened auditorium, Faye stood against the back wall, transfixed by the actors on stage.

A girl was singing, her voice surprisingly good for a high school student in an amateur production. She was joined by the male lead, who sang his character's dying words with enough emotion to bring fresh tears to Faye's eyes.

As the curtain fell and the lights came up, she clapped along with the audience. Her chest tightened as she saw Joelle run onto the stage. Her sister-in-law's once red hair was now a shimmering white as she took a happy bow alongside the performers.

Faye then scanned the crowd until she spotted her brother Rowan in the audience. He was clapping enthusiastically for his wife, a wide smile splitting his face from ear to ear.

Moving toward him, she had the terrible realization that it would likely be his last genuine smile for quite a while.

As if he'd sensed her presence and could read her mind, Rowan turned his head and met her eyes.

His smile faltered.

Snaking his way through the dispersing crowd, he walked slowly toward her, his expression dark with emotion as if he somehow sensed what she was about to tell him.

She and Rowan were twins after all, just as Nicole and Natasha had been, and they'd always had an uncanny ability to pick up on each other's thoughts and emotions.

"Is it bad?" Rowan asked once he stood in front of her.

Faye nodded as a tear escaped one eye and rolled slowly down her cheek.

"It's Nikki," she said, swallowing hard. "They found her in the woods. She's dead."

"No!"

The strangled word came from behind her.

Spinning around, Faye saw that her sister-in-law had found them in the crowd.

Joelle Prescott was standing as if frozen in place only a few feet away, her face drained of all color.

"No! That's not true, Nikki can't be dead!" she cried out, shaking her head in denial. "I...I just saw her this morning."

Reaching out a hand, Faye tried to grasp her sister-in-law's arm, but Joelle pushed her away.

"No! You're a liar!"

Her shout echoed through the auditorium, silencing what remained of the dwindling crowd.

All eyes turned toward the two women facing each other.

After a moment of tense silence, the sound of hurried footsteps could be heard tapping across the concrete floor.

Faye recognized Joshua Corwin as he hurried toward them. The man had been one of Joelle's theater students not long ago, and now he was the school's new principal.

She wondered numbly how the years had all passed so quickly.

"Mrs. Prescott, what seems to be the problem?"

The principal's initial look of reproach quickly morphed into a look of concern as he took in Joelle's pale, stricken face and wild, tear-filled eyes.

"We've received some bad news," Rowan said, suddenly stepping forward as if the question had released him from a spell. "I need to get Joelle home."

His voice shook as he took his wife's arm and guided her toward the door. Joelle walked stiffly beside him, her initial outburst of angry denial having given way to stunned and silent disbelief.

Faye looked back at Joshua Corwin.

"Consider this her notice of bereavement leave," Faye told the principal. "I'd say she'll be out for the rest of the week. Maybe longer."

Not waiting for a response, she turned and hurried after her brother and his wife, ignoring the stares and whispers that followed them to the door.

* * *

The house on Forester Way was dark as Faye pulled into the driveway behind Rowan's truck. She hurried up the path, cursing under her breath as she tripped over Joelle's gardening clogs which had been left lying on the porch.

She lifted a small fist to knock on the door, then changed her mind and tried the handle.

It turned easily in her hand.

"Rowan?" she called as she peered into the dark foyer.

Raised voices sounded from somewhere down the hall but before Faye could step inside, footsteps crunched on the gravel path behind her, and a shadow fell over her.

"Faye, is that you?"

Gerard Ernst stepped forward, then stopped under the porch light, allowing her a clear view of his weathered face.

She noted that while the wrinkles on his face had multiplied over the last few years, the hair around it had visibly diminished. And the little hair the man did have left had long ago turned gray.

"What are you doing out here, Ernst?" she asked, in no mood for surprises. "Joelle's not-"

"I'm here," a tear-thickened voice said from the foyer. "I called Ernst on the way home. I asked him to come."

Joelle brushed past Faye, taking hold of the old man's wrist and pulling him toward the open door.

"Elora is with me," Ernst said, stopping to gesture toward a young woman standing behind him in the darkness. "We were at Hammerling House cleaning up after the Beltane festival when you called."

The woman followed Ernst into the house, leaving a warm scent of sage in the air behind her as she passed Faye.

Watching Ernst loop a possessive arm around Elora's slim waist, Faye tried to guess her age, deciding the pretty, willowy blonde was probably young enough to be the old man's granddaughter.

"I brought the sage leaves I was saving for the solstice,"

she heard the young woman saying as if that would make everything alright. "I've got thyme, as well. My granny says it eases the transition from the living realm to the dead."

As the trio disappeared down the hall, Rowan appeared in the foyer, his face drawn and flushed with anger.

"I don't want that man in my house," he muttered, staring after Ernst's retreating figure with angry eyes. "Not until we know for sure who killed Nikki."

Faye frowned.

"You don't really think Ernst could have anything to do with it, do you?" she asked. "He's known Joelle since she joined the Circle. Longer than she's known you. And he's the high priest over there, isn't he?"

She rested a calming hand on her brother's arm, sensing he was looking for a reason to start a fight, wanting an excuse to release the grief and rage building inside him.

Considering Rowan's longstanding resentment of the Circle, she knew Gerard Ernst would make a tempting target.

Her brother had never approved of his wife's spiritual practice as a Wiccan, finding the coven's worship of Earth and nature to be in conflict with almost everything he'd been taught as a member of the Tempest Grove Baptist Church.

But as a young man, Rowan's initial, overwhelming attraction to an outspoken, self-proclaimed witch had drowned out his own voice of doubt, along with the voices of almost everyone around them.

They'd gotten married just days after Joelle's eighteenth

birthday, despite a chorus of objections from both families and, for better or worse, they were still together, four decades later.

"I don't care what that old man calls himself," Rowan said between clenched teeth. "He allows all sorts of people into that house of his. No telling what they get up to in there."

"Hammerling House is a historic home," Faye reminded him. "And the Circle of Light is a registered non-profit organization. I'm sure it isn't anything to be scared of."

In truth, she knew very little about the coven's activities, and even less about Wicca or witchcraft practices in general but she could see that Rowan was working himself up into a rage, and she wanted to diffuse the situation.

However, her brother didn't seem to be listening as the faint, woodsy scent of smoke drifted into the room.

Turning on his heel, he stalked down the hall, stopping in the doorway of the sunroom that ran along the back of the house, staring in at his wife and her guests.

Joelle used the spacious room as an art studio and herbology lab. It was the only place in the house Rowan allowed her to keep the supplies she used for performing rituals and casting charms and spells.

As Faye strained to look past Rowan's rigid shoulders, she saw Joelle lighting a small green candle by the north-facing window. The grieving mother looked over her shoulder at her husband with blazing eyes.

"I need to talk to Nikki," she said as the candle's flame began to flicker. "I'm casting my circle and I'm going to call my daughter's spirit home. I'm going to-"

Her words were drowned out by a loud bellow of anger.

"This is your doing!" Rowan shouted at Ernst. "You've caused this...this *madness*! Now, get out of my house!"

He made a move as if to lunge forward but Faye grabbed his arm, gripping it tight as she spoke next to his ear.

"Your daughter deserves better than this, Rowan. She deserves her family to give her a proper burial. Who's going to do that for Nikki if you're behind bars?"

Shaking off her hand, her brother turned to glare at her.

Their eyes met and held, then his shoulders slumped as the anger and the rage gave way to a terrible sadness.

"Please, just go," he said in a numb voice, not looking at Ernst or Elora. "Leave me to mourn my daughter."

Ernst looked toward Joelle, who stood motionless in the middle of the room, her eyes wide and full of tears.

For a minute Faye was afraid the Wiccan high priest would refuse to go, then the old man took Elora by the hand and moved toward the door.

Stopping next to Rowan, he spoke in a low voice.

"Tonight, I will call upon the Old Ones to see your daughter safely to the Summerland. There, she will find eternal peace as will we all when our time comes."

Faye waited until she heard the front door close, then exhaled the pent-up breath she'd been holding.

A long beat of silence filled the room.

When Faye spoke, her voice was sad and resigned.

"We'll go to the medical examiner's office tomorrow morning," she said. "They need us to officially identify

Nikki's body before they can issue a death certificate."

When neither Rowan nor Joelle responded, she continued.

"Once they release her body to us, we can make plans for the funeral and burial. At least this time, there will be a grave for us to visit."

Thinking back to the days after Natasha's disappearance, she tried to remember how they had coped with the not knowing. How had they ever been able to move on?

Then again, maybe none of us ever has.

Later, as she drove back to Wisteria Falls, the waxing moon seemed to follow Faye. It hung in the sky above her like an unblinking witness to her grief.

Wondering if Ernst's Old Ones might be listening, she whispered the questions that were never far from her mind.

"What happened to Natasha? Who took our girl?"

CHAPTER SEVEN

R aven lowered his head and pulled up the hood of his jacket as he approached Hammerling House. Slipping through the side gate, he kept his eyes down and moved quickly toward the back door, eager to get to work, not wanting to be seen or interrupted.

The old two-story mansion had originally been built back in the 1800s, serving as a boarding school for almost a century before Evander Hammerling and his wife Helga had purchased the property in 1969 when they'd first founded the Tempest Grove Circle of Eternal Light.

While the cozy east wing of the house now served as the living quarters for the coven's high priest, the larger west wing was used by its members to hold meetings, organize festivals, and conduct rituals throughout the year.

It was to the west wing that Raven went, hurrying down a long, dark passageway, before ascending the stairs to the second floor, and then using the pull-down ladder to climb up into the attic room where he practiced his dark magic and secreted away his tools and supplies.

Moving to the small wooden table that served as an altar, he opened a jar of dried wild sage leaves, and pulled out a handful, dropping them into a black crystal altar bowl.

He lit a black candle and held it to the leaves, watching as the fire took hold, before snuffing out the flames.

As the gray smoke from the embers began to fill the room, he picked up a vial of salt water and sprinkled it around himself, casting a sacred circle in which to work his magic.

Lighting a green candle, Raven placed it at the northern quadrant of the circle, then lit three more, placing a red at the south quadrant, a yellow at the east, and a blue at the west. One each for earth, fire, air, and water.

Finally ready to cast the banishment spell, he opened his *Book of Shadows* on the altar table, flipping through it until he found the jagged piece of paper he was looking for.

The paper had been ripped out of another book, but Raven didn't think the owner would mind.

What does a dead woman need with a banishment spell?

After closely studying the instructions, which had been written across the page in small, neat handwriting, he reached into his jacket pocket and took out a velvet pouch.

Loosening the draw string, he pulled out a lock of dark red hair. It had been tied together by a blue satin ribbon, now faded and frayed with time.

He extracted several strands of hair from the ribbon and placed them on a small piece of paper on which he'd already written the name of the spirit to be banished.

Sprinkling a pinch of ground agrimony leaves onto the paper, he folded it carefully, then lifted it to the black candle.

As he held the flame to the paper, Raven began to chant an invocation to the Old Ones, using words that had been passed down through the centuries by practitioners of dark magic who had come before him, ending the invocation with a final command.

"By the power of the Old Ones, I banish you. Be gone from this house, and from this land, and from this town, never to return."

He watched until the final embers of the paper had died out, then smiled with satisfaction.

That takes care of the dead. Now, for the living...

As he reached for the bundle of sticks he'd collected on his recent trip out to the Witch's Tree, the attic hatch opened, and a dark figure emerged from the shadows below.

Raven glanced over in alarm, then relaxed as he made out the features framed by a dark hood.

"Pass me the boline," he said, pointing to a copper knife on a shelf against the far wall.

His uninvited companion complied without hesitation, moving across the wooden floor to retrieve the knife before silently handing it to Raven.

As he began cutting the wood into smaller pieces, Raven kept his eyes on the table.

"Aren't you going to ask me what I'm doing?"

The responding voice was calm.

"I can see you've been casting a spell. And now you're making a poppet. I hate to interrupt, but I wasn't sure if you'd heard the news?"

Raven didn't reply.

"A body has been found by Moonstone Cavern. The new seeker who was supposed to attend the Circle's Beltane festival last night was found hanging in the Witch's Tree."

"Die Hexenbaum," Raven murmured.

"What did you say?"

A smile twitched on Raven's lips.

"I said *die Hexenbaum*," he repeated, sounding amused. "I prefer to use the proper name for the Witch's Tree, in case the spirit of Brunhilde Kistler is listening."

Shadows and silence filled the space between the two figures before Raven spoke again.

"There will be another investigation. I imagine rumors about the Circle and Hammerling House will circulate."

He released a dramatic sigh, although inwardly he felt little concern.

The bodies he'd hidden in the past were nowhere near the covenstead. He hadn't been that careless.

"I appreciate the warning," he snapped, suddenly impatient to get on with his task. "Now, if you don't mind, time is of the essence."

Looking up, he saw a wounded expression flash across the pale, drawn face.

"Very well, I'll leave you to your work."

Raven wondered how his mentor's expression would change if he confessed how he'd spent the previous evening.

But he resisted the temptation to share his secret.

Instead, he returned his attention to the task at hand.

It would be best to keep his mouth shut, at least for now.

And there was no time to waste.

The investigation into Nikki's death was already underway, and he would need the poppet for the next stage in his plan.

CHAPTER EIGHT

Bridget's sleep had been filled with jarring, disturbing dreams that followed her into the early morning hours like disjointed, fragmented memories. Had she really heard her mother's voice calling to her?

Is there something Mom wants me to know?

Squeezing her eyes shut, she listened, hoping to hear the little voice that had stayed with her all these years. Instead, she saw a flash of frightened blue eyes staring through a windshield at the headlights of an oncoming car.

She gasped and sat up straight, prompting Hank to jump to his feet and cross the room.

The Irish setter looked up at her in concern.

"It's okay, Hank," she said, swinging her legs over the side of the bed. "It was just another dream. Let's get you some breakfast. Then I need to pick up Faye."

But bits of her dream and thoughts of her mother stayed with Bridget as she once again drove to the outskirts of Wisteria Falls and pulled into the therapist's driveway.

Faye was already waiting on the porch wearing a black dress and dark glasses. As she hurried down the steps to the Explorer, her silvery hair gleamed in the morning sun, contrasting with the dark expression on her small, pale face.

Once she'd settled into the passenger's seat, Bridget headed toward the highway.

She had offered to take Faye to the medical examiner's office first thing that morning to identify her niece's body, and they had arranged to meet Rowan and Joelle there.

As Faye shifted anxiously in her seat, Bridget tried to think of something to say. Something innocuous that would distract her passenger during the minutes and miles ahead.

"Did you get any sleep?" she finally asked.

It was all she could come up with.

"Not much," Faye admitted with a yawn. "And you?"

Grimacing at the thought of her restless night, Bridget lifted her shoulders in a resigned shrug.

"Pretty much the same as always."

She wished she'd thought of another conversation starter. She wasn't in the mood to rehash the sleep issues and recurrent nightmares that had been the subject of so many of their sessions in the past.

Not when Faye was in the midst of a new and present crisis. And not when Bridget's own mind was still churning with questions prompted by the previous day's revelations.

Clearing her throat, she tried again.

"I didn't know that you and my mother knew each other," she said, keeping her eyes on the road. "Of course, I knew Mom had been a psychologist. That was one of the main reasons I wanted to get into psychology myself."

"But when my father recommended that I see you after

the Backroads Butcher case, he just told me that you were the most experienced therapist in town when it came to treating PTSD. He didn't mention Mom had been your schoolmate."

She gave Faye a sideways glance.

"Oh, Edith Bishop was more than that," Faye said. "Your mother was my mentor. And a very good friend, as well."

Affection warmed her voice.

"As soon as I'd gotten my license, Edith recommended me for an open position in Wisteria Falls," she said. "If it wasn't for her, I probably would have moved back to West Virginia."

"And then I wouldn't have had you to turn to when I needed a therapist," Bridget said. "It's strange to think that the actions and decisions Mom made in the past are still impacting my life now, even if I don't always know it."

Faye nodded.

"Edith Bishop was a good woman who left this world way too soon," she said with a sad smile. "Whatever she passed on to you...whatever energy she left behind, whatever impact she made...will be good, too. I have faith in that."

Although Bridget wanted to ask more questions about her mother, she sensed Faye had done all the talking she could manage for the time being, and they rode the rest of the way in contemplative silence.

"I don't see Rowan's truck yet," Faye said as they pulled into the parking lot of the bulky concrete building that housed Opal's office. "I guess we should wait inside."

Bridget agreed. She parked the Explorer and led Faye

through a glass door bearing the seal of the Commonwealth of Virginia Medical Examiner.

As they approached the reception desk, a cloying scent of chemicals and decay hinted at the dissection of the dead taking place somewhere within the building.

It was a scent Bridget had never gotten used to despite the many autopsies she'd witnessed.

"We're here to meet with Opal Fitzgerald," she told the receptionist behind the desk. "We need to identify a body that was brought in last night. The decedent's name is Nicole Webster."

Following Faye to a row of red vinyl chairs lined against the wall, Bridget waited for the therapist to sit down, then crossed to the water fountain and bent to take a sip.

She frowned as she heard familiar voices just beyond the door leading into the back. Glancing over at Faye, she saw the therapist had settled into a chair and was looking down at her phone with a forlorn expression.

Impulsively, she crossed to the door and inched it open.

Opal Fitzgerald was standing in the hallway wearing a white lab coat. Her gray curls were loose, and she was talking animatedly to a woman Bridget hadn't expected to see.

"What are you doing here, Charlie?" she asked, slipping into the hall and letting the door close behind her.

"I could ask you the same question," Charlie tossed back. "But then, Opal told me you were coming with Nicole Webster's family to identify the body."

Pointing down to an open folder in Opal's hand, Charlie

gestured for Bridget to join them.

"We were just arranging for the remains collected at the ravine to be sent over to the FBI lab for testing," she said.

"The bones we found are in pretty bad shape," Opal added. "But I'd say there's still a decent chance the lab will be able to get a DNA profile from the bone marrow."

Bridget wasn't as confident.

After all, the bones had been out in the open for a while. They might be too dried out and degraded.

And there was no guarantee they would be able to positively identify the bones, even if they did get a profile.

Nevertheless, she felt a small kernel of hope take root.

If they do manage to extract DNA from the bones, Faye and her family may finally find out what really happened to Natasha.

She thought of Faye sitting in the lobby, unaware that any bones had been found, or that both her nieces' remains might be in the building.

Hoping the discovery of the bones wouldn't be revealed until they had answers and knew for sure what they were dealing with, Bridget turned to Charlie.

"Did the evidence response team find anything else at the scene? I saw the Tempest High School jacket, but was there any other clothing? Any personal items?"

"Jason is working on the scene summary report," Charlie said. "But I don't think they recovered anything else."

She pointed to the folder in Opal's hand again.

"What I'm wondering is how old those bones could be," she said, her eyes moving first to Opal and then to Bridget. "Because we're all thinking the same thing, right? We're all thinking those bones could belong to Natasha Prescott."

Neither Bridget nor Opal confirmed or denied the statement. They both just stared, waiting for her to continue.

"But if those bones haven't been there for the last twenty-seven years, then..."

"Then they belong to some other poor girl," Opal said. "Maybe a hiker who got lost."

She exhaled, looking suddenly flustered.

"Maybe the fact that the bones were found near the site of Nicole Webster's murder suggests a serial killer is at work," she added. "It might have nothing to do with Natasha."

Bridget cocked an eyebrow.

"And the Tempest Grove High School jacket they found?" she asked. "Is that just a coincidence, too?"

Before Opal could answer, the receptionist opened the door and then stopped in surprise to find the three women standing in the hallway.

"Joelle and Rowan Prescott are here, Opal. They want to see their daughter."

* * *

Bridget followed Opal into the lobby, noting the stress on Faye's face as she stood and introduced her brother and sister-in-law to the medical examiner, and then to Charlie.

"And this is Bridget Bishop," Faye said. "She's with the FBI's Behavioral Analysis Unit and is-"

"You're Edith Bishop's daughter, aren't you?" Joelle cut in before Faye could finish the introduction. "I can see her in your eyes...and in your aura."

She stepped closer, taking Bridget's hands in hers, studying her face with wide amber eyes.

"Your mother tried to help our Nikki," she said, tears welling in her eyes. "Perhaps they are together again, now."

"Leave her be," Rowan said tersely, pulling his wife's hands away. "We're here to identify our daughter's body. Let's just get on with it."

The tension between the grieving parents was palpable as they followed Opal down the hall and into the viewing room.

Bridget and Charlie hovered in the back of the room as the couple walked up to the glass partition that separated them from their daughter.

"Faye should be with us," Joelle said, turning to take Faye's hand. "She's all the family we have left now."

The trio stood side by side looking through the glass as Opal motioned to the forensic technician who stood beside the metal gurney wearing protective overalls.

"Greg will pull down the sheet when you're all ready," she said. "Let me know when you-"

"We're ready," Rowan snapped. "Just show us our girl."

Looking to Joelle and Faye, Opal waited until both women nodded, then gave Greg Alcott the signal.

As he pulled down the sheet, Faye released a soft sob. Feeling her own eyes water at the sound, Bridget realized that until the day before, she'd never seen Faye cry.

And after years of baring her own emotional trauma to the therapist, it felt only right that she should be there to support Faye as she endured the loss of her niece.

Knowing there was little she could say to lessen the pain, she waited by the door, her anger growing as she wondered who had killed Nicole, and why.

"Is this your daughter, Nicole Prescott Webster?" Opal asked after a brief silence.

Both Rowan and Joelle nodded, and then Greg replaced the sheet and they were turning away.

"There's just a bit of paperwork to sign," Opal said. "You can wait in my office while I prepare it."

As she led them down the hall, Joelle reached for her husband's hand, but Rowan pulled away.

"I've got to get some air," he said. "I'll be back."

"And we'll wait for Opal in her office," Charlie suggested.

She watched them settle into chairs around Opal's desk, then cleared her throat.

"I know it's difficult to think about right now, but someone out there put Nicole on that table," she said softly. "I'd like to ask you a few questions, so that we can find out who hurt her, and so we can make sure they never hurt anyone else again."

She glanced over at Bridget as if seeking her help.

"Charlie's right," Bridget said, clearing her throat. "It's important for you to tell us if you know anyone who could have done this."

She met Joelle's eyes.

"Do you know anyone who may have wanted to hurt Nicole? Anyone who might have wanted to kill her?"

Joelle frowned and crossed her arms over her chest.

"I know Rowan thinks it must be a member of the Circle, but that's just not true," she said.

"Your husband believes whoever killed Nicole is associated with the Circle of Eternal Light?" Bridget asked.

"What's the Circle of Eternal Light?"

Charlie raised an eyebrow.

"Is it a church?"

"It's a Wicca coven," Joelle said, lifting her chin defiantly.

Charlie blinked.

"So, you're a witch?"

"Yes, although it isn't like you see in the movies," Joelle said. "The Circle is no different than a church or any other place of worship. Only we worship the earth and nature."

A slight frown creased Charlie's forehead.

"So, you don't worship the devil?"

Joelle looked offended.

"No, we don't," she snapped. "In fact, we believe there *is* no devil. There's just light and darkness in all of us. Some people choose to embrace their darkness. Those people are the real devils."

Sensing that she and Charlie would need to get past the woman's defenses if they were to glean any useful information, Bridget nodded.

"I can't argue with that. I've certainly met a few devils in my line of work," she said. "Now, tell me, when was the Circle founded? I'd never heard of it before yesterday."

Joelle's chin dropped and she relaxed her shoulders.

"Evander Hammerling founded the Circle back in 1969," she said. "He'd been in the war in Europe years before and a fellow soldier had introduced him to a Wiccan healer."

She let out a deep breath.

"Evander credited the herbs and natural remedies with healing his injuries. After that, he tried to learn everything he could about herbology, witchcraft, and the Wicca way of life, which was pretty new at that time. I guess you could say he was converted."

Her voice had lost its edge.

"When he came home to West Virginia, he looked for a coven to join but at the time all he could find were solitary witches who acted as healers and midwives in the community but kept their beliefs and magic hidden."

Glancing at Charlie, Joelle narrowed her eyes.

"You see, anyone who openly admitted to being a member of the Wicca community was shunned and even demonized. Anyone who dared to publicly share their beliefs was accused of satanism and devil worship.

"Eventually, Evander and his wife Helga founded the Tempest Grove Circle of Eternal Light and bought Hammerling House to be its covenstead."

Charlie frowned.

"What's a covenstead?" she asked.

"It's kind of like a church, I guess," Joelle replied. "It's a safe space for the coven to celebrate festivals, worship the

God and Goddess, conduct rituals, and practice the Craft."

"The Craft?" Bridget asked. "You mean witchcraft?"

"There's no fixed definition, really. But within the Circle we prefer the term magic," Joelle said.

All hint of defensiveness was gone as she explained.

"Our members practice ritual magic, divination, herbalism, or whatever else they want. It's pretty laid-back. In fact, we believe that everyone should act according to their own will as long as it does no harm."

Bridget sat forward with interest as Joelle continued.

"As part of our initiation into the Circle, we all take a vow to do no harm with our magic," she said.

"Do all members go through an initiation?" Bridget asked.

Joelle nodded.

"So, who defines what harm is?"

Joelle looked confused.

"What do you mean?"

"Well, during a war, most soldiers don't consider killing an enemy combatant as *doing harm* if it means saving fellow soldiers," Bridget said. "But others think any killing is *doing harm* regardless of the justification."

She considered her words carefully before continuing, not wanting to offend Joelle or disparage her beliefs.

"It's just that in my line of work, I often encounter people who justify murder by telling themselves the victim was out to do them harm," Bridget explained. "They may kill a perceived rival to protect a romantic relationship, or a competitor to protect their business."

Charlie nodded her agreement.

"Do you know anyone like that within the Circle, Joelle? Someone who pushes the boundaries? Someone who might have acted out against Nicole according to some sort of false justification that she posed a threat?"

Joelle glanced nervously at the door, and Bridget suspected the woman was scared Rowan might return at any minute. But her husband didn't appear.

"I've heard rumors about members resorting to dark magic," Joelle admitted. "They claim to be fighting fire with fire. But for the most part, they keep that hidden. Most members want nothing to do with the darkness."

"When were you first initiated into the Circle?" Bridget asked. "Was it before or after Natasha went missing?"

A faraway look washed over Joelle's face.

"I was a girl of sixteen," she said softly. "Just a child really. I was only a few years older than Natasha was when she went missing."

Suddenly, her face crumbled as if the realization of everything she'd lost had come crashing back in.

She buried her face in her hands.

"My sweet girls," she sobbed. "They're both...gone now."

As his wife began to wail, Rowan burst back into the room. Crossing to Joelle's side, he wrapped an arm around her shoulders and glared up at Bridget.

"Why don't we leave it there for now?" she said, getting to her feet. "I'm so-"

"Don't you dare say you're sorry," Rowan cut in, his eyes

blazing. "Just say you'll catch whoever did this. Say you'll do more than the Tempest Grove PD has done for my girls and all the other women who have gone missing around here."

Bridget frowned.

"What other women?" she asked.

"Don't you know about the others?" he asked, shaking his head. "Didn't Detective Landon tell you?"

He saw the answer in her eyes.

"My girls aren't the only ones who've disappeared from Tempest Grove over the last three decades," he said tightly. "And they aren't the only ones who never came back."

* * *

Rowan's words circled again and again in Bridget's mind as she tried to concentrate on the grim scene before her.

Standing beside Charlie on one side of the dissecting table, while Opal and Greg stood on the other, she looked down at Nicole Webster's lifeless face.

The medical examiner was speaking into a small recorder.

"A ligature mark is visible above the thyroid cartilage along with some displacement of the skin, which shows excoriation and grooving," Opal said. "The ligature appears to have occluded the carotid arteries and jugular veins resulting in cerebral hypoxia and asphyxia."

Opal looked at Bridget through her plastic face shield.

"Basically, the rope caused the base of Nicole's tongue to

get lodged against the back of her mouth, which blocked her airway and stopped her from breathing."

She looked down at the dead woman on the table.

"The cause of death is clearly asphyxiation by hanging. And based on the position of the rope and the bruises and contusions on the body, the manner of death is undoubtedly homicide."

Lifting a gloved hand, she pointed to a red patch of skin on Nicole's scalp.

"Hair has been ripped out of the skull," she said. "Unless Jason Chan and his evidence response team found hair at the scene, I'd say the killer has it. Lord only knows what he plans to do with it."

Bridget's skin crawled at the thought of someone keeping a lock of Nicole's dark red hair as a perverse souvenir.

Backing away from the table, she checked her watch.

"I've got to go," she said, pulling off her gloves as she moved toward the autopsy suite door.

"Where are you going?" Charlie called. "We need to talk about the profile. You are working on a profile, aren't you?"

Without slowing down, Bridget called over her shoulder.

"I've got a lunch meeting in Wisteria Falls. I'll check in with you later about the profile...and everything else."

She disposed of her gloves, protective coveralls, and booties, then hurried out to the Explorer, hoping that her hair didn't smell like decay.

Her father had called her earlier that morning, and when she'd agreed to meet him for lunch, he'd made her promise that she wouldn't be late. There would be no time to stop at home for a shower.

Merging onto the highway, Bridget drove toward Wisteria Falls. Her thoughts were on Faye, who'd gone home with Joelle and Rowan to stay for a few days while they planned the funeral, before turning to Nicole Webster.

Questions again started to swirl.

What were you doing by the Witch's Tree, Nikki? Did you figure out who'd taken Natasha? Was that who you'd gone to meet?

Could Nicole have gotten too close to the truth after her return to Tempest Grove? Could she have even been looking for the bones they'd uncovered?

And who do the bones belong to, anyway? Are they Natasha's? Or have we found one of the missing women Rowan mentioned?

Checking the clock on the dashboard, she saw that she was right on time as she pulled into the crowded parking lot outside of the Moonstone Diner.

As soon as she pushed through the door, she spotted her father's salt and pepper hair and quickly headed toward a booth by the window.

She sat down across from him and smiled.

"I'm here on time," she said triumphantly. "And I didn't have breakfast so I'm pretty hungry. You ready to order?"

"We need to wait for our other guest," Bob said, pretending to study the menu, which he already knew by heart. "I asked Earl Ripley to join us."

Bridget's smile fell away.

After her restless night, and a morning surrounded by the sight and smell of death, she wasn't in the mood to make polite conversation with her father's new investigator.

She hardly knew the man.

But Bob held up a hand to silence her objections.

"I thought it'd be a good idea for you to talk to him," he said. "Ripley worked for the Tempest Grove PD before he moved down to Richmond. He was a detective there when Natasha Prescott went missing."

Bridget gaped at her father.

"Ripley was on the force in Tempest Grove? Why didn't you tell me yesterday?"

"I just thought of it this morning when I saw him in the office. That's why I called and invited you to lunch."

He dropped his eyes.

"And I remembered something else," he said. "Ripley investigated your mother's accident. That's how I met him."

Before Bridget could reply, the diner door opened. She recognized Earl Ripley's thinning white hair, which topped a tan, leathery face.

The retired detective's overall look suggested a life spent largely in the sun. His outdoorsy appearance contrasted sharply with the ex-beauty-queen looks of the woman who walked in behind him.

Bridget waved a surprised greeting to Daphne Finch, who had been her best friend since childhood. In the last year, she'd taken on a role at Bishop & Company Investigations as an investigative intern.

"You invited Daphne, too?" Bridget asked.

"Ripley must have invited her along," Bob replied. "Or maybe she invited herself. You know Daphne."

He smiled as he watched the pair approach.

"I've partnered them up on a few cases now," he said in a low voice. "They're good together."

Sliding over to let Daphne sit beside her, Bridget was glad to see that Bob's strategy was working.

She had questioned the wisdom of pairing a novice such as Daphne with a well-seasoned investigator such as Ripley. But so far, it appeared to be a success.

As she watched Ripley take a seat beside Bob, he looked up and caught her eyes, then grunted what sounded like a greeting before plucking a laminated card off the table.

Squinting down at the menu, he grunted again before looking up at the server who was waiting to take their order.

"Just black coffee and plain wheat toast for me," he said.

Leaning back in his chair, he waited as Daphne ordered French toast with a side of grits for her and Bridget to share.

"I'd better stick with Greek yogurt and a fruit salad," Bob said, dropping his menu back on the table with a sigh. "Ever since my last check-up, Paloma's been going on about my cholesterol."

Bridget shot him a worried look.

Her father had suffered a serious stroke several years earlier that had forced him to retire from the Wisteria Falls PD. Although he appeared to have fully recovered and was now enjoying a successful second career as a private investigator, she couldn't help but worry.

Shifting under her gaze, Bob turned to Ripley as if eager to change the subject.

"Bridget's working that homicide near Moonstone Cavern," he said. "You've probably already heard there may be a connection to Natasha Prescott's disappearance."

Ripley nodded.

"A buddy at the Tempest Grove PD said they found the missing girl's twin sister hanging from a tree," he said with a slow shake of his head. "I sure was sorry to hear it."

Leaning forward, Bob trained his eyes on Ripley.

"I know it's been a long time," he said. "But I was thinking you may be able to fill Bridget in on the original investigation into Natasha's disappearance, seeing you were on the local force back then."

Ripley's back stiffened.

"It's all there in the files," he said, keeping his eyes on his coffee cup. "Just ask Detective Landon to-"

"Talking to someone who was there at the time is usually a big help," Bridget cut in. "And you've had years to think it over. I bet you've got a few theories as to what might have happened to Natasha. I'd like to hear them."

She paused as the server approached with a tray full of food. Once the plates had been delivered, she tried again.

"I know that Natasha snuck out of the house the night she went missing and that her sister went after her," Bridget said. "While Natasha was never seen again, a local farmer spotted Nicole wandering along the street the next morning and brought her home."

Ripley nodded impatiently.

"Yes, Nikki had some sort of head injury which resulted in memory loss," he said. "It seemed obvious that foul play must have been involved...that someone had attacked Nikki and taken Natasha."

"So, you never thought that Natasha could have just run away?" Bridget asked. "That maybe her sister tried to stop her, and they got in some sort of altercation which resulted in Nicole's head injury?"

She watched Ripley take another sip of coffee.

"There were similar theories going around town," he admitted. "Some folks spread rumors that Nicole was the one who attacked her sister. Said she could have killed her and hidden the body."

He shook his head.

"But there was no physical evidence to support that theory," he said. "And no motive could be found."

Bridget heard something in his voice. Was it doubt?

"In any case, after the initial search, we were pretty sure someone had abducted her."

Picking up a piece of his toast, he studied it for a long beat, then set it back on the plate without taking a bite.

"We had every police department in a hundred-mile range looking for her," he said. "There were flyers everywhere and news bulletins on every station, but no confirmed sightings. It was like she'd just vanished off the face of the earth."

"And the suspects?" Bridget prodded.

She waited patiently as he considered the question.

"There were plenty," he finally said. "The girl's mother belonged to an organization called the Circle of Light or some such. There were rumors about their members and stories about what went on during their meetings at some old mansion. Called it *Hammer House*, or something like that...

His voice trailed off as he looked away.

"It's been a long time," he said. "It's hard to remember."

Bridget studied him with narrowed eyes, sensing he was playing up his age and confusion. But from what she'd seen of him, she knew Ripley was still as sharp as a tack.

"Which members of the Circle were suspects?" she asked. "Anyone specific?"

Ripley stared down into his nearly empty mug.

"Calvin Hirsch," he muttered. "The guy was the track coach at Tempest Grove High. He had access to both the Prescott girls. And as we later found out, he was a secret member of the Circle, which at the time was a scandal."

Draining the last of his coffee, he set the mug down on the Formica tabletop and leaned back in the booth.

"The night Natasha went missing, Coach Hirsch was seen going into the woods. The witness said he was wearing a dark outfit and acting *cagey*. I think that's the word they used."

"Okay, so Calvin Hirsch was your prime suspect. What did he say when you questioned him?" Bridget asked.

Ripley shrugged his rounded shoulders.

"He said he didn't do it, of course. He claimed he was

going into the woods for some sort of festival. Said he was celebrating spring or summer or something. That's when we found out he was a member of the Circle."

"And did you charge him?"

The ex-detective shook his head.

"No, he had an alibi," he said. "A few other people at this festival said that he was with them most of the night. They backed up his story so, what could we do?"

"And that was it?" Daphne interjected in an indignant drawl. "You just let him get away with it?"

She trained accusing green eyes on Ripley.

"Not completely," he said. "You see, Hirsch *was* fired."

Now it was Bridget's turn to be indignant.

"Why was he fired if he had an alibi?"

"You'd have to ask Brian Corwin about that," Ripley said. "Corwin was the principal of the high school back then."

Bridget frowned.

"Was Brian Corwin a suspect, too?"

The question earned a sardonic laugh from Ripley.

"Almost everyone connected with the high school, the Baptist church, or the Circle was considered a suspect," Ripley said. "I guess Corwin was no exception."

"The guy was always making a show that he was a devout Baptist. And when the investigation uncovered Hirsch's association with the Circle, Corwin made it clear the school didn't want what he called *godless pagans* working there."

Looking around for the server, Ripley called for his check.

"So how has Joelle Prescott managed to keep her job as

the theater teacher?" Bridget wondered aloud. "She seems pretty open about being a member of the Circle of Light."

Ripley shrugged.

"My guess is that Brian Corwin is no longer in charge," he said. "And while she might be open about it now, I bet back then it wasn't public knowledge. I imagine admitting she was a member of the Circle cost her more than a few friends in Tempest Grove."

"And what about Hirsch?" Daphne asked.

Scooping up the last bite of grits, she stared at her partner with wide eyes.

"As far as I know, he's still in town," Ripley said. "I think I heard something about him starting up some sort of workshop outside town, although I never saw it before I moved down to Richmond."

"What about the new detective?" Bob asked as Ripley pulled out his wallet and dropped a twenty-dollar-bill on the table. "You know anything about Matthew Landon? You think he can handle this case?"

Ripley stood and stretched his back.

"Landon had just gotten out of the academy when I left for Richmond, so I didn't get a chance to see him in action," he admitted. "But from what I've heard, he's no Sherlock Holmes. Of course, he's the one Chief Aguilar assigned to the case, so he'll have to make do."

"And what about the other girls who've gone missing?" Bridget asked. "You know anything about them?"

Again, Ripley looked away, clearly on edge.

"I don't know anything about that."

He took a step toward the door.

"But what I do know is that Chief Aquilar filed away the investigation into Natasha's disappearance as a cold case, and when her sister returned and started asking questions, someone got mad and killed her."

He finally met Bridget's eyes and held them.

"If you find out who got mad, and why, you'll find Nicole Prescott's   killer."

CHAPTER NINE

Bailey Flynn peered over the tall stack of files on Charlie Day's desk, wondering how they would ever get through all the case files and folders they had carted away from the Tempest Grove Police Department's records room that morning.

Lifting a dusty manila folder labeled as *Witness Statement – Abner Chumbley* off the top of the pile, she sneezed, causing Ludwig to glance up at her in concern.

"I guess the Tempest Grove PD hasn't had a chance to digitize their files yet," she said, reaching for a tissue.

When Charlie didn't respond, Bailey tried again.

"Some of these files are almost as old as I am," she said, aiming a worried look across the desk. "You think we may be able to find something the original investigators missed?"

"Maybe," Charlie murmured, sounding distracted. "But first we need to get all this organized. If you can just take all of these files over to the–"

The impending request was preempted by Charlie's phone, which began to vibrate and buzz on the desktop.

As Bridget Bishop's name and number appeared on the

display, Charlie tapped on the screen to answer the call, then tapped again to activate the speaker.

"Bridget, I hope you're calling to tell me the BAU has a profile of Nicole Prescott's killer ready," Charlie said. "Otherwise, Agent Flynn and I are going to have to start going through all these old files we got from the Tempest Grove PD to dig up leads. And that could take a while."

She turned and started to pace the room, missing the look of alarm that filled Bailey's wide green eyes.

Filling out paperwork and reading through dusty old files was the last thing Bailey had imagined herself doing when she'd left the Florida sunshine behind to sign on to Special-Agent-in-Charge Roger Calloway's special crimes unit.

The opportunity to work with the most experienced agents in the Bureau while chasing down the most dangerous criminals in the country had been too tempting to pass up.

And it hadn't hurt that the move north had provided an escape from the painful memories that seemed to wait around every corner in Belle Harbor, the little beach town just north of Miami she had formerly called home.

"I just had lunch with a retired detective from the Tempest Grove PD," Bridget said. "His name's Earl Ripley and he's a private investigator at my father's agency now. He filled me in on the suspects they'd identified in Natasha Prescott's abduction before it went cold."

"I'm assuming he had some useful information to share if you're calling me now," Charlie said. "So, what is it? Have you got something solid for us to work with?"

Bailey held her breath, hoping she and Ludwig would be given a task. The German Shepherd needed some exercise since, like her, he'd been cooped up inside all day.

"Ripley seemed to agree with our theory that whoever killed Nicole had likely also been involved with Natasha's abduction," Bridget said. "He named the prime suspect in Natasha's disappearance as former Tempest Grove High School track coach Calvin Hirsh."

Picking up a marker, Bailey wrote the man's name at the top of a whiteboard hanging on the wall.

"According to Ripley, Hirsch was never officially charged with any crime. Apparently, he had an alibi that was corroborated by members of the Circle of Light."

Bailey leaned forward.

"Is he still alive?" she asked hopefully. "Is he still living in Tempest Grove? Should we go out there again and–"

"Hold on a minute," Charlie said, raising an eyebrow at Bailey's eager response. "Let's hear what else this Mr. Ripley had to say first."

She looked down at the phone on the desk.

"Bridget, did you ask him about the other women? The ones Rowan Prescott claimed had gone missing?"

"He didn't know anything about that," Bridget admitted.

Charlie frowned, clearly unhappy with the answer.

"Detective Landon told me he wasn't aware of anyone going missing, other than a few runaways," she said. "At least, not since Natasha Prescott. But Rowan told a different story. He said several women had suddenly disappeared."

"Are we sure they aren't talking about the same

women?" Bailey asked. "Maybe Landon considers them runaways while Rowan thinks they're missing."

She repeated her suggestion.

"Maybe we should go out to Tempest Grove. It sounds as if another talk with Detective Landon may be in order."

"I agree," Bridget said. "I think you and Charlie should go talk to Landon. Find out if there's any truth to the rumors."

Suppressing the urge to stand up and do a little happy dance in front of the whiteboard, Bailey remained seated as Bridget ended the call.

"Okay, fine," Charlie said with a sigh. "We'll drive out to Tempest Grove and talk to Landon. But I want to let Agent Hale know that we're going. He may even want to ride out there with us."

"I saw him go into Calloway's office earlier," Bailey said. "And I haven't seen him come back out yet."

Charlie stood and crossed to the door.

"Come on then, let's go," she said. "I'll stop by Calloway's office on the way out."

Jumping to her feet, Bailey picked up Ludwig's leash and hooked it to his collar, leading the dog out into the hall.

They followed Charlie toward Roger Calloway's closed door and waited as she knocked.

"What is it?" the SAC called out. "And this had better be good. I'm in a meeting."

Charlie hesitated, then reached forward and turned the doorknob. Inhaling deeply, she pushed the door open to reveal Special Agent Tristan Hale sitting across from Roger

Calloway at his big cherry oak desk.

"I just wanted to give you an update before I leave," she said, keeping her eyes on Calloway. "I'm going to check out an urgent lead in Tempest Grove and I'm taking Agent Flynn with me. There's room for Hale if he'd like to ride along. It would give him a chance to get caught up on the investigation."

She turned her head toward Hale, who looked unusually somber. He flashed Charlie a quick smile, but Bailey could see that it didn't quite reach his eyes.

"You'll have to make do with Agent Flynn for now," Calloway said brusquely. "Hale and I are expected on a call and will be tied up for quite some time. I'll expect a case report on my desk tomorrow morning. I'm sure the press will be panting at my door by then."

Charlie nodded, closed the door, and then turned around to face Bailey.

"That man is up to something," she muttered. "I just wish I knew what it was."

Bailey dropped her eyes, tempted to tell Charlie what she'd overheard earlier when she'd stopped outside Calloway's door, but decided it wouldn't be a good idea.

She'll find out the big news soon enough.

Besides, it was clearly supposed to be top secret, and Calloway would have her job if she went around sharing information she wasn't supposed to have in the first place.

As she led Ludwig out to the parking lot, Bailey wondered how Charlie was going to take the news that Hale might be leaving the Washington field office.

The relationship between the two agents was public knowledge throughout the Bureau. They had been together for a year or more from what Bailey had heard, and she could see that it wasn't just a casual fling.

It seemed inevitable someone's heart would be broken.

And I should definitely be an expert on that by now, shouldn't I?

"Come on, let's hurry," Charlie said as she headed toward her Expedition. "It looks like it's going to rain."

Charlie's forecast was accurate.

The threatening clouds overhead soon swelled and burst. Rain pelted down on the SUV as they pulled onto the slick highway and headed west.

Riding shotgun beside Charlie with Ludwig lounging in the backseat, Bailey strained to see the passing landscape as they drove further from the city.

She hadn't been in Virginia long and still hadn't gotten used to the rolling hills and thick woods.

Suddenly homesick for the flat, palm-tree-lined coastline she was used to in South Florida, she sighed and looked back at Ludwig, comforted by his presence.

"He did a good job yesterday finding those bones," Charlie said as she glanced in the rearview mirror at the German Shepherd. "It's amazing how he picked up on the scent."

"I know, I was amazed when I first went through the handler training," Bailey said. "You know that a dog's sense of smell is up to a hundred thousand times stronger than a human's sense of smell?"

She smiled back at Ludwig, who appeared to be listening.

"They can pick up on a scent that is literally a mile away on land, or even further if the wind is right," she added. "And detect a scent thirty or forty feet underground, or even further in the water."

"How long have you had Ludwig?" Charlie asked. "Was he the first SAR dog you were assigned?"

A sudden knot formed in Bailey's throat and for a minute all she could manage was a nod. Then she swallowed hard and cleared her throat.

"He wasn't exactly assigned to me," she said. "I requested Ludwig after his original handler was injured in the line of duty. It took some doing, but they let me go through handler training with him and we've been together ever since."

She kept her eyes on the window, watching the rain and trying not to embarrass herself by getting emotional.

It was still too hard to talk about what had happened back in Belle Harbor. It was easier to be a thousand miles away, focusing on the present instead of the past.

It's easier to just leave everything and everyone behind, right?

They drove along, listening to the rain beating down on the roof, until Charlie pointed to a sign up ahead.

"There's the turn-off for Tempest Grove," she said, merging the Expedition onto the exit ramp.

Minutes later they were turning onto South Street and pulling up to the small Tempest Grove police station.

Detective Landon was waiting in the lobby for them, having been alerted in advance that they were on their way by a call from Charlie.

"Did you two come back for more files?"

Bailey assumed the question was the detective's lame attempt at humor, but Charlie wasn't in the mood for jokes.

"We came back to talk to you about reports we've heard that several women have gone missing in Tempest Grove since Natasha Prescott disappeared," she said. "We came to find out if we're dealing with some sort of serial predator."

Propping her hands on her hips, she stared up at Landon.

The detective raised both hands in surrender.

"Listen, I told you before, there've been no missing person reports filed to my knowledge. I don't know who is spreading rumors, but that's all they are, just whispers and rumors."

"Not according to Rowan Prescott," Charlie insisted.

Landon shook his head and sighed.

"The man is grieving," he said. "His daughter just died and he's not thinking straight. But if he does have real information about a missing person, I'd be the first one to tell him to come on down and file a report. I'd even be happy to write it up myself."

He lowered his voice and looked around the tiny lobby as if someone might be listening in.

"You do know his wife belongs to the Circle of Light coven, right? From what I've heard, people come and go from Hammerling House all the time," he said. "And it's not uncommon for those kinds of people to just wander off. Maybe they went off to forage in the woods and just kept going. I mean, who knows?"

Shrugging his wide shoulders, he inched toward the door.

"Now, if that's all you wanted to ask about...."

Charlie shook her head.

"Actually, no, that wasn't all we came for," she said. "We also needed to ask you about Calvin Hirsch. I understand he was the number one suspect in the original investigation into Natasha Prescott's disappearance."

"I haven't spoken to Hirsch in years," Landon said, scratching at his beard. "Maybe even decades. The man may have been a suspect, but that case is no longer active. I had no reason to-"

"I'd say Nicole Prescott's body hanging from a tree is reason enough to question him again," Charlie cut in. "Agent Flynn and I will go out there now and speak to him. Then we'll swing by Hammerling House to ask if any foragers have gone missing lately."

Landon frowned.

"Well, now, Calvin Hirsch has become a bit of a recluse in the last few years," he said. "He may not welcome you two strangers showing up at his property without warning."

He shook his head.

"No, I better speak to him myself. I'll ask him about Nicole and see if he has an alibi. I'll let you know what he says."

Charlie looked as if she was about to protest, then nodded.

"Okay, then we'll head straight out to Hammerling House. Maybe we can find out if anyone's gone missing."

CHAPTER TEN

Charlie was still inwardly fuming over their encounter with Landon as she followed Bailey and Ludwig back toward the Expedition. The rain had stopped but the sudden, heavy downpour had partially flooded the road, and they had to wade through ankle-deep muddy water to get back to the vehicle.

"Are we really going to Hammerling House?" Bailey asked as she snapped on her seatbelt. "Because I think it's a good idea. And since we're already out here..."

"Yes, we'll go see what we can find out," Charlie agreed.

She suspected Bailey was thinking about the pile of folders waiting for them back in D.C. and would suggest going to meet the devil himself if she could find a way to avoid the tedious process of wading through them.

The soothing voice of the Expedition's satnav system directed Charlie to continue down South Street until she reached Shackleton Highway and then headed north.

Ten minutes later they were turning onto Arcana Avenue, a wide, shady street that snaked its way through thickly forested hill country.

"That must be it," Bailey said.

Pointing to a wrought iron gate, she leaned forward and peered eagerly through the car window.

"Wow, the place is kind of creepy," she murmured.

Charlie had to agree.

The sprawling Victorian mansion sat back from the road, its steep, gabled roofs adding height to its two-story frame. The towers, turrets, and dormers on the exterior were paired with stained-glass windows for a maximum dramatic effect.

"Let's just hope they let us in," Charlie said, suddenly uneasy at the thought of entering the coven's property unannounced. "If not, we can try again later, or..."

Before she could finish her thought, the gate in front of them began to swing open.

For a minute, Charlie thought that someone in the big house had seen them arrive, perhaps through a security camera feed, and was allowing them entry.

Then she saw the car coming down the driveway and realized it was leaving the property.

Waiting until the car had exited through the open gate, Charlie steered her big SUV onto the long drive, making it safely through just as the gate swung shut behind them.

"Do you think this qualifies as trespassing?" Bailey asked, looking around at the grounds with interest.

Charlie ignored the question as she navigated the Expedition around a fountain in the courtyard, noting a five-pointed star engraved in the thick white stone.

Coming to a stop in front of the wide wraparound porch, she tried to recall if the symbol was called a pentagram or pentacle but couldn't remember.

She checked the ammunition in her Glock, then opened the door and stepped onto the driveway.

Treading carefully through a series of puddles left by the rain, she opened the back door for Ludwig, who eagerly jumped out, splashing muddy water over her boots and pant legs as he ran to take his place beside Bailey.

With one hand on her holster, she crossed to the porch, leaving muddy boot prints on the steps as she approached the front door and knocked.

Footsteps sounded somewhere inside, and she could sense movement beyond the window.

A deadbolt turned, and then the door squeaked open to reveal a young woman with long blonde hair that had been woven into a silken braid.

"Seekers of the light must use the west entrance," she said. "Just follow the driveway around that-"

"I'm Agent Day with the FBI," Charlie interrupted. "And this is Agent Flynn. We're investigating a homicide and need to ask some questions about the Circle. Are you a member?"""

The woman hesitated, then nodded.

"Yes, I'm Elora and I live here, actually," she said. "With Ernst. He's the coven's high priest. Why don't I go get him?"

She turned and hurried down a wide dark hall, leaving the door open behind her.

With a shrug to Bailey, Charlie stepped inside.

Scanning the dark floorboards and old-fashioned

wallpaper, she wondered if anything had been updated in the house since Evander Hammerling and his wife Helga had moved into the place more than half a century earlier.

"Can I help you?"

The man's voice came from shadows, and Charlie's hand instinctively moved toward her Glock.

"I'm Gerard Ernst," the man said, stepping into the block of sunlight streaming in through the open door. "Elora said you're with the FBI?"

His tall frame was slightly stooped with age, although Charlie could see that he moved nimbly enough for a man of his age and that his eyes were sharp and curious.

"Yes, I'm Agent Day and this is Agent Flynn," she said. "We're investigating a homicide."

Ernst's eyes flicked past her to where Ludwig stood on the porch. The German Shepherd remained still and alert as if he knew he was now on duty.

"Are you here to perform a search?" Ernst asked.

The high priest didn't seem to be unduly alarmed by the idea, only curious about the dog's presence.

"We're only here to ask a few questions," Charlie said. "Ludwig just came along for the ride."

"Search and rescue dogs really are amazing," Ernst said. "Although what you're looking for in this house can't be scented or even seen."

Charlie raised an eyebrow.

"I'm sorry?"

"Sometimes the truth is the hardest thing to find. Much more difficult than tracking down something solid, such as a body. Don't you think, Agent Day?"

Before Charlie could formulate a response to the strange statement, he turned to Elora.

"Bring our guests some tea, my dear," he said. "And some water, I think, for Agent Ludwig."

"No, we can't stay," Charlie said, suddenly eager to get out of the house, which had an earthy, smoky scent that she couldn't quite place. "I just have a few questions for you."

Producing a placid smile, Ernst inclined his head.

"Ask whatever you like, Agent Day. You said you were working on a homicide? And you think it has something to do with me or with Hammerling House?"

"A woman was killed on Monday night," Charlie said. "The victim's identity hasn't been officially released yet, but her name has already been leaked by the media, so..."

Ernst held up a hand to stop her.

"Let me save you the ethical dilemma," he said. "I am dear friends with Nicole Prescott's mother and I'm painfully aware that the poor girl has been killed."

He leaned closer as if he was about to share a secret.

"Nicole was going to join the Circle, you know. Of course, she was a new seeker and had many questions. But I'm sure she would have followed in the footsteps of her mother and her sister if the Goddess had granted her more time."

"Nicole was preparing to join the coven?" Charlie asked. "And what do you mean by *following in the footsteps of her sister*? Are you saying that Natasha was a member, too?"

The old man nodded.

"Yes, Nicole had come back to find out what happened to

her sister and came to Hammerling House seeking answers."

"And did she find the answer here?" Charlie asked. "Could that be why she was killed?"

Ernst sighed.

"And here it goes again. History repeating itself," he said.

His voice was no longer placid.

"Do some seeking of your own and you'll find that the Tempest Grove police already looked within our little group when Natasha went missing," he said. "But they should have been looking at those who are working against us."

Charlie wasn't sure she understood.

"Are you saying Natasha was taken by someone with a grudge against the Circle? And that's why Nicole was killed?"

Before Ernst could reply, Ludwig lifted his nose into the air and barked once, then lunged off the porch before Bailey could tighten her hold on his leash.

As the leash was pulled out of her hand, she made a grab for it but lost her footing on the rain-slick porch.

"Ludwig!" she called as she went down on one knee.

Scrambling back to her feet, Bailey ran after the German Shepherd, following him around the corner of the house.

After a momentary hesitation, Charlie ran after them.

By the time she caught up to Bailey, the handler was leading an excited Ludwig back toward the front of the house.

"He was barking at the fence back there," she said,

nodding to a wooden fence at the edge of the property that bore a large *No Trespassing* sign. "But he hadn't signaled yet. He must have picked up on a scent somewhere beyond it."

She looked hopefully at Charlie.

"Can we find a way to get over it?"

"I wouldn't suggest that."

Charlie turned around to see Ernst and Elora.

"That fence separates our property from Chumbley's Organic Farm," Ernst said. "Abner Chumbley owns the farm, and he doesn't abide trespassers. He carries a gun to make sure everybody knows it."

He rolled his eyes.

"Old Chumbley has also made it quite clear that he doesn't like *witches and devil-worshippers*, as he calls us. There's no way he'd let any of us in there."

"Abner's a lost cause," Elora agreed. "But his son Vern has always been nice to me. You could see if he'll let you in."

Bailey turned eager eyes to her at the suggestion, but Charlie was already shaking her head and reaching for her phone, which had started buzzing in her pocket.

Her pulse jumped as she read the incoming message.

"If we need to search the Chumbley Farm we'll get a search warrant," she said, backing toward the driveway. "Now, we've got to get going."

Hurrying Bailey and Ludwig back to the Expedition, she waited until they were settled in, then showed Bailey the text she'd gotten from Opal Fitzgerald.

We got DNA back on the bones from the ravine. I think you're going to want to see this right away. And then you're going to want to call one of your emergency task force meetings.

* * *

Charlie stood at the front of the BAU conference room, staring down at the open folder, still stunned by the results of the DNA analysis of the bones collected from the ravine.

After reading Opal's text the previous afternoon, she had raced back to her office to review the startling results.

Just as the M.E. had predicted, she had immediately requested Calloway's approval to pull together a task force.

She'd then spent the rest of the day arranging an emergency kick-off meeting with the team of agents and forensics experts she had hastily assembled, jumping at Terrance Gage's offer to use his department's conference room at Quantico.

Now, as the task force members began to file into the room and take their seats around the table, Charlie shuffled through the stack of folders on the podium.

Opening a file labeled *Crime Scene Photos: Nicole Webster,* she flipped past a collection of horrifying images. Still shots of the body hanging from the old Witch's Tree were mixed in with images of the surrounding woods and nearby highway.

She studied a photo of the historical marker off Shackleton Highway, then impulsively turned and wrote *Operation Hexenbaum* on the smartboard at the front of the room.

"Okay, I think everyone is here, so let's get started," Charlie said, looking around the table.

Bridget, Gage, and Argus filled the chairs along the left side of the conference table, while Baily Flynn, Vivian Burke, and Jason Chan filled the seats on the right. Opal Fitzgerald was at the end.

"We've got a few task force members who are joining us via conference call," Charlie added.

She gestured to two video feeds on the screen behind her.

"Chief Fitzgerald and Detective Kirby are joining us from Wisteria Falls," she said. "And Detective Landon is joining us from Tempest Grove."

Cecil lifted a hand in greeting while Kirby sat beside him wearing a stoic expression. Landon appeared to be scrolling through his phone and didn't look up.

"We'll start off with the main reason I called this meeting," Charlie said. "It's also the main reason Calloway approved this task force."

She cleared her throat.

"The DNA results came back from the bones we recovered in the ravine out by Moonstone Cavern," she said. "And I've asked Vivian Burke to review the findings with us."

Motioning for the forensics examiner to join her at the podium, she waited as Vivian got to her feet and carried a thick folder to the front of the room.

"I should first remind you that the bones we recovered had been in the ravine for many years," she said, placing the folder on the podium. "They had been picked over by the local wildlife, and scattered, so we didn't have a complete set of skeletal remains to work with."

"Luckily, we did recover a femur that had been covered by a solid layer of dirt and debris. The lab was able to extract DNA from the femur and a profile was obtained and entered into CODIS. I'm pleased to say a match was found."

The forensics examiner paused as a murmur of excitement sounded around the table.

"The DNA extracted from the femur was an exact mitochondrial DNA match to Nicole Webster," she added.

"How could the profile exactly match Nicole?"

Landon had finally looked up from his phone.

"In the case of sisters, or with a mother and daughter, their mitochondrial DNA sequences are identical," Vivian explained. "So, the DNA match to Nicole tells us that the femur belonged to either her mother, a sister, or a daughter."

"Nicole's mother is alive, and she had no children, so they must be her sister's remains," Bridget said, sounding relieved. "We've finally found Natasha. Of course, it's terribly sad but it gives her family closure, and-"

Vivian cleared her throat, glaring at Bridget.

"I'm not finished," she said, adjusting her glasses. "The femur wasn't the only bone that yielded DNA. There was also a jawbone recovered that contained mitochondrial DNA from a second unrelated female. And a tooth from a third."

She paused and looked around the room.

"In total, we believe the ravine contained the remains of

at least three different females, only one of which was a DNA match to Nicole Webster. There was no match to the other two women in CODIS."

A startled silence fell over the room as the task force members processed the information.

"The lab is working to date the remains in an effort to determine how long they've been in the ravine," Vivian said. "They should also be able to estimate how old the victims were at the time of their death, but it could take a while."

"And the evidence response team wasn't able to find any clothing other than the high school jacket?" Bridget asked, turning to look at Jason Chan. "Or anything else that might help us identify these other two women?"

The evidence response team leader shook his head.

"Unfortunately, the area is full of wildlife," he said. "It was a miracle we found that jacket intact. We could go back and dig down further, maybe look in burrows and nests, but I'm not sure it would do any good."

The room fell silent at the grisly image his words conjured, and then Terrance Gage spoke up for the first time.

"So, we've got a serial killer in Tempest Grove," he said bluntly. "I'm betting our unsub killed Nicole because she found out who abducted and killed her sister. Or maybe she was just getting close. Do you have any viable suspects yet?"

He was looking at Charlie.

"The prime suspect in Natasha's disappearance was a

man named Calvin Hirsch," Charlie said. "He was a coach at Tempest Grove High when she and Nicole were freshmen."

Looking at the video feed on the screen, she saw Landon appeared to be back on his phone.

"Detective Landon, what did Hirsch say?" Charlie asked. "Did he have an alibi for Monday night?"

Landon glanced up with a frown.

"Uh, I didn't get a chance to go out there yet," he said. "I was planning to go talk to him after this meeting. I'll let you know how it goes."

Doubting he would do any such thing, she turned to Argus Murphy, who was typing away on his computer.

"Argus, I went into my office this morning and my desk was practically empty. I thought I'd been robbed," Charlie said. "Then I heard you'd come by and picked up some files."

Bridget's fellow profiler and behavioral analyst looked up from his keyboard with a distracted frown and scratched at his thatch of ginger hair.

"Sorry, I guess I should have told you I was taking the files," he said. "But you weren't there, and I wanted to get started entering the data from the Tempest Grove PD."

He lifted an impatient hand to push back his glasses.

"I need the data from the initial investigation into Natasha's disappearance as well as the current investigation into Nicole's homicide," he explained. "That way I can run a cluster analysis on both. It'll help us identify connections between the crimes and victims so we can come up with a list of possible suspects."

"Well, you're welcome to the files if it'll help us identify suspects," she said, noting the look of relief on Bailey Flynn's face at the thought of the pile-free desk. "And I'm hoping we'll be getting a profile soon, too."

She checked her watch and looked around the table.

"Okay, anything else before we close out the meeting?"

Opal raised her hand.

"We'll need to tell Natasha's parents," she said.

Looking at Bridget, Charlie raised an eyebrow.

"Are you up for another trip out to Tempest Grove?" she asked. "Joelle and Rowan Prescott need to be told."

"Yes, and Faye, as well," Bridget agreed. "She's at her brother's house now. They're planning Nicole's funeral."

"And when are you planning to hold a press conference?" Opal added. "Once the news gets out about the bones in that ravine belonging to Natasha, as well as two other victims, the press will go wild. News of a Tempest Grove serial killer will be everywhere."

She shot a heaven-help-me glance at Charlie.

"Cecil told me a radio DJ over in Tempest Grove was the first news source to identify Nicole Webster as the victim found in the Witch's Tree. The guy completely ignored our request to wait for next-of-kin to be notified."

"You must mean Spike Oswald over at WARP 102.5 FM," Landon interjected. "That man's got a few screws loose."

The detective shook his head.

"I was fresh out of the police academy when Natasha went missing," he said. "I remember listening to Spike most mornings. It's hard to believe he's still kicking around."

He leaned forward as if he'd had a sudden idea.

"You know, it was Spike who got people worked up about the Circle. I think he likes to stir up trouble. In fact, he was one of the main voices calling for blood back when Natasha Prescott went missing.

"He blamed the Circle for her disappearance and did everything but gather a mob and grab a pitchfork trying to run the group out of town. No one really knew anything about them until Spike Oswald started spreading rumors."

Charlie cocked her head.

"What kind of rumors?"

"Oh, just crazy stuff, like the Circle must have sacrificed Natasha and burned her body," he said. "Most people would know better, but some people may believe it."

As the task force meeting came to an end and the members began to gather their belongings, Charlie jotted down a note to herself to follow-up with Spike Oswald.

The man had a morning show, a horde of fervent listeners, and a bitter grudge against the Circle and its members, which included Joelle Prescott and her daughters, both of whom were now dead.

I'd say that definitely makes Spike Oswald a person of interest.

CHAPTER ELEVEN

Bridget slid her laptop into her bag and slung the strap over her shoulder as she stood and headed toward the conference room door. She stopped next to Charlie, who was gathering files from the podium, intending to ask where Hale had been over the last few days, then hesitated.

The agent had been prickly lately when it came to Hale, and she likely wouldn't want to discuss her love interest's absence in front of the rest of the team.

"I'll head out to the Prescott house now," Bridget said instead. "Then you'll be free to hold that press conference."

Charlie nodded.

"The sooner the better," she agreed. "The news about Natasha's remains and the DNA results won't stay quiet for long. Although, you shouldn't go out there on your own."

She turned to the video feed from the Tempest Grove Police Department's conference room, which was still active.

"What about you, Detective Landon? Are you available to go with Bridget to notify Natasha's next of kin?"

Landon's eyes widened and he quickly shook his head.

"I already promised you I'd go question Coach Hirsch," he said quickly. "I was just on my way."

As Landon quickly switched off his feed, Charlie turned her attention to the second video feed, which still showed two figures seated behind the long wooden table in the Wisteria Falls Police Department's conference room.

"Cecil, I realize Natasha Prescott's parents live in Tempest Grove," Charlie said. "But their daughter's body was found in Wisteria Falls' jurisdiction, so maybe you or Kirby should go along with Bridget?"

Cecil nodded his approval without glancing at the woman beside him. He took no notice of Kirby's sullen expression or the way her back had stiffened.

"That's a good idea, Charlie," the police chief said. "Bridget, you let Detective Kirby know what time you'll arrive at the Prescott place, and she'll meet you over there."

Irritation flashed in Kirby's eyes, and for a minute Bridget thought the detective might object, but she remained silent.

"Good, then it's settled," Charlie said. "And in the meantime, I'll work on scheduling the official press conference. Until then, no leaking and no giving unauthorized interviews to the press."

Sensing she'd been dismissed, Bridget hurried into the hall after Terrance Gage. Her boss had seemed distracted during the task force meeting, not saying much, and he jumped as Bridget put a hand on his arm.

"I know I was the one who volunteered to notify Natasha's parents about the DNA results," she said once she had his attention. "But I was thinking you could come with me. We can discuss the profile on the drive out to Tempest Grove."

Bridget didn't add that the drive would also give her a chance to ask him about Estelle Malone's parole hearing.

She'd been meaning to follow up with him since their conversation on Monday but had been preoccupied with the investigation into Nicole Webster's murder.

Once they were in Gage's big Navigator heading away from Quantico, she turned to him and studied his tense profile.

"You seemed distracted in the task force meeting," she said. "Are you worried about Estelle's hearing?"

Shooting her a sideways glance, he raised an eyebrow.

"You're a psychologist, but you're not *my* psychologist," he said. "If I need a therapy session, I'll go see Faye."

He cracked a thin smile to soften the sarcastic remark.

"In any case, I'm fine."

It was Bridget's turn to lift an eyebrow.

She'd worked with Gage for years and knew him well enough by now to see that he was anxious.

"Maybe you're fine," she said, deciding to try a different tactic. "But what about Russell? How's he handling this?"

The question prompted a heavy sigh.

"That's hard to say," he admitted. "For the last two years, I've taken Russell to see his mother on a regular basis, at his insistence. But lately, something's been off."

"What do you mean?" Bridget asked.

Gage rubbed a nervous hand over his smooth head.

"Well, he's been really quiet after the visits," he said. "I've tried to talk to him, but he's not telling me anything."

There was a hint of panic in his voice.

"I'm not sure he's ready to live with Estelle again," he said. "And I'm not sure I'm ready to let him go."

Reaching over the console, Bridget put a hand on his arm.

"You're going to be fine. And so is Russell," she assured him. "He's a resilient kid. And if Estelle does get out and is granted custody of Russell, she'll need a strong support network. You and Kyla can still be a big part of Russell's life."

Gage didn't argue, but as he merged onto the highway, she saw doubt in his eyes and knew he hadn't been convinced.

They used the next hour to walk through the details of Natasha's disappearance and Nicole's murder in detail.

As they pulled onto the exit for Tempest Grove, Gage suddenly leaned forward to get a better look out the window.

"Isn't that the guy Opal mentioned in the meeting?" he said, pointing up to a billboard for WARP 102.5 FM on the side of the road.

A twelve-foot-tall man with a white crewcut and a thick handlebar mustache stared down at Bridget.

"Looks as if Spike Oswald is quite the celebrity around here," Gage said as he switched on the radio.

Tuning it to WARP 102.5 FM, he quickly lowered the volume as Spike Oswald's voice boomed through the vehicle.

"...and local police have yet to name a suspect in the murder of Nicole Webster, whose body was found near Moonstone Cavern on Monday morning."

A shiver of distaste ran up Bridget's back at the DJ's aggressive, derogatory tone.

"Why is it that our police force had to call in the FBI?" he barked. "Why can't they take care of business in their own backyards? All you listeners out there know who's really got to be behind this, don't you? Cause I sure have my suspicions."

Gage pointed to the speaker and sighed.

"Wait for it..."

"Tell me, have the Tempest Grove PD even talked to the witches or warlocks or whatever they want to call themselves over at the Circle of Light? Cause in my mind, they've been behind this whole thing from the very start."

Impulsively reaching forward, Bridget switched off the radio. She'd heard enough of Spike Oswald's angry rant.

She needed a few minutes of quiet and calm. She needed to prepare herself for the task ahead.

* * *

The driveway leading up to the Prescott house was filled with cars when Gage pulled onto Forester way.

"Park along the curb," Bridget instructed as she looked around for Detective Kirby's official vehicle. "I don't think Kirby's here yet. Let's go wait on the porch."

By the time they made it to the front door, Kirby's black Dodge Charger was pulling in behind Gage's Navigator.

"You sure you're ready for this?" Bridget asked the dark-haired detective as she approached.

Kirby didn't respond. She just leaned past Bridget and rapped twice on the door.

Seconds later a red-eyed Faye was opening the door, revealing a roomful of people behind her.

"Joelle and Rowan have had non-stop visitors all day stopping to pay respects and leave casseroles," Faye said.

Stepping back to let the newcomers inside, she leaned forward and lowered her voice as Bridget stepped inside.

"You'd think these people would know better," Faye said. "It's as if they think we're having a party, and-"

Her words were interrupted by an icy voice.

"We're leaving now."

Bridget saw that a trio of women had come up behind Faye. Based on their stony expressions, it was clear they'd overheard the therapist's remarks.

"Oh...yes, well, thank you for bringing over the casserole," Faye said, suddenly flustered under the women's offended gaze. "I know Rowan and Joelle appreciate your prayers."

As the visitors left, Faye rolled her eyes.

"They work with Joelle at the high school," she muttered. "Principal Corwin was here, too. Likely came to find out when she'll be back at work. All her students love her class."

When she looked up, Faye finally noticed the look of

empathy and regret on Bridget's face.

"What is it?" she asked. "What's happened?"

Leading the therapist onto the back porch, Bridget gathered Rowan and Joelle, and once again told them that a body had been found.

"DNA results have confirmed it's Natasha," she said. "We're still trying to determine how long she's been there but...well, now you'll be able to lay her to rest."

Joelle looked at Rowan, who stood stoically by her side, then took his hand.

"We'll have a double funeral," she said. "After all these years, our girls will finally be back together."

As Bridget started to turn away, wanting to give the family privacy, Kirby stepped forward.

"I'm sorry for your loss, Mr. and Mrs. Prescott. But I need to ask you a few questions."

Putting a protective arm around his wife's shoulders, Rowan frowned at the detective, then looked toward Bridget.

"Who is *she*?"

"I'm Detective Kirby with the Wisteria Falls Police Department. Our department responded to the call about your daughter, Nicole. We were with the FBI when they discovered Natasha's remains."

Bridget put a hand on Kirby's elbow.

"Why don't we give them time to-"

"No," Rowan said, glaring at Kirby. "I don't want *time*. I want to know who killed my daughters. Can you tell me that, Detective? Can you tell me who killed my girls?"

Taking an involuntary step backward, Kirby bumped into Gage, who reached out to steady her.

"The investigation is ongoing," she said, shaking off Gage's hand. "And any information you have could help us. Do you know who may have harmed your daughters?"

Rowan gave an angry laugh.

"I already told the police what I knew," he said. "But they didn't do anything about it. I told them it was probably Coach Hirsch. The man was at the school with Natasha every day. And he also attended Circle meetings, although he kept that a secret. Did anyone ever ask him why?"

Stepping away from her husband, Joelle shook her head.

"Coach Hirsch wouldn't hurt a fly," she protested. "I know the man. I'm not sure who started that rumor, but I bet it was that idiot Spike Oswald. He's the one who got everybody in town worked up about the Circle, too."

She turned to Kirby.

"If you want to know who killed my girls, then go talk to the folks at the Tempest Grove Baptist Church. They all hate the Circle. Maybe someone got mad when Natasha quit the congregation. Maybe Pastor Parnell didn't want the rest of his flock following her example."

Joelle ignored the dirty look her husband was giving her.

"That's insane," Rowan said. "He's been the senior pastor for almost twenty years without complaint. Are you seriously suggesting he *killed* Nikki?"

"I'm saying that I always had a bad feeling about Pastor Parnell. But you never would listen," Joelle replied, refusing to back down. "Sure, he's a pillar of the community. But that only means he'd have a lot to lose if anyone found out he was involved with Natasha's disappearance."

Clenching his fists in frustration, Rowan opened his mouth to reply, then snapped it shut again.

Without another word, he crossed the back lawn and pushed through the gate.

CHAPTER TWELVE

Terrance Gage slipped on his dark sunglasses and followed Bridget and Kirby back to the street, ignoring the stares they were getting from a group of the Prescotts' neighbors and friends who had congregated on the porch. Stopping next to his Navigator, he turned to Kirby.

"You need to work on your timing, Detective. Those people in there just lost two of their children. Can you even imagine what they're going through? The loss they must be feeling?"

He inhaled sharply as an image of Russell came to mind. His foster son was about the same age as Natasha had been when she'd gone missing. What would it be like to lose him?

It's likely I'll know soon enough if Estelle has her way.

He pushed back the thought as Kirby's face turned pink.

"I was just trying to do my job," she said. "That's what they want. They don't care about nice manners and nice words. They want us to find whoever killed their daughters."

"Let's just get going," Bridget said before Gage could

respond. "I want to follow-up on the information Detective Kirby got out of Joelle."

Gage cocked his head.

"And what information would that be?"

"Joelle said that she suspects Pastor Parnell or someone at his church might have had a motive to harm her daughters."

She turned to Kirby.

"Would you like to come with us to the church?" Bridget asked. "You seem to have a knack for getting people to say what they think. It could come in handy."

"Are you serious?" Gage asked. "You really want to go question the local pastor?"

Bridget nodded.

"I saw in the case files that Andrew Parnell was the youth pastor when Nicole and Natasha were teenagers," she said. "From what I remember, he was fresh out of the seminary when Natasha disappeared. He was questioned multiple times when she first went missing."

Glancing over at Kirby, she raised an eyebrow.

"So, you want to join us at the church?"

"I can't," the detective said. "I've got to get back to Wisteria Falls. I've got another conference to get to. This one's at my kid's school."

She flashed a wry smile and headed for her car.

After watching the detective's Charger disappear around the corner, Bridget turned to Gage.

"Okay, then. Let's go to church."

Fifteen minutes later, Gage was turning the big gray

Navigator onto Liberty Parkway.

He spotted the tall, graceful spire of the church in the distance and followed the winding road toward a large white building, which was surrounded by neatly arranged flowerbeds and tall, shady trees.

Following Bridget into the hushed interior of the sanctuary, Gage looked around at the empty altar and pews.

When he crossed to the church office and pushed open the door, an older woman with bright blue eyes, snow-white curls, and soft, finely lined skin smiled a greeting.

The nameplate on her polished wooden desk read *Merry Corwin, Church Secretary.*

"Good morning, Ms. Corwin," Gage said. "We're with the FBI and we need to speak to Pastor Parnell."

The church secretary's smile didn't falter as she stood.

Gage noted that the woman didn't seem to be surprised by the sudden arrival of two FBI agents.

It's almost as if she was expecting us.

"Pastor Parnell is in his office," Merry said. "Follow me."

As she padded down the carpeted hall leading into the administrative offices, she spoke over her shoulder.

"The police interviewed the pastor a dozen times or more when Natasha Prescott first went missing, you know," she confided. "So, when I heard they'd found her sister hanging from the Witch's Tree, I figured he'd be questioned again, although it's really just a waste of your time. He knows nothing about it, I'm sure."

She tutted in disapproval.

"I knew there'd be trouble when that girl came back."

"What girl?" Bridget asked. "You mean Nicole Webster?"

Merry shrugged.

"Doesn't matter if you call her Nicole Webster or Nikki Prescott," she said. "She was clearly a very disturbed young woman right from the start. There were even rumors that she had done something to her own sister, although I never could bring myself to believe it."

Gage bit back a sharp reply.

Spike Oswald is likely responsible for spreading the rumors, not Merry. The woman is only repeating what she's heard.

"It's just such a *shame*," Merry continued. "But you don't think the pastor could have..."

A long shadow fell over them before the church secretary could finish her sentence.

Pastor Parnell stood in the doorway to his office.

He was tall and lanky in a dark suit and white button-up shirt that washed out his pale, freckled skin. Shaggy brown hair fell over his forehead and skimmed his starched collar, clashing with his otherwise clean-cut appearance.

"These folks are from the-"

"I know who they are," Parnell quickly cut in. "You can go now, Merry. I'll take it from here."

He led them into his office and waved them toward chairs at a cherrywood table by the window, waiting until the door had closed behind Merry before speaking.

"Agent Bishop, it's an honor to meet you in person," he said with a thin smile, although he didn't offer his hand. "I feel as if I should already know you after seeing you on the news again and again in the past few years."

Bridget returned the smile and then cleared her throat.

"Yes, well, this is my boss, Special Agent Terrance Gage with the FBI's BAU," she said. "As you've probably heard, a woman's body was recently discovered in the woods near Moonstone Cavern. We've identified her as Nicole Webster."

Gage remembered Merry's words.

"Of course, you may remember her as Nikki Prescott," he said. "Back when you were her youth pastor."

Parnell gave a solemn nod of his head.

"Yes, I did hear on the radio that poor Nikki was found out in the woods late Sunday evening," he admitted. "Our only comfort is knowing she's with our heavenly father now."

Closing his eyes, he moved his lips in silent prayer.

A look of impatience tightened Gage's face.

"I understand Nicole and her sister Natasha both attended this church regularly when you were the youth pastor," Gage said as soon as Parnell had lifted his head. "And that you were questioned in Natasha's disappearance at the time."

The statement was met with silence. After an awkward pause, Parnell frowned.

"Was that a question?" he asked. "I thought you said that *Nikki* had been found. Why are you asking about Natasha?"

He squared his shoulders and straightened his jacket.

"You know, when Natasha went missing, the local police questioned me. More than once actually. I think you'll find they determined I had *nothing* to do with her disappearance. Just like I had *nothing* to do with Nicole's death."

, Bridget jumped in before Gage could reply.

"We're not accusing you of anything, Pastor Parnell. We're just investigating every angle."

She kept her tone calm and matter-of-fact.

"We have to consider that whoever abducted Natasha may have targeted her sister. You knew them both, is that right?"

The pastor nodded.

"Yes, I did," he agreed. "Rowan Prescott has been a lifelong member of the church and the twins had been in the youth group since they were able to walk."

He produced a sad smile.

"But in the weeks leading up to her disappearance, Natasha had stopped coming to our youth activities. There were rumors she'd gotten involved in *the Circle*."

The words were accompanied by a grimace of distaste.

"Then, after Natasha went missing, Nicole stopped coming to the church altogether. She got lost somewhere along the way," he said. "Her body was still here in Tempest Grove, but her heart was gone, along with her sister."

"When was the last time you saw Nicole?" Bridget asked.

Parnell dropped his eyes and fidgeted with the sleeve of his jacket as if stalling for time.

"She came to service last Sunday," he finally admitted. "I recognized her right away. I was surprised to see her."

"And did you speak to her?"

Watching his eyes, Bridget thought she saw a flash of emotion. Was it irritation? Or maybe guilt?

"I didn't get a chance," he said. "We never spoke. But I'm sure it was her. She was definitely there."

"Do you have any idea who may have abducted Natasha Prescott?" Bridget asked, suddenly angry at the pastor, although she couldn't say why. "Or who may have killed Nicole?"

Parnell hesitated, then shook his head.

"You don't like the Circle, do you, Pastor Parnell?" Gage asked as they headed toward the door. "In fact, from what I've heard, you think they're all sinners. Maybe even devil-worshippers. Am I right?"

"I think they're misguided," Parnell corrected. "And considering my calling, I worry for their immortal souls."

He excused himself as Merry appeared to show them out.

"You're wasting your time here," Merry said as she stood by the door. "It's Calvin Hirsch you should be visiting, not the pastor."

She looked over her shoulder as if to make sure her boss wasn't listening in, then lowered her voice.

"I hate to spread rumors. I mean, I have nothing against Mr. Hirsch. He and my husband used to work together. Of course, that was years ago, before Brian retired."

"But I'm sure you already know that Coach Hirsch was a suspect in Natasha's disappearance, and when I saw him talking to a woman last week, and then realized it was Nikki...well, I thought maybe I should tell someone. And who better to tell than the FBI?"

Gage frowned down at Merry.

"You saw Nicole and Hirsch together last week?"

Nodding eagerly, Merry followed them onto the sidewalk.

"I guess I should have said something at the time," she admitted. "It's a bit too little, too late now, isn't it?"

Gage didn't reply as his phone buzzed in his pocket.

His stomach dropped as he checked the display.

"I've got to go," he said to Bridget, already moving toward the parking lot. "I'm needed at home."

* * *

After dropping Bridget off at her Explorer, Gage steered his Navigator back toward Stafford County, trying not to overthink Kyla's text.

I'm worried about Russell. We need to talk ASAP.

The text could mean almost anything. She was probably having the same fears and worries about Russell that he had.

After all, Gage and Kyla had managed to create a new family for Russell out of the wreckage Estelle had left behind.

Now, Estelle was threatening to tear the boy's world apart again. No wonder Kyla was panicking. She was his aunt, and the only connection Russell still had to his father.

If Estelle banished her from Russell's life it would be like she'd banished Kenny from his life, too.

And Russell had already dealt with enough mental anguish and trauma for a boy his age. There was no telling

127

what he might do if pushed into another unstable situation.

Teenagers could be erratic and unpredictable at the best of times, unable to make connections between actions and the possible consequences.

And if Gage was honest with himself, he'd been worried about Russell for several weeks.

His foster son had been acting strangely even before he'd learned his mother might be paroled. But he now seemed more withdrawn and secretive than ever.

Gage was still brooding when he turned into the driveway on Mansfield Place and saw Argus' white SUV.

"*What the hell is he doing here?*" he murmured to himself as he nosed the Navigator into his garage.

Hurrying into the kitchen, he saw that Argus had settled himself at the table by the window, along with his laptop and a stack of files.

Kyla stood at the sink refilling Sarge's water bowl although the big tomcat was nowhere to be seen.

"Where's Russell?" Gage asked.

"He's in his room," Argus said.

He didn't look up from his computer.

"I wasn't asking you," Gage snapped. "And what are you doing here, anyway?"

"You said we could work on the profile this afternoon, but you weren't in your office so I figured we could work here."

Gesturing to the stack of files, he beamed at Gage.

"It's taken most of the day, but the data set is complete."

"That's going to have to wait for later," Gage said as he

saw the look in Kyla's eyes. "I need you to go."

Argus stared at him in surprise, then jumped up from the table. He spoke quickly as he shoved his computer in his bag and gathered his files.

"My initial algorithm is pointing to a suspect," he said. "It's the guy Charlie was talking about earlier. That track coach Calvin Hirsch. It seems that all the data points to him."

"Okay, I've got it," Gage said. "We'll go through everything later. Right now, I need some space."

Once Argus had gone, and they were in the room alone, Gage crossed to the sink and pulled Kyla against his chest.

"I'm worried about our boy," she said, letting her head fall onto his shoulder. "I have a bad feeling about this parole hearing. I have a feeling we could lose Russell forever."

"It'll be okay," Gage soothed. "Everything will be fine."

Pulling back, he looked down into her sad, brown eyes.

"Why don't I pour us some wine and we can talk through everything? We can come up with a game plan."

He gestured toward the hall.

"You can choose the music while I get the wine."

Kyla nodded and headed into the living room.

As Gage crossed to the wine rack, he saw Argus had dropped a folder. It fell open as he bent to pick it up.

The high school yearbook photo of Natasha Prescott that had been used in her missing person poster slipped out.

He studied the photo of the fourteen-year-old teen who he now knew had been killed and dumped in a ravine not long after the photo had been taken.

You never know what might happen. Sometimes the people you love walk out your door and they're never seen again.

Dropping the folder onto the table, he thought of what Argus had told him, then reached in his pocket for his phone.

If there really was a chance the track coach was the one who'd killed the teenager in that photo, he couldn't just sit on the information. He needed to let someone know.

Charlie answered on the second ring.

"Argus tells me his initial algorithm points to Hirsch," Gage said. "I think you should bring him in for questioning."

"You and everyone else I've spoken with," she said. "Hale and I are actually heading over to Hirsch's place now to meet up with Landon. I'll let you know what I find out."

CHAPTER THIRTEEN

Calvin Hirsch tightened a length of rope around the small bundle of black walnut branches and secured it with a slipknot. Hefting the bundle onto his shoulder, he looked up at the sprawling branches, idly wishing for the fall, when the Goddess would send down a rain of hard-coated walnuts for him to gather and eat.

Turning on the worn wooden heel of his boot, he started back through the forest, satisfied that the gathered branches would make a profitable batch of handcrafted wands.

Each branch had been selected based on its unique pattern of knots, burls, and blemishes. They would each be stripped of bark before he carved, sanded, stained, and sealed them.

Prior to selling the finished products, he would consecrate each wand by purifying and energizing it with the four elements of earth, air, fire, and water.

The process would take weeks, but he was in no rush. His life was no longer dictated by alarm clocks, time clocks, daily planners, or yearly calendars.

Not as it once had been when he'd been a teacher and

track coach at Tempest Grove High School.

That had ended long ago, and now he operated on the earth's clock. The rising and the falling of the sun was his only reference to passing hours and days, while the blossoming and then withering of the forest informed him as to the passing months and years.

He moved east at a quick pace and was soon back on Arcana Avenue, nearing the gate to his own property.

Lowering the bundle of branches, he secured it under one arm, then opened the latch.

Before he could step through, a voice spoke up behind him.

"Mr. Hirsch? Can we have a word with you?"

He turned slowly, careful to make no sudden moves, and saw Matthew Landon standing a few yards away.

The fit young man who had once run a 400-meter race at a respectable best of 50.5 seconds, looked as if he had grown soft and slow in the last three decades.

Hirsch decided he'd be able to outrun him if it came to that, although the gun under Landon's jacket made it unlikely he'd get away if the man really wanted to stop him.

"I'm Detective Landon with the Tempest Grove PD," he said as if the two had never met. "And this is Special Agent Charlie Day with the FBI and her colleague Special Agent Tristan Hale."

"And what does the FBI want with me?" Hirsch asked although he was pretty sure he already knew the answer.

The blonde agent stepped forward.

"We're in Tempest Grove investigating the recent

homicide of Nicole Webster," she said. "And we've had a report that you were seen with her last week."

"Nicole's...dead?"

The words stuck in his dry throat.

"When did that happen?" he asked. "I saw Nicole in town...not long ago, and she..."

He shook his head, trying to think, trying to remember how many sunrises had come and gone since then.

"I'm not sure exactly when..."

Landon nodded as if he understood.

"Perhaps we can go inside," he suggested. "Maybe you can tell us what you two spoke about?"

Stepping back, Hirsch allowed Landon and the two FBI agents to walk past him through the gate.

He followed them to his small bungalow and then fumbled with the lock. He rarely had visitors anymore and remembered too late that he only had two chairs, so they all remained standing.

"What did you talk about with Nicole?" Landon demanded.

The question was clearly an accusation.

"She said she'd come back to find out what happened to her sister," Hirsch said in a weak voice, already knowing he wouldn't be believed. "She told me she knew someone had taken Natasha and that...that it wasn't me."

He saw doubt in the three faces before him.

Three is a powerful number.

The thought echoed nonsensically in his mind.

"So, you didn't take Natasha?" Landon asked, stepping

close enough for Hirsch to smell his pine-scented aftershave. "And you weren't the one who killed her?"

"Natasha's dead?" Hirsch asked. "You finally found her?"

Landon hesitated, but the truth was written on his face, and in the angry looks the FBI agents were aiming his way.

Dropping his head into his hands, Hirsch squeezed his eyes shut, trying to block out images of the two lovely young sisters who had ruined his life, through no fault of their own.

Now they were both dead, unable to speak the truth, and he was a lonely old man who would once again be accused of terrible crimes he hadn't committed.

Nikki Prescott had been one of the only people in town who hadn't wanted to come after him with a pitchfork after her sister went missing. One of the only ones who had defended him when people like Spike Oswald had been calling for his head.

And when he'd found out she'd returned to Tempest Grove the previous winter, he'd been tempted to go see her. He'd been tempted to tell her about his suspicions.

Suspicions that had grown over the years as he heard tales of other young women from the Circle going missing. Tales that had come from certain members of the Circle he'd kept in touch with despite his self-exile from the group.

It had all started almost a decade after Natasha had gone missing. A young redhead using the craft name Faustina had joined the coven and then had vanished suddenly without a word of farewell to anyone, leaving her meager belongings behind.

Rumor had it that she'd gone out foraging and had never come back to Hammerling House.

Then, years later, came Zephra.

The woman had looked much younger than her twenty years and her dark red hair had reminded Hirsch of Natasha.

He'd heard from a trustworthy source that the woman had vanished after celebrating the summer solstice. She'd last been seen in front of the high altar in Hammerling Hollow.

A *Book of Shadows* had been found weeks later discarded under a honeysuckle bush. No name had been written inside and no one knew for sure if the book belonged to Zephra.

Although the two women were the only ones he was sure about, he suspected there must have been others.

But Hirsch was no longer an active member of the Circle, and in no position to substantiate the rumors.

And based on the unearned reputation he had as a predator, he was certain that no one in law enforcement would believe him if he told them what he knew.

Certainly not the Tempest Grove PD who had persecuted him unfairly for years and not these FBI agents who had arrived in Tempest Grove decades too late to save Natasha or the other women.

Lifting his head, he raised bitter eyes to Landon.

The man was useless. He and his FBI friends should be hunting down the real killer, but once again they were wasting time harassing the nearest easy target.

"If you have nothing to hide, you won't mind if we look around the place, will you?" Landon asked.

Gesturing to the bundle of branches he'd dropped on the floor when they'd come in, and to the few modest possessions in the small room, Hirsch shrugged.

"Look all you like," he said. "I have very little."

Landon nodded to the agents, and they spread out around the little house. After finding nothing of interest, just as he'd expected, they went out to the yard and began to walk the perimeter of his property.

"I told you, there's nothing to be found," he said, as they circled back to the gate. "I have nothing to hide."

"What about your workshop?" Agent Hale asked. "You mind if we look in there?"

Hirsch thought of his *Book of Shadows*, hidden in the workshop cupboard. What would they think if they found it?

"You okay with us looking in the workshop?" Hale asked again. "Because if you're not, we can–"

"Go ahead," Hirsch said with a sigh. "Just be careful in there. There are several projects I'm working on."

He watched them disappear into the wooden structure where he made his wands and mixed up his potions and tinctures. Sure, there were a few jars of dried herbs and such, but it was all basically harmless.

But at the sound of excited voices, he walked to the doorway and peered inside.

"What's this?" Landon asked.

He held a small poppet in his hand.

The strange doll-like figure was made of sticks and twigs and wore a faded pink dress. A lock of dark red hair had been attached to its tiny walnut head.

"I've never seen that before," Hirsch said slowly, suddenly confused. "Where did you find it?"

"It was lying on this workbench," Charlie said.

She pointed to the poppet, then frowned.

"Put it down, Landon," she ordered. "It may be evidence."

The detective dropped the poppet on the table.

"That looks like human hair," Charlie said. "And hair was missing from Nicole's scalp when her body was found."

"It's just a little poppet," Hirsch said. "They're made to use in spells. I have no idea where that one came from. It isn't mine."

But he could see that they didn't believe him, and this time he couldn't really blame them.

Obviously, someone had left the poppet there for a reason.

It had been meant to be found.

"Calvin Hirsch, I'm arresting you on suspicion of the murder of Nicole Webster," Landon said as he pulled out his handcuffs. "You have the right to remain silent. Anything you say can and will be used against you in a court of law. You have a right to an attorney. If you cannot afford an attorney, one will be appointed for you."

But as Hirsch looked back at the poppet, he had a feeling it was too late for a lawyer and too late to save himself.

* * *

Hirsch woke up the next morning in a jail cell, his back stiff, and his mind foggy after a nearly sleepless night.

What little sleep he had managed had been plagued by nightmares of living poppets with flames for hair.

"Calvin Hirsch?"

A guard stood in the open door of his cell.

"Get your stuff and come on," the man said. "It's your lucky day. You've made bail."

Hirsch knew of no one who would want to bail him out, but he asked no questions as he followed the guard through a series of metal doors and concrete hallways.

After he'd signed a few papers and changed back into the clothes he'd been wearing the day before, a guard waved him through a wide metal door.

He stepped outside, lifted a hand to shield his eyes from the morning sun, and then turned as he heard a voice he thought he recognized.

Joelle Prescott had been waiting for him.

"You aren't here to shoot me, are you?" he asked. "Cause I want you to know that I'm sorry to hear about your daughters. But I had nothing to do with that."

"I know you didn't kill my girls," she said. "And I need you to help me find out who did. That's why I bailed you out."

Hirsch shook his head.

"Oh, no. I can't stay in Tempest Grove," he said. "Not with the curse on me."

"The curse?"

Joelle raised an eyebrow.

"Someone made a poppet and left it in my workshop," he explained. "I guess it must be some kind of curse. The police found it and that's why they arrested me. They plan to use that poppet as evidence I killed your girls."

"What kind of evidence?" Joelle asked.

The idea of telling the woman in front of him about the red hair made him feel sick to his stomach.

"Listen, I need to go home and get some rest," he said. "After that, I'll come find you. We'll talk."

He watched as she turned and walked away, not sure if it was a good idea to tell her about the poppet.

Maybe I should just follow my first instinct and leave town.

But he couldn't leave without his *Book of Shadows*. All the spells, potions, tinctures, rituals, and secrets he had were documented in that book.

No, he would have to go back to Arcana Avenue, despite the curse. And once there, he would try to cleanse the house, to see if he could dispel the dark magic.

But when he pushed through his gate an hour later, he was tired and dehydrated from the long walk home.

"I'll have a cup of tea, and then lie down," he muttered to himself, heading inside. "Once I'm rested, I can cleanse the house and decide what to do next."

Moving to the cupboard, he studied his collection of mason jars, reaching for the feverfew tea, which he often used as a pain killer and sedative.

He heated the water in his kettle over an open flame,

then poured it over the dried tea leaves, inhaling the pungent scent with a wrinkle of his nose.

After letting the leaves steep for a good ten minutes, he drank the hot golden liquid quickly, eager for a nap.

His eyes were heavy and hard to keep open by the time he crawled into his bed.

He didn't wake up when the front door opened, or when his uninvited visitor tripped over the bundle of branches he'd collected the day before.

No, Hirsch didn't wake up until the rope had tightened around his throat. And by that time, it was much too late.

.

CHAPTER FOURTEEN

Fern Creek Road was quiet as Hank pulled Bridget along the sun-warmed sidewalk toward home. Despite the arrest of Calvin Hirsch the day before, she sensed the investigation in Tempest Grove was far from over. There were too many questions still unanswered to consider the case closed just yet.

As she followed Hank up the driveway to her red brick house, Bridget's mind returned to the West Virginian town, running through possible scenarios of the events that had played out on a fateful night almost three decades earlier.

Not the night Natasha Prescott had gone missing but the night her own mother had lost her life in a car crash.

Bridget knew very little about the accident. Only what her father had told her. He said his wife had been coming home late after visiting Nicole at the hospital in Tempest Grove.

She'd lost control of the car and had veered off the road, slamming into a tree. The first responders had been unable to save her, and she'd been pronounced dead at the scene.

Questions swirled through Bridget's mind as she let Hank into the house and followed him into the kitchen.

Why did Mom veer off the road? And what did she know about the man who'd abducted Natasha Prescott? Did she suspect the girl was dead and that Hirsch was her killer?

Pouring Hank's breakfast into his bowl, she listened to his contented munching and allowed herself to contemplate how things would have been different if her mother had lived.

It wasn't a pastime she indulged in very often.

Little good could be done by dwelling on the past, which could never be changed. But she sighed as she pictured her mother sitting at the table beside her.

Would they be discussing the details of the case? Maybe working together on a profile?

Or maybe Mom would have helped Nicole remember what had happened that night. Maybe she would have solved the mystery way back then and Nicole would still be alive now.

Realizing suddenly how quiet and empty the house felt, she reached down and put her hand on Hank, seeking comfort from the warmth of his soft red fur.

Although the Irish setter was good company, she was glad Santino was on his way back from New York. He would be surprised to hear they'd made an arrest in the case already.

She checked the clock on the wall, then retreated to her bedroom, staring into her closet for a long beat before pulling out a spring-green blouse, slim gray pants, and a matching jacket. Thinking of the forecast for rain later in the day, she scooped up a pair of low-heeled boots.

Once she was dressed, and Hank had finished breakfast, they headed to her father's office on Ashburn Avenue.

Earl Ripley was standing outside her father's office talking on the phone when they arrived. The investigator nodded at Bridget as she and Hank slipped past him to the front door.

Stepping inside the office, Bridget saw Daphne sitting behind the reception desk.

"Yes, I'm playing secretary again," her friend complained. "And yes, Paloma is running late...*again*."

Daphne opened the desk drawer and pulled out a treat for Hank, then turned her sea-green eyes on Bridget.

"I don't know what good it is having a hotshot FBI profiler for a best friend if she won't share any inside info with me," she said tartly. "It isn't fair."

She cocked her head.

"I've had to stream the local news from Tempest Grove to find out the latest updates," she complained. "Spike Oswald at WARP 102.5 FM knows more about the case than I do."

Bridget failed to look contrite.

"Did you hear the station is offering a ten-thousand-dollar reward for information leading to the arrest of Nicole Webster's killer?" Daphne asked.

She sighed as she bent to pour water into a bowl for Hank, who had settled in by the window.

"What I want to know is why the station isn't offering a reward for Natasha's safe return?" Daphne asked. "Or are they assuming she's already dead?"

Bridget shrugged.

"I have no idea what Spike Oswald or his bosses over at

WARP 102.5 are assuming," she said, raising an eyebrow in Daphne's direction. "And I'm not going to give you insider information about the status of the investigation, so you can stop fishing."

The door behind her opened, and Ripley stepped inside. Crossing to the desk, he looked down at Daphne with an impatient scowl.

"When's Paloma going to get here?" he asked. "We're supposed to be running surveillance on Mr. Wilson now."

Daphne rewarded the question with her sweetest southern smile. It was a smile Bridget knew well. One that usually preceded a caustic reply.

"I think you need to cool your britches, Ripley."

She punctuated the comment with a flip of her blonde hair.

"I know how much you love those exciting insurance fraud cases, but you're going to have to wait a few more minutes."

Exhaling loudly, she flicked her eyes back to Bridget.

"Some people would rather be tracking an insurance cheat than a murderer," she said. "I just can't understand it."

Her voice rose an octave as if she wanted to make sure Ripley could hear her.

"You know, if I were to find Nicole Webster's killer, I could collect that ten-thousand-dollar reward."

She glanced at Ripley to gauge his reply, but the older man was already shaking his head, unmoved by the temptation.

"I've got my pension and a half-decent paycheck," he muttered. "That'll do me...at least for now."

With a huff, Daphne stood and grabbed her purse.

"Paloma should be here any minute," she said sourly. "I'll go and powder my nose so I'm ready to go."

As she left the room, Ripley turned to Bridget.

"There was something I thought of after our last conversation," he said, speaking in a low, somber voice. "Something I've been wanting to tell you."

His serious tone worried Bridget, and she immediately thought of her father, wondering if perhaps Bob had confided something to the man about his health.

"What is it?" she asked. "Is it my Dad? Is he-"

"No," Ripley said. "It's nothing like that."

Footsteps sounded on the porch and the door swung open to reveal Paloma, loaded down with shopping bags.

"Well, is anyone going to help me?" she asked as both Bridget and Ripley turned to stare at her.

With a grudging scowl on his weathered face, Ripley stomped to the door and allowed Paloma to load most of the bags into his outstretched arms.

He turned and piled them onto the desk just as Daphne came back into the room.

"Ripley, what did you want to tell me?" Bridget asked.

The investigator cocked his head and frowned.

"You know, it's slipped my mind again."

Lifting his hands in frustration, he sighed.

"Getting old is a pain in the you know what," he said. "But I'll remember eventually."

Bridget nodded, sensing the older man didn't want to talk in front of Daphne and Paloma.

"Okay, well don't forget to call me when you do."

As she walked back to her Explorer, her phone buzzed in her pocket with an incoming text.

She climbed back in the driver's seat and fastened her seatbelt before checking her phone.

Her heart skipped a beat at the message on the display.

Hirsch is gone. Looks like he skipped town.

* * *

Bridget stood beside Charlie outside the Tempest Grove police station, waiting for Santino and Decker to arrive.

"I was looking forward to Santino getting back from New York today," Bridget said, checking her watch. "I didn't realize he'd be called back into action so soon."

The comment elicited only a distracted nod from the FBI agent, who was tapping on her phone.

"Are you doing okay?" Bridget asked as Charlie looked up.

"Yes, I'm just scheduling that press conference," she said. "Tomorrow morning we will officially announce that Natasha Prescott's remains have been found."

She grimaced.

"And we'll likely also have to say that her suspected killer is loose and on the run."

"Well, I'm glad we're releasing the information," Bridget said. "It's getting impossible to keep it under wraps. But that wasn't what I meant when I asked if you're okay."

Putting a hand on Charlie's arm, she tried again.

"I was asking if you're doing okay. You seem on edge and...well, not like yourself lately. Is something wrong?"

"It might be," Charlie replied with a grim smile. "But that's still up in the air."

She shifted her troubled gaze toward the empty street.

"Calloway has asked Hale to head up a new unit," she said. "An undercover unit assigned to a top-secret, long-term investigation. If he takes the job, he'll be deep under for months. Maybe years if he gets in deep enough."

Charlie's brisk tone belied the hurt and pain Bridget sensed just under the surface.

"I haven't been told all the details," she said. "I'm not *authorized*, I guess. But it sounds dangerous."

Summoning a sad smile, she finally met Bridget's eyes.

"Hale loves undercover work."

Her voice had softened. It was almost wistful.

"If his cover hadn't been blown, he would never have given it up to begin with," she said. "And now that he has another chance, can I really ask him to give up an opportunity to go back to what he loves?"

"He loves you," Bridget said. "And he'd be miserable going undercover without you."

Swallowing hard, Charlie nodded.

"You're right," she agreed. "He *does* love me. He *will* be miserable if he leaves. But he'll also be miserable if he stays."

A flash of red appeared at the end of the street, catching

Bridget's eye. She turned to see a red Chevy coming toward them and was able to make out Santino's dark head in the driver's seat and a blonde head beside him.

"It'll be okay," Bridget said as the truck drew closer.

She gave Charlie's hand a reassuring squeeze.

"You'll figure it out together."

Hoping she was right, Bridget smiled at Santino as he parked the Chevy along the curb and climbed out.

Both he and fellow deputy marshal Howie Decker stopped on the sidewalk to stretch out the stiffness caused by the plane, train, and truck rides they'd endured during the previous eight hours.

"You guys aren't too tired for your new mission, are you?" Charlie asked with no hint of compassion. "Because we need you to hunt down Calvin Hirsch and bring him back."

As she followed Charlie and the deputy marshals into the station, Bridget wondered what she would do if she faced Charlie's predicament.

How would I handle Santino going away for months or years at a time with no contact, and no guarantee he'd ever return?

Her question went unanswered as they filed into the meeting room, taking seats next to Cecil, Kirby, and Landon.

Just as Charlie began to review the status of the investigation with Santino and Decker, Argus Murphy stuck his head into the room.

"Sorry I'm late," he said with an awkward wave. "Gage asked me to fill in for him. Something's come up."

As Argus made his way around the table to an empty chair, Charlie looked down at the folder in front of her.

"Okay, where were we?"

"You were saying that yesterday you arrested Calvin Hirsch," Santino replied. "And then this morning he jumped bail. You want us to bring him back in. Is that about right?"

Charlie nodded.

"That's right," she said. "We went to Hirsch's house this morning and he was gone. We looked around his property and around town, but there's no sign of him."

"Is he armed?" Decker asked. "Did you see any weapons in his house that would make you think he'll put up a fight?"

This time Landon jumped in.

"We did a brief search of his place yesterday," he said. "I didn't see any weapons. Unless you consider his wood carving knife a weapon?"

Leaning back in his chair, Decker shrugged.

"I guess that depends on how big the knife is, and if he knows how to use it in combat."

"The man's accused of killing two women," Santino said. "We have to assume he's dangerous. Now, is there any reason you think he might still be in town?"

Argus raised his hand.

"I doubt Hirsch is dumb enough to hide out in a public place," he said. "But based on the information I read in the files on Hirsch, I don't think he'd go far."

"And why is that?" Santino asked.

The question wasn't a challenge. Bridget could see that Santino was genuinely curious. He knew he needed to understand Hirsch if he hoped to catch him.

"Well, he never left Tempest Grove, despite decades of suspicion, ostracism, and open hostility," Argus said. "So, I'd say it's unlikely he'd leave now. I think he'll stay close to his comfort zone. I think he'll try to lay low."

CHAPTER FIFTEEN

The rain that had been threatening all day started to drizzle onto the windshield just as Santino turned the red Chevy onto Arcana Avenue. He drove past an old-fashioned, wrought iron fence, which bordered a large Victorian house, before passing a sturdy stone wall, which bore a sign reading *Chumbley's Organic Farm.*

As he reached the row of thin, unpainted boards that made up the fence surrounding Calvin Hirsch's property, he wondered why the people living along Arcana Avenue felt the need to erect such obtrusive walls and fences around their properties.

What or who are they all trying to keep out?

Parking the truck along the curb, he turned to Decker, who had fallen asleep in the passenger's seat during the short drive, and shook one big shoulder.

His fellow deputy marshal had the annoying ability to fall asleep almost anywhere or anytime he chose as Santino had learned during the many assignments they'd handled.

"Let's go, Decker, we're here," he said, wishing they'd gotten a chance to rest and recuperate after their last assignment. "Let's go find Hirsch."

He yawned as he looked around at the empty street, then checked the Glock in his holster as Decker sat up.

"There's not much room in there to hide," Santino said, surveying the top of the small building visible beyond the fence. "But I guess he could be holed up lying in wait."

Santino knew better than to underestimate any of the fugitives he was assigned to bring in. Hirsch would be considered dangerous and treated as such until he was safely back behind bars.

"You ready to go knocking?" Decker asked, sounding cheerful after his power nap. "I think we'll have to-"

His words were cut off by the buzzing in Santino's pocket.

Pulling out the phone, Santino tapped to answer the call, then activated the speaker, and propped it on the dashboard.

"What's up, Charlie?"

"The hair on that creepy doll is human," she said, bypassing a greeting. "Vivian Burke just called me."

Raising an eyebrow, Santino looked over at Decker, who was staring back at him with wide blue eyes.

"She said the roots were even still attached," Charlie added. "The lab was able to extract a DNA profile. They confirmed that the hair is a match to Nicole Webster."

Santino felt the tension building in his shoulders.

The pressure to find Hirsch would be intense once the news came out that the dead woman's hair had been found in the fugitive's possession.

"Why are you guys at Hirsch's place?" Charlie asked as

152

an afterthought. "I told you we already checked there."

"And I heard you," he said. "But Ivy could find no signs that Hirsch left town. There's no trail to follow, no crumbs of information. Nothing to point us in the right direction."

He exhaled in frustration.

"The guy hasn't used his phone, or any credit cards, and his broken-down truck is still sitting in his yard."

"Who's Ivy?" Charlie asked.

Santino pictured the tiny woman who spent her days sitting behind a big computer monitor pecking on her keyboard in an endless quest to locate fugitives on the run.

"Ivy Savoy is our research specialist. And if Hirsch leaves any sort of trail online, she'll find it," Santino said. "But so far there's nothing. No financial activity, no social media activity, no posting from family or friends."

He stretched his back, leaning closer to the phone.

"That means we've got to start at the last place we know for sure he's been," Santino said. "And that's his place."

"Well, you know best," Charlie said, although she sounded doubtful. "Once you finish searching Hirsch's place you might want to go down the street to Hammerling House. It's an old Victorian mansion that serves as the headquarters for the Tempest Grove Circle of Eternal Light."

Decker shifted in his seat, restless now that he was awake.

"What's that? A church?" he asked.

"No, it's a coven," Charlie said. "They're a Wicca group."

The startled look on Decker's face melted into a smile.

"So, now we're witch hunters?" he laughed. "You want me to go get a pitchfork and light up a torch?"

Santino didn't share in Decker's amusement.

"It seems that Hirsch kept his affiliation with the Circle secret," Charlie continued, either ignoring or unaware of Decker's comments. "After Natasha Prescott disappeared, he was outed as a member and fired from his job as a high school track coach. There's no indication he's still involved with the group."

Her blunt summary of events had Santino almost feeling sorry for the guy. It sounded as if for all practical purposes, Calvin Hirsch had become an outcast and a recluse.

"Without friends or family in town, it's unlikely anyone will take him in," he said. "Which makes me more convinced than ever that he must be hiding on the property or in the woods behind his house."

Deciding it was time to make a move, he motioned for Decker to check his weapon.

"We're going up to Hirsch's house now," he said. "If we don't find him inside, we'll start searching the woods."

"Okay, and I'll send over some help," Charlie said.

Before he could ask what she meant, she ended the call.

"Stop your cackling," he said, glaring at Decker, who was still chuckling. "If you're going to watch my back in there, you better have your game face on, not that stupid smile."

Opening the Chevy's door, he climbed out onto the street and headed toward the fence, ignoring the rain on his face, and confident that Decker would be right behind him.

When he got to the thin wooden gate, he tried the latch

and found it unlocked. Shouldering it open, he raised his Glock into the ready position with both hands and stepped into the yard.

He moved swiftly up the path to the front door, where he leaned his shoulder against the doorframe and listened for noise inside.

Hearing nothing, he took one hand off his Glock and tried the handle. As soon as the door swung open, he was inside the house, moving swiftly from room to room, looking in closets and under furniture.

Within minutes the little house was clear.

An hour later, the yard and the workshop had also been searched and cleared, as had the old truck in the yard.

"That just leaves us the woods," Decker said. "And then we're going to have to come up with a new plan."

They turned as a black SUV pulled up to the fence.

It looked like one of the vehicles Bridget occasionally borrowed from the pool of cars the FBI kept on hand, but he didn't recognize the female agent who stepped out of the driver's seat.

She wore a black tactical vest with the letters *FBI* emblazoned across the front. Her alert green eyes stared out from under a black cap, and her dark blonde hair was pulled back into a ponytail.

Opening the SUV's back door, the agent ushered out a black and tan German Shepherd and snapped on a leash.

As the dog ran forward, practically pulling his handler after him, she smiled and stuck out a hand.

"I'm Special Agent Bailey Flynn," she said. "And this is

Ludwig. He's trained in search and rescue. Charlie Day thought you may be able to use him."

Decker nodded enthusiastically as he took her hand.

"We were just getting ready to search the woods," he said. "You two arrived just in time."

"If you're looking for the man who lived in this house, we can use an item of his clothing to give Ludwig a scent," Bailey said. "That'll be the quickest way to see if he's hiding in the woods. Ludwig will smell him a mile away."

Santino nodded, suddenly hopeful their trip out to Tempest Grove wasn't going to be a waste of time after all.

"There are sheets on the bed," he told Bailey. "Looks as if they were recently slept in."

"That should do it," she said. "Bring me a pillowcase and we'll see what Ludwig can find."

Jogging back to the little house, Santino pulled a pillowcase off the bed and returned.

Bailey took the thin material and held it out to the German Shepherd, allowing the dog to sniff it.

"Find it, Ludwig," Bailey said. "Go find it!"

The dog lifted his nose high into the air and issued a high-pitched bark, then scrambled toward the fence.

Racing along the outside, he headed toward the woods as Bailey chased after him with Decker and Santino close behind. He took care not to slip on the rain-slick ground or trip over tree roots and fallen branches.

They were all panting with exertion and dripping with rainwater by the time Ludwig came to a sudden stop ahead and began to bark again and again at the base of a sprawling black walnut tree.

Motioning for Bailey to stay back, Santino again lifted his Glock, suddenly aware that they were exposed in the forest, and that Hirsch may be hiding in or around the tree.

He crept forward as Ludwig continued to bark with his nose lifted in the air and his paws scratching frantically at the muddy ground.

As he drew closer, Santino squinted through the rain, not sure if his eyes were deceiving him as he made out a man's figure standing still under a thick branch.

No, not standing. He's hanging.

Running forward, he saw the blue discoloration of the old man's face and noted the slack hang of his arms and legs.

The hunt for Calvin Hirsch was over.

Their fugitive would not be returning to jail.

"Good boy!" Bailey said as she grabbed up Ludwig's leash and pulled the German Shepherd away from the tree and the dead man hanging in it. "Good boy, you found it!"

Her encouraging words for the dog contrasted sharply with the troubled expression Santino saw on the handler's face as she led the dog away.

It took almost an hour for back-up to arrive from the local station, and then another for the medical examiner to arrive.

By the time Opal Fitzgerald stood next to him at the base of the black walnut tree, the rain had stopped, and the sun was setting.

"You think he did this to himself?" Santino asked.

"I'm not sure," Opal admitted. "Could be self-inflicted,

or it could be a homicide. We'll need to review all the evidence."

She watched as Greg Alcott snapped photos of the rope twisted around Hirsch's neck.

"It looks like the same type of rope used to hang Nicole Webster," she said. "And there's definitely some sort of tissue under his nails."

Santino frowned.

"So, you're saying someone did this to him?"

She shrugged.

"It's possible," Opal said. "Although, sometimes people who hang themselves change their minds at the end. They'll rip off their fingernails trying to loosen the rope they put around their own necks."

She gestured toward the dead man's fingers.

"There's only one sure way to tell. We need to get the tissue under his nails over to the FBI lab. Vivian Burke will be able to tell us if we've found our killer or if he's still out there."

CHAPTER SIXTEEN

The next morning Raven woke early, his body stiff and sore from his exertions and activities the day before. Sliding out of bed, he made his way to the bathroom and opened the big cabinet where he kept his colorful selection of jars, bottles, and vials.

Reaching for a small glass jar, he unscrewed the top and dipped in a finger, scooping out a small dollop of the special salve he'd made by infusing oils and herbs, and mixing the concoction with melted beeswax.

The salve would help heal the deep scratches on his arm. The ones left by Calvin Hirsch when the old man had made one last, desperate attempt to escape his fate.

But then no one escapes their true fate without help from the Old Ones. The wheel of destiny is beyond human control.

Luckily, Raven knew how to commune with the Old Ones, as well as the spirits who dwell in darkness.

As a novice, Cypher had reluctantly taught him the basics of dark magic, always warning him to be cautious, trying to hold him back.

But over the years Raven had studied and practiced the dark craft on his own until his power and knowledge had exceeded that of his mentor.

Now he was the determiner of fate and the decider of destiny for those who crossed his path.

He had been the one to decide that Calvin Hirsh would make the perfect sacrificial lamb.

His will alone had made it happen. And now his salve would help heal the wounds that Hirsch had left behind.

Pulling on his dressing gown, Raven descended the stairs and went into the kitchen.

After preparing his morning cup of tea, he carried the cup into the living room and turned on the television.

He flipped through the channels until he found what he was looking for. An official press conference was being held at the Wisteria Falls City Hall.

Police Chief Cecil Fitzgerald stood at the podium next to Special Agent Charlie Day from the FBI.

"...the joint task force looking into the homicide of a woman out by Moonstone Cavern earlier this week has officially identified the victim as Nicole Prescott Webster, a resident of Tempest Grove, West Virginia," Cecil said.

The police chief held up a photo that showed Nikki as an adult woman, not as the angry, awkward teenager Raven had tried and failed to kill in 1996.

I had to wait almost three decades for another chance...but the sight of Nikki swaying in the Witch's Tree was well worth the wait.

As soon as he'd heard that Nikki was back in Tempest Grove, he'd known he had to kill her. It was her fate.

Especially once she'd started asking questions and it

became clear that she was beginning to remember who she'd seen that night. Clear that she was getting closer to the truth.

He couldn't just sit back and allow her to tell everyone that he'd lured Natasha out to the woods for the Beltane festival.

That he'd been the one who had killed her sister. Not when he'd worked so hard to point the investigation in a different direction.

Sipping at the hot tea, Raven watched as the police chief held up a second photo. He turned up the sound on the television as he recognized Natasha Prescott's high school yearbook photo.

"During the course of the investigation, the task force discovered the remains of another body, which had been disposed of in a nearby location," Cecil said. "DNA analysis has confirmed that the remains belong to a teenage female reported missing from Tempest Grove, Virginia in 1996."

He cleared his throat.

"Next-of-kin has been notified and we can now officially identify this second victim as Natasha Prescott."

A scowl settled over Raven's face as a murmur of surprise rippled through the gathered media and onlookers at the press conference.

The discovery of Natasha and the other women in the ravine hadn't been part of his plan. He hadn't intended or expected the bodies to ever be found.

Not after all this time.

He'd assumed the weather and wildlife would have

cleared away the evidence long ago.

And he'd taken care to dump them outside of Tempest Grove, over the state line, in an area where Natasha's disappearance had long since been forgotten.

Keeping his eyes on the screen, he wondered if details about the other two bodies in the ravine would be revealed.

Or would the FBI keep the secret as he had all these years?

Of course, the news would have to come out eventually, which was a shame. After all, he'd been so very disciplined and discreet, only allowing himself one girl every three years.

Three was a powerful number.

That's what Cypher had taught him, and he'd found it to be true. Thus far his adherence to the three-year rule had served him well.

At least, it had until Nikki had come back into his life.

Setting his teacup down on the table, he scrolled through his mental list of the lives he'd taken.

It had all started with Natasha.

After taking her life that night, he'd found himself drawn to women who reminded him of Natasha whenever he was making his selection.

Not wanting to draw too much attention to his own hometown, only two of the women had been taken from Tempest Grove.

Both Faustina and Zephra had been fledgling members of the Circle. Both were young, with the same fiery hair as Natasha, and both had been too tempting to resist.

All the others had been taken from covens in towns as far away as Louisville or Memphis when he'd had the opportunity to travel out of town.

But Cecil didn't make an announcement about the other bodies. Instead, he moved back from the podium wearing a solemn expression as Agent Charlie Day stepped forward.

"Earlier this week, a Tempest Grove resident named Calvin Hirsch was declared a person of interest in the death of Nicole Webster. He was arrested and subsequently released on bail."

Charlie spoke slowly, looking directly into the camera.

"Yesterday, after Mr. Hirsch was reported to have violated his bail conditions, a search was conducted by U.S. Marshals in the woods behind his home and a body was found."

She ignored the murmurs and gasps from the crowd.

"The body was confirmed to be that of Mr. Hirsch," she said. "An investigation into his manner of death is ongoing. No further information will be released at this time."

Raven turned off the television with an uneasy sigh.

He'd known Hirsch's body would be found eventually.

In fact, his plan relied on it. Only he had expected it to take longer. Everything seemed to be moving faster than he'd expected and he wasn't sure if that was a good thing or bad.

Soon they would find evidence cementing Hirsch's role in Natasha's disappearance and Nicole's death.

Evidence that would convince everyone that the ex-coach had killed himself to avoid prosecution.

The case would be closed, and Raven's will would be done.

CHAPTER SEVENTEEN

Bridget sipped at her coffee, keeping her blue eyes glued to the little television screen, watching as Charlie stood at the podium. The agent had likely just set off a media firestorm with the announcement that Natasha Prescott's body had been found and that the man accused of her abduction and murder was dead.

"Who's that with Cecil?" Santino asked.

He was sitting at the breakfast table beside her, starting in on his second bagel, while Hank lounged at their feet.

"That's Landon's boss," Bridget said. "Chief Aguilar."

She studied the man, who was outfitted in a crisp uniform that had been perfectly tailored to his athletic physique, then looked for Landon on the podium, but it appeared that the detective hadn't shown up to support his chief.

"He looks as if he's hoping to get some good press out of this," Santino said as he spread strawberry jam onto the bagel. "He thinks we've closed a missing person cold case that's been on his books for twenty-seven years."

"And what do you think?" Bridget asked.

Santino shrugged.

"I think we need to wait for the lab results," he said. "If the tissue under Hirsch's nails isn't his, then..."

He was distracted by a rasping voice coming from the television. Bridget followed his gaze to see a stocky man in a black WARP 102.5 FM t-shirt and white crewcut speaking to a reporter.

"...taken the Tempest Grove PD way too long to solve this crime. We knew back in '96 that there was something fishy going on with Hirsch and that group of devil worshippers he was hanging out with over at Hammerling House."

Bridget grimaced as she realized the man must be Spike Oswald. Picking up a tiny remote on the table, she shut off the television, silencing the radio host's angry voice.

"We better get going," she said. "I told Charlie we'd meet her over at the Hirsch crime scene once she was done with the press conference. And it looked pretty done to me."

She followed Santino and Hank out to Chevy, replaying what she'd seen of the press conference in her mind.

"Spike Oswald worries me," she said as they crossed over the Shenandoah River on the way out of town. "He's a danger to the community. Whether he's just spreading unrest or doing something worse. I don't trust him."

Santino gave her a sideways glance.

"If your intuition is telling you not to trust him, then you shouldn't," he said. "And it wouldn't do any harm to look into his past and see if he's got a record."

Bridget nodded, but her thoughts had already moved on from the angry DJ to the image of Charlie standing with Cecil at the podium.

The agent had been immaculately dressed in a navy-blue suite with her golden blonde hair pulled back into a low bun.

She'd come across as confident and professional. But Bridget couldn't help but notice that her face had been drawn and her eyes looked tired.

"Can you keep a secret?" she asked, looking over at Santino. "If I tell you something in confidence?"

Lifting a curious eyebrow, Santino nodded as he kept his eyes on the road ahead.

"It's just that Charlie told me Hale's been asked to go back undercover," she blurted out. "It's some big case where he'd be gone for however long it takes. That's why she's been so distracted. I guess she's worried."

Santino glanced over at her.

"It sounds as if you're worried, too," he said.

"It's just...I know how I'd feel if I were in her place, and you were going off for God knows how long."

She turned her eyes to the window.

"How would you feel?" he asked in a soft voice that made her heart beat faster. "Would you miss me?"

Reaching over the console, he took her hand.

"Cause I know I'd miss you like crazy."

Bridget smiled and gave his hand a squeeze.

"And I don't blame Charlie for being concerned," he added. "In my experience, few agents go deep uncover and come back intact. Those kinds of assignments can break an agent...and a family."

With a sigh, Santino pulled back his hand and put it on

the steering wheel as he merged the Chevy into the exit lane.

"But then, nothing lasts forever, no matter how much we wish it would," he said almost as an afterthought. "Life moves on, with or without our consent."

Bridget felt a sense of foreboding at the softly spoken words. Was the wistful comment some sort of warning that he, too, was preparing for a change?

The troubling thought was replaced by more pressing concerns as they approached Calvin Hirsch's property to see Charlie, Bailey, and Ludwig standing outside his gate.

As she climbed out of the truck, Bridget called for Hank to jump down, then snapped on his leash, unsure how Ludwig might react.

"Ludwig's cool with other dogs," Bailey called over. "He's been trained to work solo or as part of a team."

As if to prove her right, the German Shepherd remained calm as Hank trotted over and began sniffing around him in a hopeful, friendly way.

Smiling down at the budding friendship, Bridget didn't see Jason Chan and Matthew Landon exit the front door of Hirsch's house until they were standing at the open gate.

The response team leader held up a see-through evidence collection bag which appeared to contain a stack of old photographs.

"I found these in Hirsch's dresser drawer," Jason said. "Looks as if they're all pictures of the same girl."

Stepping closer, Bridget peered down to see that the image on top showed a teenage Natasha Prescott.

The photo appeared to have been taken through the girl's bedroom window.

"There's the proof we've been looking for," Landon said. "Those photos are proof that Hirsch was our man."

Bridget frowned down at the unsettling evidence, not sure she was convinced, although she could understand the detective's eagerness to find Hirsch solely responsible for Nicole and Natasha's murders.

Proof of his guilt would effectively end the case. And with Hirsch no longer around to defend himself, there wouldn't even be a trial to put the family through.

But something was bothering her.

She walked back to Santino and spoke in a low voice.

"Didn't you and Decker search the whole property yesterday?" she asked. "Do you think you could have missed these photographs?"

Running a hand through his dark hair, Santino shrugged.

"I certainly didn't see any photos or even a camera when I was here," he admitted. "But, I can't be sure without talking to Decker. Could be that he saw something."

But he sounded doubtful, and as Bridget turned and surveyed the little house, she again had the sinking sensation that the investigation wasn't over yet.

* * *

It was noon by the time Bridget was ready to leave the crime scene on Arcana Avenue, which quickly filled with reporters, news vans, neighbors, and gawkers after the information released at the press conference had begun to circulate around town.

Moving past a bulky satellite van that was attempting to parallel park along the already crowded road, Bridget picked up a snippet of a live news feed that was likely being broadcast around the country.

From what she could hear, the reporters were making it sound as if Calvin Hirsch's role in Nicole's hanging, and Natasha's abduction and murder, had been confirmed, and that the case against him was watertight.

As she skirted the big news van, Bridget caught a glimpse of Chief Aguilar giving an interview to a reporter. She winced as she overheard a statement that was destined to become a soundbite on the evening news.

"We're glad we caught this monster among us before he could hurt anyone else," the police chief said. "Now we're just hoping to put this nightmare behind us."

Moving quickly toward the Chevy, Bridget was relieved to see Santino standing on the sidewalk. Before she could ask him where Hank was, she caught sight of the Irish setter lying beside Ludwig in the grass.

"I want to update Joelle and Rowan Prescott on the true status of the investigation," Bridget told Santino.

She scanned the swelling crowd with worried eyes.

"They need to know the case is still open, and that Hirsch's guilt hasn't been proven yet, despite what they may be hearing on the news."

She felt obliged to tell the Prescotts that their daughters' killer may still be out there, although she doubted they'd be happy to hear it. Everyone seemed to want the case closed.

As Bridget snapped on Hank's leash, Bailey came up behind them.

"Are you guys leaving now?"

She bent to scratch the Irish setter behind the ears.

"Yes, although I'm sure Hank would rather stay," Bridget said. "He doesn't often get the chance to make a new friend."

"Ludwig's the same," Bailey said.

She brushed at a tiny white blossom that had fallen onto the German Shepherd's black and tan coat.

"His original handler trained him to work well within a team," Bailey added. "And I can tell he really likes being around other dogs."

Bridget detected a hint of sadness in the agent's voice and wondered what had happened to Ludwig's original handler.

Why had the search and rescue dog been reassigned?

But her questions would have to wait for another time.

Right now, she needed to get to the Prescott house.

As the Chevy pulled onto the road, Hank stuck his head out of the window and looked back at Ludwig, while Bridget entered the address for the Prescott house into the GPS.

Twenty minutes later they turned onto Forester Way.

Santino parked the Chevy in the driveway behind a white Cadillac with tinted windows and expensive-looking rims.

They left Hank in the truck as they walked up to the porch and knocked on the door.

Footsteps sounded and then the door swung open to

reveal Rowan Prescott's haggard face and red-rimmed eyes.

"Come on in," he said, stepping back to allow them to pass. "We're sitting in the living room."

They followed Rowan down the hall to where a man in a dark gray suit sat on the sofa holding what appeared to be a glass of ice-tea.

"Pastor Parnell is here," Rowan said. "We've been discussing the funeral service for the twins."

Bridget nodded a greeting. She recognized Andrew Parnell from her previous visit to the Tempest Grove Baptist Church.

"It's good to see you again, Pastor," she said, stepping further into the room. "This is Deputy Marshal Vic Santino. He's been working with the FBI and the local police to-"

"Are you the one who took down Calvin Hirsch?" Rowan cut in. "If you are, I owe you a great deal of thanks. I've been waiting for someone to prove that man took my little girl for decades."

Bridget winced inwardly.

The man wouldn't want to hear that Hirsch may not be their daughters' killer. That he may have been a victim, too.

"I'm sorry, Mr. Prescott, but we need to speak to you and your wife about the investigation," she said, glancing at Parnell. "Preferably in private."

A scowl fell over Rowan's face.

"Joelle isn't here," he said curtly. "She's at Hammerling House with those-"

"Excuse me," the pastor said, pulling out his phone and getting to his feet. "I need to make a call. I'll go outside."

Once he'd left the room, Rowan sucked in an angry breath.

"You'll have to excuse me if I don't want my wife hanging out with those people over at Hammerling House," he said. "Hirsch belongs to that group of miscreants. He used to be one of them, and he killed both my girls. But Joelle just won't see it. She's been blind to their evil for years."

Searching for the right words, Bridget cleared her throat.

"Mr. Prescott, I came here to update you on the investigation. It's important that you hear the truth. Not just what the press is saying."

Rowan frowned.

"What do you mean by the truth?" he asked.

He crossed his arms defensively over his chest.

"The truth is that the case is still open, and the investigation is ongoing. We can't be sure yet if Calvin Hirsch was the man who abducted Natasha or killed Nicole."

Wondering how much she should share with Rowan, she looked to Santino, who nodded slightly as if encouraging her to tell all to the grieving father.

"We also have reason to doubt that Hirsch committed suicide," she continued. "That doesn't necessarily mean he wasn't involved with what happened to your daughters, but there's a possibility he may have been a victim himself."

Her revelation was met with stunned silence.

Before Rowan could gather his thoughts, a deep voice spoke from the doorway.

"Calvin Hirsch was a known pagan," Pastor Parnell said as he stepped into the room. "I have no doubt he's guilty, and that his eternal soul is roasting in hell as we speak."

Bridget turned to glare at the pastor but before she could ask him to leave the room, her eyes landed on the loveseat behind him.

A doll-sized poppet was propped in front of one of the pillows. Its dark red hair gleamed in the sunlight coming in through the window.

"What's that?" she asked.

Rowan followed her gaze.

"Joelle brought that ugly thing home this morning," he said impatiently. "I told her to throw it out, but she refused. She said someone at the Circle made it for her special. She said it reminded her of our girls."

CHAPTER EIGHTEEN

Charlie stood outside the wrought iron gate which protected Hammerling House and its grounds from anyone who didn't have a passcode for the electronic security system. Taking out her phone, she reread the message she'd gotten from Bridget an hour earlier.

Meet me at Hammerling House ASAP.

A photo had been attached to the message.

Charlie opened the photo and looked down with wide gray eyes at the image of a small figure constructed out of dark sticks and twigs.

The poppet's stick body had been tied together with a blue satin ribbon and its small walnut head was adorned with a silky lock of dark red hair.

The sound of tires on asphalt announced the impending arrival of Santino's red Chevy pickup truck.

Bridget jumped out of the passenger seat as soon as the truck stopped beside Charlie.

"Did you bring the creepy doll?" Charlie asked.

Bridget held up a brown paper evidence bag.

"It's in here," she said. "I found it at the Prescott house when I went to speak with Joelle and Rowan. Apparently,

Joelle brought it home from Hammerling House this morning. Rowan claims someone gave it to her as a gift."

Leaning forward, Charlie carefully opened the brown paper bag and peered inside.

She shivered as she looked in at the red-headed poppet.

"It matches the other one," she said. "At least the hair looks the same from what I can tell, although I guess we'll have to send it to the lab to find out for sure."

Bridget nodded and then looked up at the gate.

"So, how are we supposed to get up to the front door?"

Santino spoke up behind her.

"I could always use my Glock," he said, putting a hand on the butt of the weapon in his holster.

From the expression on his face, Charlie wasn't sure if the deputy marshal was being serious.

"Let's try the intercom first," she said, nodding toward a stainless-steel box affixed to the side of the gate. "Maybe we can save ourselves a bullet."

Reaching forward, Charlie pressed a button on the box.

Several seconds passed before a buzz sounded behind them. Charlie turned to see that the gate lock had disengaged.

"I guess that means we've been invited in," Santino said, quickly pushing open the gate as if suspecting that the lock might reengage at any minute.

Charlie left her Expedition parked along the curb, climbing into the backseat of the Chevy's cab alongside Hank as Santino steered the truck up the driveway and parked in front of the mansion's elaborate wrap-around porch.

Climbing out to stand in front of the big house, she looked up at the turrets and towers, deciding the mansion would have made a good setting for the cheesy horror movies she'd always loved as a child.

As she followed Bridget and Santino up the porch steps, Gerard Ernst opened the door before they could knock.

"Agent Day, how nice of you to come back so soon," Ernst said. "After that delightful press conference you held this morning, I had a feeling we'd be seeing you again."

Deciding to skip the pleasantries and small talk, Charlie took the brown paper bag from Bridget and held it out to the old man.

"We need to know where this came from," she said. "You can look inside but don't touch the contents. It's one of those creepy dolls. I think it's called a puppet."

After a moment's hesitation, Ernst took the bag and peered inside. He frowned and raised both eyebrows.

"It's not called a puppet," he corrected. "It's a poppet."

He held on to the bag and cocked his head.

"Where did you get this?" he asked. "The figure looks like Elora's work but the hair...well, I haven't seen that before."

"May we speak to Elora, then?" Charlie asked. "That *poppet* was given to Joelle Prescott, and we need to ask whoever gave it to her a few questions."

Soft footsteps sounded on the stairs.

Charlie looked up to see Elora standing on the landing. Her long blonde hair had been plaited into two braids, and she wore a flowing green dress that nearly reached the floor.

"Did you make a poppet for Joelle?" Ernst asked, looking up the stairs. "Did you give it to her this morning, dear?"

Moving down the wide staircase with graceful ease, Elora showed no surprise at having the FBI show up at her door to ask about her craft work.

She took the brown paper bag from Ernst, peeked inside it, and then nodded agreeably.

"Yes, I made it," she admitted. "And I gave it to Joelle when she stopped by this morning."

She handed the bag back to Charlie.

"I knew the poppet would be special when I made it," Elora said. "You see, the other night I was having a hard time falling asleep, and I came downstairs to get some herbs for a sleeping potion out of the herbology room in the west wing."

A disapproving grimace flashed across Ernst's face, then vanished just as quickly.

"It was after midnight," Elora continued. "I remember the clock striking twelve. And I heard the door close. But when I went into the room, no one was there."

She pointed to the bag.

"But that hair was lying on the table," she said. "I liked it. It felt so real and so soft. And it reminded me of Joelle, so I made it into a poppet. I hoped it might comfort her."

"Do you often make poppets?" Bridget asked.

Elora nodded.

"I enchant them and sell them online to seekers," she

said. "Joelle offered to give me money for the one I made her, but I told her it was a gift. I think she liked the hair, too."

She cocked her head.

"Ask her if you want. She's in the courtyard now."

Waving for them to follow her, Elora led the trio down a hall and out to a courtyard garden, fragrant with the scent of flowers, herbs, and spices.

Joelle had just dropped a handful of fresh leaves into a small basket when she saw Elora and their visitors emerge.

Her eyes found Bridget's.

"What's happened?" she asked. "Who's dead now?"

"Calvin Hirsch," Bridget said. "He was found hanging in a walnut tree in the woods behind his house."

Joelle's face fell and her shoulders sagged.

"I'm sorry to hear that," she said. "That poor man wouldn't have hurt a fly if it had landed on his nose. And he certainly didn't kill my girls."

Her voice hardened.

"The real killer is still out there," she said. "And you've got to find him."

* * *

Charlie watched Santino's red Chevy disappear around the bend before climbing back into her Expedition and carefully setting the brown paper bag in the seat beside her.

Joelle had given her permission for the poppet to be sent to the FBI lab for testing. The woman had been adamant that the hair on the poppet was not from one of her daughters.

"*I brushed my daughters' hair every night for the first ten years of their lives. I know what it feels like in my hands. If I close my eyes I can feel it now. And that hair didn't come from my girls.*"

Deciding it was pointless to argue, Charlie had taken the bag, knowing the lab would determine the truth.

As she sped down Shackleton Highway, she pictured the stack of photos Jason Chan had discovered in Hirsch's drawer, and impulsively made a sharp turn onto Fairview Avenue, heading west toward Tempest Grove High School.

While several of the photos had obviously been taken by someone standing outside Natasha's bedroom window, there were also a dozen or more that had been taken at various high school track meets.

Jason Chan had pointed out that, if you looked closely, you could see Coach Hirsch in the background of several photos.

So, how could Hirsch have taken the photos if he was in them?

Did Hirsch ask someone to take photos with his camera? Did an accomplice assist him with his crimes? Could someone have planted the photos in his drawer?

The possibilities swirled through Charlie's mind as she approached the school.

Perhaps there would be some clue in Hirsch's employment record. Maybe there was something in his file that would prove he'd shown an unhealthy interest in Natasha.

Maybe some of the staff still remembers Hirsch.

After pulling into the lot, Charlie searched for the email she'd recently received from Argus Muphy.

The profiler and analyst had combed through the original files and created a list of everyone the Tempest Grove PD had considered a possible suspect during the initial investigation.

While Argus had identified Calvin Hirsch as being the prime suspect, based on the information he found in the files, Charlie remembered that the principal of the high school had been questioned several times as well.

Scrolling through the attachment Argus had prepared, Charlie stopped at the name Brian Corwin.

The principal was the only other person besides Hirsch at the school who'd been on the suspect list.

But it had been a long time ago. Hirsch might not be the only dead suspect on their list, and there was only one way to find out.

Charlie opened the car door and walked through the nearly empty parking lot toward the school office.

Based on the lack of students and activity, she could see that classes had already ended for the day.

Luckily, the school office was still open, and a clerk was sitting at the attendance desk tapping on a keyboard.

"Can I help you?"

The woman looked up with a suspicious frown.

"I'm Special Agent Day with the FBI," Charlie said, pulling her credentials out of her pocket and holding them up. "I need to speak to Principal Corwin."

With a look at her watch, the clerk picked up the receiver on her desk phone, held it to her ear, and punched in an extension.

"Mr. Corwin, I've got an Agent Day in the attendance office asking to speak to you. Should I bring her back, or-"

She listened for a long beat, then dropped the receiver back into place.

"He said he'll come out to you," she said, then lowered her voice. "But he didn't sound very happy about it."

Charlie turned as footsteps sounded down the corridor.

The man who walked toward her was too young to have been the principal of a school back in 1996.

"Brian Corwin?" Charlie asked in a doubtful voice.

The man shook his head.

"I'm Joshua Corwin," he said. "Brian's my dad. But if you're looking for him, you're in the wrong place. He retired more than ten years ago."

He glanced over at the clerk, who was watching their exchange with interest, then moved closer to Charlie and lowered his voice.

"What do you want with my father?" he asked.

"I wanted to ask him about Calvin Hirsch," Charlie said. "They used to work together and I'm sure you've heard that Mr. Hirsch was arrested in connection with several homicides, and...well, now he's dead. So, if you know where your father is now..."

Joshua reluctantly checked his watch.

"Dad's usually on the golf course around this time on a

Friday," he said. "You might catch him on the back nine of the Tempest Grove Country Club if you hurry."

The door to the attendance office had already closed behind Charlie when he came after her.

Looking over his shoulder to see if the clerk was watching, Joshua cleared his throat.

"Why is the FBI still investigating the case if Hirsch is dead?" he asked. "You don't think my father had anything to do with those girls' deaths, do you?"

Charlie raised an eyebrow.

"Is that what you think, Mr. Corwin?"

The man looked shocked.

"No, of course not," he said. "It's just, I remember the day Dad came home from work and told me and my mother that Natasha was missing. He was torn up about it."

Joshua's face tightened.

"That's when the police started questioning him and...well, I don't want him to have to go through that again. I was hoping it was all over."

"Maybe it is over," Charlie said. "But we have to be sure no one else is in danger. And until we are, the investigation will stay open."

CHAPTER NINETEEN

lora hurried down the staircase and crossed the polished oak floor to the kitchen. Slipping through the wide, swinging door, she passed the butler's sink and antique gas-burner stove on her way to collect her woven wicker basket from its wooden hook on the wall.

Letting herself out onto the back lawn, she held the basket with one hand and used the other to hold her long green skirt as she ran toward the gate.

The sun had already started its inexorable journey toward the horizon, and she wanted to forage for mushrooms before all the natural light was gone in hopes she'd have something savory to throw in the pot for that night's dinner.

She planned to make a special anniversary meal in order to soothe Cypher's smarting ego.

The high priest hadn't been happy to hear she'd been out roaming in the west wing after midnight again, although he'd tried to hide his jealousy from the blonde FBI agent.

He'd never completely forgiven Elora after he'd found her in the crystal room with another man's name written on a piece of paper as she'd prepared to cast a binding spell.

Funny how a man as old and wise as Cypher still suffered insecurity and petty jealousy over a woman's affections.

But it was their six-month anniversary, and she didn't want to have to endure his sulking all evening. Better to prepare a warm mushroom stew paired with a fresh valerian root salad to lull him into an early sleep.

Perhaps she'd find her way to the crystal room to try the binding spell again once Cypher was safely tucked into bed and the clock had struck midnight.

Raven still hadn't succumbed to the first one she'd tried, but Elora wasn't the type to give up easily.

Her mother had successfully raised her and her seven siblings in the Appalachian foothills by sheer force of will, using the midwifery knowledge she'd learned at Granny Effie's elbow to support them, and supplementing the household's erratic income by foraging for herbs and roots to sell and barter.

When Elora had discovered the Circle of Eternal Light's message board online the year before, she'd instantly felt that she'd found a new spiritual home.

She'd set off for Tempest Grove with little hesitation, despite her mother's fervent warnings and objections. And she'd quickly been welcomed into the fold, and into the high priest's inner sanctum, once she'd arrived.

During her initiation into the coven, Gerard Ernst had revealed his craft name to her, warning her that she should never call him Cypher outside the coven's inner circle.

He had also helped her select her own craft name, but she hadn't wanted to save it only for the coven.

She'd taken to using the name Elora all the time, much preferring it to the more standard Mary Jane she'd been given at birth.

Now, as she made her way up Hammerling Hill, she bent to inspect a pair of morel mushrooms that had sprouted up under a sickly-looking elm tree.

Taking out the little knife she always carried with her while foraging, Elora cut the two mushroom caps from their stems and dropped them into her basket.

She moved on quickly, her eyes scanning the damp shady ground for more mushrooms, stopping to peer in tree stumps and in logs, soon finding herself at the edge of High Hollow, the secluded clearing where the coven had created their high altar on a smooth granite boulder.

The altar was used during the solar and fire festivals celebrated throughout the year, as well as initiation ceremonies for new members and various rituals.

Resting her basket on the altar, she looked up to the sky and sucked in a deep lungful of the fresh spring air.

She turned as she heard a branch crack. Listening closely, she could make out the soft, stealthy approach of footsteps. Someone was coming.

Had Cypher decided to come looking for her?

Elora arranged her face into a smile, expecting to see the high priest's large frame and craggy face emerging from the trees at any minute.

They often spent lazy afternoons alone by the altar, making good use of the High Hollow's seclusion.

But the figure that emerged wasn't Cypher.

A figure appeared at the edge of the tree line wearing a dark ceremonial robe with a wide hood that covered the head and hid the face in shadow.

Based on the broad shoulders and wide stance, Elora could tell it was a man. But he wasn't tall enough to be Cypher.

"Who are you?" she called out, unsure what the man wanted. "The High Hollow is reserved for the High Priest."

When the man didn't reply, she took an instinctive step back, sensing hostile energy in the air.

"Others will be coming soon," she said as she took another small, backward step. "You really can't..."

Her voice faded away as she saw the man was holding something in one big fist.

Is that a rope?

Images of Nicole Webster flashed through her mind. The woman who'd come to Hammerling House asking so many questions had been found hanging by a tree only a thirty-minute drive from where Elora stood now.

Without warning, the silent figure began moving across the clearing, coming toward her with frightening speed.

Spinning around in panic, careless of the direction she was heading, Elora dropped her basket and ran toward the cover of the trees, not daring to look back for fear she would trip and fall over a root or plant on the forest floor.

At the edge of the clearing, she ducked under a large branch and then plunged into the dense forest, skirting around trees and jumping over bushes as she tried to evade her pursuer, who seemed to be getting closer with every step.

Then she heard a grunt and a crash.

Looking over her shoulder, she could see that the hooded figure had tripped on a root and gone down on one knee.

Not waiting to see how long it would take for him to get back on his feet, Elora looked to the fading sun for guidance and then veered south, heading for Hammerling House.

She moved as quietly as possible, keeping her head down and her eyes on the ground in front of her as she made her way through the growing darkness of the trees around her.

The sound of angry footsteps and muffled curses echoed in the shadows, first growing nearer and then receding.

Elora forced herself to draw in a calming breath as she stopped and listened carefully.

Who was the man and why was he chasing her? Had she lost him in the forest? Had he given up and run away?

Not willing to trust the hope that was growing bigger and heavier in her chest, she continued moving in a southerly direction, knowing that eventually, she would come to Arcana Avenue, where she could find people and help.

Cypher will be waiting for me. He'll be worried.

The thought kept her feet moving, and soon Elora found herself facing a six-foot tall stone wall with barbed wire running along the top.

This must be the Chumbley place. I can follow the fence around. I can find Vern and ask him to...

The thought was cut off by the sound of movement behind her. The man was coming, and he was traveling fast.

Not sure which way to go, she stood still, frozen in place

by terror and indecision.

Maybe he knows where I live. He might try to cut me off at the pass if I go left. But if I go right, where will I end up?

Closing her eyes, she followed her memory down Arcana Avenue. Tried to visualize the street and remember where it ended. She decided the woods would take her to Burdock Bend, and from there she could flag down a car.

Then the rustle of tree branches to her right made her doubt her decision. With a resolute sigh, she headed left, keeping one hand on the fence as she worked her way back toward Hammerling House.

When her hand brushed against smooth metal, she stopped and looked down, her heart jumping as she saw a metal latch securing a small gate set into the wall.

She tried to pull the latch back, but it was locked.

Resisting the urge to scream for help, she forced herself to suck in a deep breath.

If I call out, the man will know where I am. He may get to me before anyone else does. I have to find another way.

The thought calmed her, and she dropped her eyes to the ground, looking for a makeshift tool or a rock.

She saw a fist-sized stone that had gotten dislodged from the wall and picked it up.

Gripping it with both hands, she brought it down hard against the rusted latch, which fell away.

Not waiting to see if the loud crash of stone against metal had alerted her pursuer, she wrenched open the gate and lunged through, trying to pull it closed behind her.

But the latch had been broken, and she was forced to

leave the gate swinging in the breeze as she frantically scanned the property for a place to run or hide.

Choosing the closest option, she sprinted toward the backside of a big red barn and slipped inside.

A soft beam of light shone in the side window, which framed the setting sun, and as Elora looked through it toward the fence, she saw a dark head peek around the gate.

She swallowed back a scream of fear and scurried toward the back of the nearly empty barn, not sure where to hide, finally crouching behind a bale of hay.

Holding her breath, she tried not to move as she waited and listened. Then her eyes fell on a pitchfork that had been discarded by the hay and she grabbed it with shaking hands.

This time the witch is the one holding the pitchfork.

Fortified by the thought, she exhaled.

After several minutes of silence, she peered around the hay, wondering if the man had decided not to take the risk of trespassing on the farm after all.

Perhaps he hadn't come in through the gate.

Could he really be gone?

Another five minutes passed. And then ten.

Sucking in a steadying breath, Elora stood and stepped out from behind the hay. Moving slowly and cautiously, she approached the barn door and peered out.

Before she could step out into the dusky air, a dark figure was in front of her, grabbing the pitchfork from her hand, and aiming three steel tines at her heart.

CHAPTER TWENTY

Dusk had fallen over Wisteria Falls by the time Bridget and Hank got back to the red brick house on Fern Creek Road. Santino had dropped them off on his way back to his apartment in Arlington, and Bridget was more than ready to spend a quiet night at home, reviewing case files and unwinding after the stressful week.

She eyed a half-full bottle of the Napa Valley Merlot that she and Santino had started on the night before, then checked her watch.

It wasn't quite cocktail hour yet, so she decided a cup of herbal tea would do for the time being.

Making her way into the kitchen, she filled Hank's bowl with fresh water and then set the kettle on the stove.

As she reached for a teabag, her phone buzzed on the counter and Vivian Burke's name appeared on the display.

The forensic examiner rarely texted her directly, so Bridget figured she either had a complaint to make or important results from the lab to share.

Her eyes widened as she read the message.

I've got results on the creepy doll. Will be in the lab for another hour if you can make it by then.

Knowing timing would be tight with Friday night traffic, Bridget texted a reply.

Will be there ASAP. On my way.

Glad now that she hadn't started in early on the wine, she poured food into Hank's bowl and then ran for the door.

Ninety minutes later she was walking into the lobby, relieved to see Vivian walking toward her.

"I was just leaving for the weekend," Vivian said. "I've got a big date tonight. So you're lucky you caught me."

"Thanks for calling and letting me know," Bridget said, trying not to sound impatient. "What did you find?"

Vivian dug through the bag over her shoulder and pulled out a thin file folder.

"The DNA came back from the tissue under Calvin Hirsch's fingernails," she said.

She handed the folder to Bridget.

"Based on what I've heard in the news, I'd say the results are unexpected. I figured you'd want to know right away."

The forensics examiner made no move to walk away as Bridget scanned through the DNA results.

"So the DNA under Hirsch's fingernails wasn't his own," Bridget murmured as she read.

The report went on to state that the extracted DNA profile was from an unknown male with no match in CODIS, the nationwide DNA database.

As Bridget processed the information, Vivian spoke again.

"If you go to the next page, there's more," she said. "I

also managed to slip the hair from that creepy doll at the Hirsch crime scene into the front of the line for testing."

She produced an exaggerated shiver.

"I wanted that spooky doll out of my lab," she explained. "It turns out the hair attached *was* human. Unfortunately, only the hair shaft had been attached...no roots."

Bridget frowned.

"So, you couldn't extract any DNA for a profile?"

"Without the roots, we couldn't get *nuclear* DNA, but *mitochondrial* DNA was extracted," she clarified. "The subsequent profile did have a match."

She nodded toward the file.

"As you'll see in the report, the hair on the doll was taken from Nicole Webster or one of her direct female relatives."

"So, you can't be sure if it's Nicole's hair or Natasha's?" Bridget asked.

Vivian shook her head.

"Not with mitochondrial analysis," she said. "As I explained before, with a mother and daughter, or with two sisters, the mitochondrial DNA sequences are identical. They are indistinguishable."

"So, the hair on the poppet could have come from Joelle Prescott or either one of her daughters," she said. "And there's no way to determine if the contributor of the hair had been dead or alive?"

The question earned an eye roll from Vivian.

"No, unfortunately not."

"And have you told Charlie Day about these results?"

Bridget asked.

Slinging her bag back over her shoulder, Vivian nodded.

"Yes, and for my trouble she dropped off another one of those creepy dolls. It's in the lab now waiting to be tested."

With another visible shudder, Vivian stepped around Bridget and headed toward the exit.

* * *

Before heading home, Bridget decided she might as well stop by the BAU and check in with her boss.

She'd been worried about Gage ever since he'd been a no-show at the Hexenbaum Task Force meeting the day before.

As she walked down the BAU hallway, she stopped outside Gage's office. The door was closed, but she could hear his deep voice coming from within.

Assuming he was on the phone, she hesitated, then knocked softly.

"Come in," Gage called, sounding annoyed.

Bridget pushed open the door and stuck her head in.

"I can come back once you're off the phone," she said.

But Gage waved her inside.

"Come in," he urged, still holding the phone to his ear. "It's Russell. I'll be off in a minute."

He continued his conversation as Bridget took a seat across from his desk, trying not to listen in to his call, but unable to prevent herself from picking up on the fact that Gage's foster son had gotten into some sort of trouble at school.

Once Gage had ended the call, he dropped the phone on the desk and looked at Bridget with tired eyes.

"Something's not right," he said, allowing his broad shoulders to sag. "I can't get through to him. And he won't listen to anything I say."

"Maybe you need to be the one listening," Bridet said before she could stop herself.

Gage cocked an irritable eyebrow.

"I'd love to be the one listening," he snapped. "But he won't talk to me either. If I left it up to him we'd just be sitting there in silence."

"Sometimes that's enough," she said. "Sometimes that's all kids really need. Just to have you there, supporting them."

Leaning back in his chair, he shook his head.

"Don't use that psychology BS on me. I'm trying to figure out what's going on with Russell while I still can. I need him to tell me what's wrong *now* before Estelle gets paroled and it's too late."

He cocked his head.

"Maybe he'll talk to you. You've counseled him in the past. Maybe you can get through to him."

Bridget detected a hint of desperation in his voice.

"The parole hearing is on Monday and if Estelle gets out, she's going to seek custody," he said. "I've got to make sure Russell is ready for that."

Suspecting Gage was the one who needed to be prepared, Bridget refrained from sharing the thought.

"Why don't you come by for dinner tonight?" he suggested. "You can bring Santino with you."

A voice sounded in the doorway and Bridget turned to see Argus Murphy holding his usual stack of files.

"You having a dinner party tonight, Gage?" he asked. "I'm not doing anything if there's an empty chair at the table."

"No, it's not a party," Gage said, ignoring the hopeful look on Argus' freckled face. "But there's an empty chair right there next to Bridget, so sit down."

As Argus' face fell, Gage looked toward Bridget.

"I'm assuming you came here to see me on a Friday evening because you had some sort of news?" he asked.

Bridget was about to shake her head, then her eyes fell on the file of DNA results in her hand.

"Yes, I was going to tell you that the lab came back with the DNA results for the tissue collected from under Calvin Hirsch's fingernails."

Both men turned to stare at her with interest.

"It isn't Hirsch's DNA," she said. "There was another person there when Hirsch died. He didn't kill himself."

Argus looked crestfallen.

"I was sure Hirsch was our guy," he said.

"He could still have killed Natasha and Nicole," Gage said. "Maybe someone found out and decided to make him pay."

But Argus didn't look reassured.

"We'll have to run the data through the algorithm again," he said. "The results clearly showed that the same

196

person was highly likely to be responsible for the deaths of Nicole Webster and Calvin Hirsch. The same rope was used, and the same knot..."

He shook his head.

"These results may change everything," he insisted. "The data will have to be updated and the algorithm-"

"What's the problem?" Gage cut in. "If Hirsch isn't the one who killed Nicole and Natasha, don't you want to know?"

"Of course, but it's bad news for us all," Argus said.

"What do you mean?" Gage asked.

Bridget answered before Argus could reply.

"If Hirsch wasn't our guy then we've still got a killer to find," she said. "And eventually, another woman will go missing, and another body will be found."

"So, you're sure he'll kill again?" Gage asked.

Glancing over at Argus, she saw that her fellow profiler was nodding along with her.

"Based on the two unidentified bodies that were found in the ravine with Natasha's remains, I'm sure of it," she said. "He may be telling himself he's on a mission to avenge some sort of wrong, but that's just an excuse to justify the kill. He likes it. And he won't stop."

"I'd have to agree," Argus said. "And with such a long time between killings, I'd bet there have been more than just those two, perhaps at another disposal site. It's possible he's been killing for decades without detection."

Gage raised an eyebrow.

"So, the unidentified remains in the ravine...have we

made any progress in finding out who they are?"

"I have been doing some online research and analysis," Argus admitted. "And I think I'm onto something."

He nodded down to the files he'd brought with him, which were now piled on Gage's desk.

"I've been researching all the Wicca groups in the area, along with their affiliated websites and message boards," he said. "The number of users on these sites has grown over the last few decades, but it's still a small, manageable number compared to mainstream sites."

He opened a file and flipped through the contents, producing a summary data report.

"Luis Cortez helped me access the backend database for several of the websites. That let me run some queries on the data and build my own algorithm."

A startled expression appeared on Gage's face.

"The sites didn't ask you for a warrant?" he asked.

Argus shook his head.

"No, although I did get permission from the site administrators. The sites all seem to be pretty open and casual," he explained. "Just message boards sharing spells, recipes, and info about events."

"Besides, people posting on Wicca and witchcraft sites don't use their real names. They use craft names, so their real identity is hidden. But most craft names are fairly unique, at least within a single coven or Wicca group, so I figured I could identify changes to users' activity patterns."

Gage looked lost as Argus continued.

"I've identified a dozen or so specific users who, over the

last two decades, had been active in the online Wicca community and have one thing in common," he said. "Each of these users has at one point abruptly vanished from the online community."

"What do you mean by vanish?" Bridget asked.

Argus pointed to the report in front of him as if the data on it would back up his assertion.

"These were all regular users who frequently visited the sites and often made posts. Then at one point, each of them abruptly stopped all activity and never logged on or posted anything again."

Widening his eyes for emphasis, he looked back and forth between Bridget and Gage.

"When I looked closer at their activity, I saw they had received unanswered messages and people on the site were posting messages asking about them," he said. "And right before their activity stopped, seven of them had been communicating with a user named Raven."

"Seven?" Bridget said, feeling her stomach drop.

"Yep," Argus confirmed. "And two out of the seven had been logging on regularly to the Tempest Grove Circle's message board before they vanished."

He looked down at his folder.

"A user named Faustina had been one of the first to post on the Circle's online message board when it started," he said. "She logged on or posted pretty much daily until May of 2005 when she disappeared from the boards for good."

Scrolling down the list, he tapped another name.

"Almost ten years later Zephra was a regular poster on

the Circle's board until she, too, just *stopped*. She never logged on to any of the sites again. That was in 2014."

Bridget frowned.

"You said there were seven altogether. What about the other five women?"

She saw the answer in Argus' grim eyes.

"The pattern is pretty consistent," he said. "An active engaged user has suddenly vanished from the online community once about every three years. They all seem to have disappeared in May, and none of them have ever been seen online again."

"Can you find out who the users were in real life and if they're okay?" Bridget asked. "And can we find out who Raven is?"

Argus shrugged.

"I'm working on it," he said. "But like I said, most of the people frequenting these sites don't use their real names."

"Could we post a message on the boards asking for information?" Bridget suggested. "Maybe we can pose as someone wanting to join the Circle."

"Sure, if we want our guy to know we're on to him," Argus said. "We might lure him out into the open, or we could scare him into hiding."

He looked pensive.

"And I have a bad feeling that's what Nicole Webster tried to do when she returned to Tempest Grove," he said. "And look where it got her."

CHAPTER TWENTY-ONE

Full night had fallen, and Gage's stomach was loudly rumbling in response to the delicious aromas coming from the kitchen, when Bridget and Santino finally arrived for dinner. Their knock at the front door sent Sarge scrambling toward the hall. The tiger-striped tomcat obviously wasn't in the mood to host visitors.

Opening the door, Gage stepped back to let the couple enter just as Kyla hurried into the room wearing a figure-hugging red dress that complemented her dark hair and smooth brown complexion.

As he stood in the doorway, Gage almost felt like a normal family man who was simply having friends over for a Friday night dinner party.

At one point in his life, not too long ago, he had despaired of ever having a family of his own. But now that he had Russell and Kyla with him, the big house on Mansfield Way had finally started to feel like a home.

No wonder he was starting to panic at the thought of losing Russell. The idea of returning to the lonely life he had lived before was hard to contemplate.

"Dinner will be ready in a few minutes," Gage said as he

took Santino's jacket and hung it on the rack. "And I hope you both like red wine. I've opened up a bottle of Chianti to go with the pasta."

Pulling Bridget to the side, he lowered his voice.

"Russell is in the backyard kicking around a soccer ball," he said. "I was thinking maybe you could talk to him out there while we get dinner on the table?"

Bridget followed him through the kitchen, stopping to admire the spicy red sauce bubbling on the stove, then slipped out onto the back porch, where Rusell was sitting on the steps, scrolling through his phone.

Unable to help himself, Gage held the door open just a crack and strained to listen to their conversation as Bridget sat down beside the teenager.

"I thought you were supposed to be kicking around the soccer ball," Bridget said. "What's on that phone that's so interesting? Anything you want to share?"

She made a show of staring down at the little screen and Russell quickly tucked the device away in his pocket.

Now that there was no phone to command his attention, the teenager turned his eyes to Sarge.

The cat had slipped out after Bridget and was halfheartedly trying to catch a lizard hiding in the flower bed.

"So, your Uncle Gage tells me that your mother's parole hearing is coming up soon," Bridget said.

Russell didn't look at her.

"He's not really my uncle."

The soft words felt like a punch to Gage's stomach.

"Who's been saying that?" Bridget asked.

"My mom told me to remember he's just a family friend," Russell said. "She said I shouldn't get too attached because when she gets out of jail, it'll be just the two of us again."

Resisting the urge to throw open the door and charge out onto the porch, Gage forced himself to remain quiet.

I knew it. I knew that woman was planning to take him away from the only stable home he's known since Kenny died.

He shook his head in outrage as he stuck his eye to the crack in the door and tried to see what was happening, but all he could see was the back of Russell's red sports jersey.

"How have you been feeling about the parole hearing?" Bridget asked. "Are you worried about what might happen after it's over? Are you concerned about where you'll live?"

Russell nodded.

"Yeah, but it's not up to me," he said. "At least, that's what my mom told me. She said I've got to do what she says."

His voice wavered a little on the words.

"And what is it she wants you to do?"

The question hung in the air, and for a minute, Gage didn't think Russell was going to answer.

"She wants me to listen to her, I guess," he finally said, looking away. "And she doesn't want me to let Dad down."

"How would you do that?" Bridget asked.

Russell shrugged his thin shoulders.

"By turning my back on her...and not being loyal."

Holding back an indignant objection, Gage wondered

what Estelle could be thinking.

How could she try to manipulate her son and make him feel guilty when she's the one who committed a crime?

Gage strained to hear what Bridget said next, but suddenly Kyla was standing behind him in the kitchen.

"Is this how the FBI gets its information?" she asked in a dry voice. "By listening to private conversations through a crack in the door?"

Grabbing his arm, she pulled him into the room and gently closed the door behind him.

"Now, you've got a table to set and pasta to serve," she reminded him. "And don't forget the wine. I definitely need a glass. Or two."

As she went back to the living room, where Santino sat by himself on the sofa, Gage wondered if he should tell Kyla what he'd overheard.

He doubted she would be as calm and collected as she was now if she knew what her sister-in-law had been saying and what she was planning.

And will she still want to stay here with me once Russell's gone? Will I lose them both?

The question nagged at him as he went to the stove and began to stir the steaming red sauce.

His mind was still mulling over the question when Bridget and Russell came through the back door.

"That smells really good, Uncle Gage," Russell said as he walked across the room. "I'll go wash up and then I'll come back down and help set the table."

After the teenager had left the room, Gage looked back at

Bridget, trying not to let his face reveal the fact that he'd overheard most of their conversation.

"He is conflicted," she said before he could ask any questions. "And I think he should see a therapist. Someone who specializes in teenagers and blended families."

She held up a hand before he could protest.

"I can't lie and tell you it's going to be easy to work with Estelle once she's out," she said. "But if you have a therapist who can advocate for Russell with the court, it could help."

Before he could ask any questions, his phone buzzed in his pocket. Digging it out, he saw a reply to his earlier text had come in.

"It's Charlie," he said, looking up at Bridget. "I told her what you and Argus said about Hirsch. If he isn't the one who killed those women, then she should expect more bodies soon. She just replied."

Bridget raised an eyebrow.

"And what did she say?"

He held up the phone and read Charlie's reply aloud.

Message received loud and clear. We'll be investigating Hirsch's death as a homicide. Task force resources are canvassing the area around Hirsch's property now. Will keep you updated.

CHAPTER TWENTY-TWO

Bailey Flynn settled into the passenger seat of Matthew Landon's Ford Interceptor and yawned. It had been a very long day so far, and it wasn't over yet. Glancing back at Ludwig, who was sitting in the backseat, she could see from the German Shepherd's heavy eyes that he was also starting to get fatigued.

Charlie Day had called her just as Bailey was about to head back to D.C., and she'd readily agreed to go with Landon to canvas the area around Calvin Hirsch's house.

After all, there was no one waiting for her in the tiny apartment she rented in the city. But she wasn't complaining. She'd been lucky to find a place she could afford on her own, with Ludwig as her only roommate.

And now that Hirsch's death had been determined to be a homicide, they would need to talk to as many people as possible in the area to see if they could find a witness who may be able to point them in the right direction.

"I guess we should start at the next-door-neighbor's place," Bailey said as the Interceptor approached Hirsch's house. "They would be the most likely ones to have seen someone coming or going that night."

She looked over at Landon, but the Tempest Grove detective didn't appear to be listening.

"Stop!" she called out, pointing toward the *Chumbley's Organic Farm* sign on the fence. "This is it. It's directly adjacent to Hirsch's property."

As the big SUV jerked to a stop, Bailey surveyed the sturdy wooden fence that surrounded the farm, which lay between Calvin Hirsch's dry strip of land and the lush woods west of Hammerling House.

Before she could open the door, Landon put a restraining hand on her arm.

"Hold on, now. We can't just go totting up there without a plan," he said as he checked his holster. "Abner Chumbley's a strange breed. He's always carrying a gun wherever he goes, even on his own property. Although his boy Vern is harmless enough."

Following his lead, Bailey reached for her Glock, quickly checked the chamber, and then returned it to her holster.

"Old Abner better not try anything funny," Landon said, running a hand through his thick beard while making no move to get out of the car. "I'm not going to take any of his craziness tonight, I'll tell you that."

Bailey glanced over at the detective, wondering if the big man was nervous. Was he working up his courage to get out and go up to the gate?

She'd spent most of her relatively short career in the FBI partnered with agents in Miami and D.C. who were seasoned and jaded. She couldn't remember seeing any of them show signs of fear or hesitation.

Perhaps in Tempest Grove, Landon hadn't developed the hard shell that came from facing danger and death day after day. Maybe he'd been sitting behind a desk a little too long.

"Why don't I go up to the gate and just see if they'll let me in?" Bailey suggested. "You can stay here with Ludwig and cover me from the street."

When Landon nodded, Bailey opened the door and stepped out, leaving her gun in her holster, but keeping her hand near enough to pull it out if old Abner Chumbley came out with both barrels blazing as Landon seemed to fear.

Approaching the gate, she gave a tentative push on the latch but saw right away that it was locked tight and appeared to be operated by some sort of pulley system that would slide the gate open if activated.

She examined a small metal box mounted on the gate and pushed the red button on the front to see if anything would happen. Nothing did.

As she looked closer, she saw the cables at the back of the metal box had been disconnected and appeared to be rusting.

Footsteps sounded somewhere behind the fence.

"Hello?"

When no one answered, she tried again.

"I'm Agent Flynn with the FBI and I'd like to ask you a few questions," she yelled, feeling vaguely foolish.

Suddenly, a loud screech sounded, and the gate creaked open to reveal a muscular man in jeans and a clean blue work shirt. His broad face was free of facial hair, and he stared at Bailey with wide, friendly eyes.

"I'm Vern," the man said, lifting his hand in a quick wave.

Before Bailey could respond, a loud horn blared behind Vern, causing him to jump. The man looked to Bailey with wide, scared eyes as a white truck roared up to the gate and skidded to a sudden stop.

"That's Pa," Vern said. "He's leaving for the market."

Bailey put a protective arm in front of Vern, nudging him back toward the edge of the driveway as the door to the white truck swung open and an old man stepped out.

"What do you want?" he asked, his eye resting on the butt of Bailey's gun, which was visible under her jacket.

"Abner Chumbley? I'm Agent Flynn with the FBI, and..."

She looked back at the Interceptor and saw Landon stepping out of the vehicle.

"And that's Detective Landon with the Tempest Grove PD," she added. "We'd like to ask you a few questions about a homicide we're investigating."

"I won't be answering any questions without my lawyer present," Abner said, watching Landon approach with hostile eyes. "I know how y'all work. First, I start talking and next thing you know I end up in one of those cells of yours."

He pointed to the gun hanging on a rack in the back window of his truck.

"Now get off my property before I get my gun," he said. "And just y'all try to come back with one of them warrants and we'll see what happens."

Stomping back to the truck, Abner got into the driver's

seat and slammed the door shut.

He made a move as if to reach for his gun, and Bailey prepared to pull her own weapon, but then dropped her hand as the old man put the truck into gear and sped away.

As Abner's tail lights disappeared down Arcana Avenue, a tentative voice spoke up beside Bailey.

She had almost forgotten Vern was still there.

"Sorry about my Pa," he said. "He's always like that."

He pointed to the Interceptor.

Landon had left the interior light on, and Ludwig's head was visible behind the thick glass.

"Is that one of them rescue dogs like they have on TV?" Vern asked. "I always wanted to see one of them in real life."

"Yes, that's Ludwig," Bailey said. "If you like, I can bring him out here and let you meet him. Then maybe we can ask you a few questions about Calvin Hirsch."

Cocking her head, she tried to make eye contact with the man, but he quickly looked away.

"Pa told me never to talk to the police."

Vern scratched at his short, dark hair.

"He said y'all can't be trusted," he added. "But he's always saying stuff like that."

"I'm not actually with the police," Bailey said. "I'm with the Federal Bureau of Investigation. And I just want to ask you a few questions about Mr. Hirsch."

Looking over at the Interceptor, the man hesitated.

"You'll let me meet that dog if I answer your questions?"

Bailey nodded.

"Okay, then, but I don't know much. At least, that's what Pa always says to me. He says I'm simple. But then, he's always saying stuff like that."

Deciding she liked Abner Chumbley even less than she first thought, Bailey asked Vern a series of questions about what he'd seen the day Hirsch had been killed.

It was clear he hadn't seen Hirsch or anyone else on the property that day, but he attempted to answer each question as earnestly as a child.

"Coach Hirsch is a good man," Vern said. "My Pa says he's no good trash and told me to stay away from him, but I didn't listen. I like him."

Bailey wondered if the man knew Hirsch was dead.

"What about your other neighbors?" Bailey asked. "Do you know the people who live in Hammerling House?"

"I sure do," he said.

His eyes lit up with pleasure.

"I've got lots of friends there. My Mama used to go over there all the time back before she went up to heaven."

The light in his eyes seemed to dim.

"Did you ever meet a woman named Nicole at Hammerling House?" she asked on impulse.

Vern nodded soberly.

"But Pa told me she's dead just like Mama," he said. "And she had a twin sister, too. Pa said it was a real shame what happened to her."

Bailey exchanged glances with Landon.

"Do you know what happened to Nicole's sister, Vern?"

He nodded again.

"She disappeared," he said. "Just like magic."

A shiver worked its way up Bailey's spine.

"Okay, well, thanks for answering our questions, Vern."

She was turning away when he put out a hand to stop her.

"What about Ludwig?" he asked. "Can I meet him?"

"Sure, I'll bring him out and let him stretch his legs before we go," she agreed. "He's had a long day."

She left Landon with Vern, jogged back to the interceptor, and opened the rear door.

As soon as Ludwig jumped to the ground, he lifted his head and sniffed at the air.

Before Bailey could snap on his leash, he let out a loud bark and took off running toward Landon and Vern.

The detective jumped back as the German Shepherd raced past him through the gate, while Vern stood grinning after the dog as if enjoying the show.

"What's he after?" Vern called out as Bailey sprinted past him, chasing after Ludwig.

By the time she caught up to the dog, he had made it all the way back to the big red barn at the rear of the property.

She stopped at the open door and stared in at what appeared to be a shadowy figure inside.

Not sure what she was seeing, she took out her phone and activated the flashlight, shining it into the barn.

A woman in a green dress hung from the rafter. Streaks of blood had stained the dress and formed a puddle at her feet.

Running footsteps sounded behind Bailey, and she turned

to see Landon and Vern approaching.

Both men stopped and stared at the dead woman.

"Elora?" Vern asked in a strangled voice.

Before Bailey could catch him, he fell to the ground.

"I think he fainted," she called to Landon. "Check his pulse while I call for back-up."

CHAPTER TWENTY-THREE

T he gate outside Chumbley's Organic Farm was closed when Bridget and Santino arrived, but a crowd of reporters and press were already gathering in the street despite the late hour, and a stocky man in black leather pants and a white crewcut stood by the gate.

"...once again the Tempest Grove PD arrived too late to stop one of our citizens from getting slaughtered," the man rasped into his microphone. "And it won't surprise any of our loyal listeners to learn that the scene of the latest murder is within spitting distance of Hammerling House..."

Bridget recognized Spike Oswald from the billboard she'd seen on Shackleton Highway.

"He looks a lot smaller in person, doesn't he?" she murmured to Santino as a uniformed officer opened the gate and ushered them inside where Detective Landon was waiting to take them to the body.

After pulling baggy protective coveralls and booties over their clothes and shoes, they headed off toward the back of the property.

"I have to warn you it's pretty gruesome," Landon said, leading them past an old farm house and into the back garden. "The guy who lives here actually fainted when he saw her. That's how bad it was."

Sensing that Landon was still slightly traumatized by the scene he had witnessed, Bridget suggested that he go back to the gate and wait for Charlie, who was on her way.

She and Santino continued walking toward the flood lights up ahead. As they approached a red barn, Bridget could see that Opal Fitzgerald and Greg Alcott had already arrived.

The M.E.'s white van sat outside the barn door, and a gurney had been rolled inside the big building.

"You work fast," Bridget said when she saw that the body was already on the gurney. "Did you make an ID?"

"According to the man who lives here, her name is Elora," Opal said. "But we were able to go next door and speak to her partner. A man named Gerard Ernst. He said her real name is Mary Jane Johnson."

Bridget's eyes widened in surprise.

"Elora?"

She crossed to the gurney and gently pulled down the sheet. The green dress the young woman had been wearing earlier in the day was now stained with blood, and her blonde hair had broken free of her braids and fell over the side of the gurney in tangled waves.

"At first I thought she had been stabbed three times by a very long knife," the M.E. said, gesturing to the wounds on the woman's chest. "Then I saw the pitchfork."

Bridget looked past Opal to see Jason Chan taking photos of a large pitchfork with three stainless-steel tines and a thick wooden handle.

The murder weapon was lying next to a pool of blood.

"It appears he stabbed her with the pitchfork first, then hung her up on the rafter, perhaps for dramatic effect, since she was likely already dead at that point."

Walking over to where Jason was working, Bridget looked down at the pitchfork.

"There's blood on the handle," Jason said.

He pointed to several red swirls on the wood.

"And fingerprints in the blood."

"You think some of that blood could be from the killer?" Bridget asked. "Could he have hurt himself?"

If so, they might be able to get DNA.

"We'll find out," he said. "And we'll run the fingerprints through AFIS as well. Who knows, maybe we'll get a hit."

Bridget nodded, eager to know what the Automated Fingerprint Identification System would tell them.

As she and Santino were about to leave the barn, Jason called them back.

"We've found something up in the loft."

The evidence response team leader pointed toward a ladder leading up to a loft that ran along the side of the barn.

One of his crime scene technicians was standing at the edge of the loft looking down, waiting for them to climb up.

"I guess I'll go first," Bridget said.

Climbing up the thin wooden ladder, with Santino only a few rungs behind her, she reminded herself not to look down.

As Bridget climbed onto the wooden platform, she stared in surprise at the telescope positioned by the window, its lens focused on Hammerling House.

The house where Elora had lived up until that afternoon.

"I'd say someone spent a lot of time up there based on the supplies we found scattered in the hay," Jason said.

Bridget looked back at Santino.

"It could be one of the men who live here," she said. "One of them could have been watching Elora. They could have lost control and killed her."

"Why do it in their own barn?" Santino asked.

She shrugged.

"Maybe they didn't expect company," she said. "Maybe it was some kind of ritual they didn't get a chance to complete, and they didn't count on Ludwig catching their scent."

CHAPTER TWENTY-FOUR

Charlie Day studied the two men sitting across the table from her with growing frustration. After arriving at their farm and viewing the crime scene in the barn, she had insisted on bringing Vern and Abner Chumbley down to the Tempest Grove police station, threatening to arrest them both if they refused.

It was now after midnight, and she and Hale had been questioning the father and son in separate interrogation rooms for over an hour but had failed to get any useful information out of either one of them.

She had finally decided to sit them down together and take one last shot at it.

"Okay, let's go through this again, Mr. Chumbley," she said, staring at Abner. "When you left your farm earlier today, you didn't know a woman's body was hanging from your barn rafter, is that what you're trying to tell us?"

Abner pressed his lips together, refusing to answer.

"And the reason you didn't want to let Agent Flynn onto your property had nothing to do with the dead woman?"

Again, Abner looked away.

Turning to stare at Vern, she cleared her throat.

"What about you, Vern? If you and your father had nothing to do with Elora's death, do you expect us to believe you didn't see anyone bringing her body onto your property?"

Vern looked at his father, obviously anxious to talk, wanting to give them what they wanted so he could go home.

Abner lifted a finger to his lips and mimicked the motion of a key being turned in a lock.

"We know you were watching Hammerling House through your telescope, Vern," Hale said, slamming his hands on the table between them. "Why were you watching the house? Were you watching Elora? Were you stalking her?"

"No!" Vern said, shaking his head vehemently. "She was *nice*. All the folks at Hammerling House were nice. That's why I was watching them."

He glanced at his father, then quickly looked away, ignoring the man's stern look of warning.

"I just liked to pretend I lived there," he said in a small voice. "I made believe that was *my* house and that those folks were *my* family. I didn't mean any harm."

Charlie met the man's pleading eyes and sighed.

No matter what the evidence was telling her, she couldn't picture the man in front of her as a killer. Couldn't see the earnest, scared man wielding a pitchfork.

And Abner was old and in poor health. Would he really have had the strength and ability to subdue Elora and hoist her over the rafter?

Whoever had killed Elora had been both able-bodied and evil, and neither of the men before her fit the profile.

"I'd like you both to submit a DNA sample," she said. "That will allow us to eliminate you from our inquiry."

Abner snorted.

"That's the oldest trick in the book," he said. "And neither one of us is going to give you a damn thing."

"Then we'll consider you both as suspects," Charlie said. "And I'd advise you to start looking for a lawyer."

* * *

Charlie slept in late, exhausted from the long night she'd spent working the crime scene out at Chumbley's Farm.

Waking with a start, she sat up and looked around the room, then relaxed as she saw Hale standing by the side of the bed, smiling down at her.

When he saw that her eyes were open, he sat down next to her on the bed.

"Calloway wants my answer on Monday morning," he said softly. "If I accept, I'll be gone by the end of the month."

His words pierced the quiet room.

"So, I guess I'll have to turn him down."

He managed a rueful smile.

"There's no way I'll be able to walk out of here and leave you behind, not knowing when or if I'll ever..."

She lifted a finger to his lips to stop the words, unable to bear the regret she heard behind them.

Leaving her would hurt, but so would staying and giving up his chance to be part of something important.

"Don't decide anything yet," she said. "Let's talk about it tonight. Let's make sure we know what we're doing before you tell Calloway anything."

He smiled.

"I like it when you use the word *we*," he said.

Pushing a strand of hair back from her face, he bent over to kiss her, then sighed and pointed to her phone.

"There's a text on there from Bailey Flynn," he said. "You're probably going to want to read it."

Charlie hesitated, then reached for the phone, simultaneously irritated, and impressed that the task force's new agent was working on a Saturday.

Her gray eyes narrowed as she read the message.

Abner Chumbley has a felony record for assault. He served time in Rock Ridge, and his DNA is in CODIS. He isn't a match to the DNA under Hirsch's nails.

Her mind instantly switched to work mode.

Picking up her phone, she tapped on Bailey's name in her recent call list.

The agent picked up on the second ring.

"What do you mean Abner's not a match?"

"I mean the tissue found under Calvin Hirsch's fingernails isn't a DNA match to Abner. He didn't kill Hirsch."

Charlie couldn't pretend she was surprised.

The old man hadn't seemed spritely enough to take down Calvin Hirsch or anyone else for that matter.

"The DNA isn't a partial match either," Bailey went on. "So, Vern Chumbley's also off the hook for Hirsch."

"That doesn't mean he didn't kill Elora," Charlie said without conviction. "There was blood on the pitchfork handle...and fingerprints. So we'll have to wait and see."

There was a pause on the other end of the connection.

"Of course, we will," Bailey finally said as if placating an unreasonable child. "I've already been by the lab this morning. I spoke to the forensic examiner working on the evidence taken from the scene at Chumbley's Farm."

Charlie raised both eyebrows in surprise.

"Vivian Burke was in the lab this morning?" she asked. "She was actually working on a Saturday?"

"Yes, and she was very accommodating," Bailey assured her. "She said she should have the profile of the blood sample on the pitchfork later today. She offered to run it through CODIS right away."

Accommodating was a word few people used when describing Vivian Burke. Either Bailey was being sarcastic, or she'd managed to catch the notoriously prickly forensics examiner on a good day.

"Although, I doubt the DNA will find a hit in CODIS," Bailey cautioned again. "Not if Elora's killer is the same man who killed Nicole Webster and Calvin Hirsch."

Staring over at Hale, who was slowly getting dressed, Charlie knew Bailey was right.

"And don't forget Natasha Prescott," she said in a glum voice. "She's a victim, too. We now have four homicide victims and zero viable suspects."

Ending the call, she tried to think.

"DNA is getting us nowhere fast," she said, watching Hale strap on his holster. "We're running in circles. If the guy isn't in CODIS, we're going to need another way to find him. We need to know who we're looking for."

TWENTY-FIVE

Raven stood beside the bleachers, listening to his fellow spectators gossiping. He watched with interest as another batch of runners sprinted past him at full speed, their arms and legs pumping with youthful energy as parents and friends urged them on.

Tempest Grove High School had always held their track meets on Saturday mornings, and the sights and sounds of the event always brought back memories of Natasha Prescott.

He'd been standing on the sidelines that fateful day long ago, watching the girl laugh with her friends after the race.

In fact, if he remembered well, he'd been standing on that very spot when he'd first felt the urge to kill her.

She'd been hauntingly beautiful with her pale, delicate complexion and her dark red hair gleaming in the sun.

A sigh hovered on Raven's lips at the memory.

Too bad that underneath the girl's lovely exterior, she'd had a heart of ice. A witch's heart.

Perhaps the flame-colored hair should have warned him, but foolishly Raven had ignored the warning signs and had willingly allowed himself to fall under her spell.

Only later had he realized she must have used a love charm or enchantment on him, although she never would admit it.

The surprise in her startled eyes when he'd declared his love had seemed genuine. She'd put on a very good show.

But the look had morphed into fear as he'd explained that he'd been watching her. That he'd seen her at the Circle. That he had been captured by her spell.

"Raven?"

He turned in surprise at the sound of his craft name.

Gerard Ernst stood before him, looking stooped and sad.

"Watch your words," he said sharply, looking around to see who else may have heard. "You of all people should know better that to use my craft name outside the Circle. You're the one who taught me the rules."

It had been many years since the high priest had explained to him that craft names were used to maintain privacy and avoid religious discrimination.

Based on Ernst's advice, he had selected the craft name Raven at the time of his initiation, and he'd only shared it with a few selected members of the Circle since then.

Holding up a hand in apology, Ernst raised red-rimmed eyes to Raven. His face was pale and haggard.

"I can't believe Elora is dead," he said numbly. "I mean, why her? She never hurt a soul."

"Yes, it's terrible," Raven said as his heart started to thump hard in his chest. "I'm sure you must be devastated."

He took Ernst's arm and pulled the high priest toward

the side of the bleachers, not wanting to be seen with the man, not wanting to provide fodder for spectators in the stands.

"You know they found her hanging in the barn, don't you?" Ernst said as he shook his head mournfully. "I just can't stop thinking of it..."

A thrill rolled through Raven's body at the remembered image of Elora's body swaying below the rafters, her long, fair hair hanging over her shoulder in silken strands.

He hid his excitement as he dropped Ernst's arm.

"Yes, it's terrible," Raven repeated. "Such a shame."

"I'd like to kill the bastard who did it," Ernst said, clenching his fists by his side. "You think it was Abner? Or maybe even Vern?"

Raven pictured Abner and Vern Chumbley being driven away from their farm in a Tempest Grove PD cruiser.

"I'd say they're definitely prime suspects," he agreed.

"The FBI came to search her room this morning," Ernst added. "Just like they do on TV. When they were leaving, they said it looked as if she left the house of her own free will."

Nodding gravely, Raven guided Ernst back toward the parking lot, impatient to be rid of the older man.

"Are you going back to Hammerling House?" he asked as he looked over his shoulder. "I'm sure the rest of the Circle will gather there once they hear the news. You'll want to be with the coven."

"Her identity hasn't been released to the public yet."

Ernst sounded forlorn.

"So, I came out to let her friends know that she's...gone."

His voice wavered and he dropped his eyes as if embarrassed by the display of emotion.

"Once I've spread the news, I'll go home."

"Yes, that's probably the safest bet," Raven agreed. "Too many people have gotten killed in this town lately. It seems no one's safe anymore."

He watched Ernst disappear into the crowd, then turned and made his way toward the parking lot, returning several greetings from track meet spectators along the way.

He'd have to go now if he wanted to get to Hammerling House and find a way into Gerard Ernst's private living quarters before the old man returned.

If the crime scene team was done with their initial search of the house, he may have a chance to get inside unseen.

Walking quickly back to his car, he drove home, preferring to make the journey on foot through the woods.

It was less likely he'd be noticed that way, and less likely that questions would be asked.

He made his way quickly through the thick forest, avoiding the path to the high altar, just in case others from the coven might be out and about.

But he saw no one as he approached the gate and slipped into the back garden. He moved confidently around the side of the building to the east wing's private entrance, hurrying up the back stairs in search of Elora's room.

The door to the small bedroom was open, and Elora's scent hung in the air, summoning thoughts of the first time

Raven had seen her.

Their eyes had met when Ernst wasn't watching, and at the first opportunity, she had murmured an invitation.

"Meet me at the high altar at midnight."

She'd been startled by his refusal.

"I know your secret. I know who you really are."

Her whispered words echoed now in the empty room as Raven remembered how he'd followed her into the woods.

His secret had to be kept at all costs, even if the cost was another woman's life. And now he needed to make sure that she hadn't shared the secret with anyone else.

There was one place a witch might document such things.

One book that might hold the truth.

A book that the FBI might have already found.

But from the look at the room, which was neat and tidy, it appeared that the search they'd performed that morning had been cursory. Likely just an effort to make sure there hadn't been a struggle, and that Elora hadn't been abducted from the house.

Later on, as the investigation continued, the investigators might return to conduct a more thorough search.

Raven would need to make sure the book was gone before that could happen.

Moving toward the head of the bed, he picked up Elora's pillow and looked underneath. Her *Book of Shadows* lay beneath it, just as he'd expected.

As he flipped through the pages, he saw that much of the

book had been written in her own hand.

She'd recorded favorite spells, herbal recipes, and notes on her experience within the Circle of Eternal Light.

Near the end of the book, a yarrow twig had been stuck between the pages. Raven paused as he saw his own name written in Elora's now familiar childish script.

Below his name, she had added several smudged lines.

> *Once I discovered that the blood of our creator fills his veins, I wrote his true name on a piece of paper, tore it into tiny pieces, and scattered it to the four winds while invoking the blessings of the Old Ones. I trust in the spirits that our destinies are now entwined.*

He had no doubt the woman had written his name and used it in a binding spell, attempting to snare him in her trap.

But if she had known the extent of his secret, she would also have known that you can't charm the devil.

Closing the *Book of Shadows*, he hurried out the door.

CHAPTER TWENTY-SIX

Sunlight shone through the back window of the red brick house on Fern Creek Road as Bridget refilled Hank's water bowl and added fresh food to the dish beside it. Pouring herself another cup of coffee, she moved to the back door and stepped out onto the porch.

Out of the corner of her eye, she caught a flutter of red above the fence. A bright-red bird with a black patch around its face and beak landed lightly on the wood, then flew down to the bird feeder to peck at the sunflower seeds she'd set out just that morning.

"Look, Hank. It's a cardinal," Bridget called over her shoulder. "They're supposed to be a sign of good luck."

She looked back through the door to see that the Irish setter wasn't listening. He was busy eating his breakfast.

Moving to the top of the steps, she stopped and held onto the rail, overcome by a sudden pang of longing as she flashed back to a similar spring day when her mother had spotted a cardinal in the yard of her childhood home.

The wind lifted Edith Bishop's chestnut brown hair around her happy face as she pointed to the tiny red bird in the tree.

"Cardinals bring good luck, Bridget," she said, taking the six-

year-old by the hand. "Some people even think they bring us good wishes and messages from loved ones who've died."

Bridget turned her face up to her mother, meeting the blue eyes that so closely matched her own, trying to see if her mother was teasing. If she was being serious, who could have sent the bird?

Could her grandfather have sent her a message from wherever it was that dead people went? She knew he'd gone into the hospital and had never come back. Her father said he'd gone to heaven, but Bridget wasn't sure where that was.

"Do you think Grandpa is sending us a message?" Bridget asked, hopefully. "Did he send the cardinal from heaven?"

She frowned as she saw the happiness leave her mother's face. Had she said something wrong?

"You never know, Bridget."

Edith smiled, though her eyes had gone bright with tears.

"Sometimes, magical things can happen."

Her mother's words hung in the air as Bridget watched the cardinal flutter from branch to branch. She wondered how she could fix whatever she'd done to make her mother cry.

"Maybe we can send a message back?" she said uncertainly. "We can ask the cardinal to tell Grandpa we miss him. Can't we?"

Pulling her small daughter in for a hug, Edith nodded.

"Of course, we can, sweetheart," she agreed softly. "All we have to do is whisper a message into the wind, and the cardinal will carry it to Grandpa wherever he may be."

As the memory faded, Bridget became aware of a harsh buzzing from her pocket.

Sinking onto the top step, she pulled out her phone and looked down to see Charlie's number on the display.

"We need your help," Charlie said as soon as she heard Bridget's voice. "According to the DNA results, Hirsch didn't kill himself. And he didn't kill Elora. I'm convinced he didn't kill Nicole or Natasha either. So, we need to know who we should be looking for. We need a profile, and fast."

The tension in her voice was palpable over the phone.

"Well, Argus and I have been working on a profile," Bridget said. "So far we've reviewed most of the data from the original investigation into Natasha's disappearance."

"Okay, that's good," Charlie said. "So, what can you give us as far as a profile? Who should we be looking for?"

Bridget thought back to all the files she'd read, and the data Argus had sorted through, and sighed.

"I'd like to speak to Earl Ripley again before I complete my initial profile," she said.

"Who's Earl Ripley?" Charlie asked.

Seeing that the cardinal had flown away, Bridget turned and walked back into the kitchen.

"He was a detective on the Tempest Grove PD when Natasha went missing," she said. "He's retired now, but he works as a private investigator for my father. I've already spoken to him about the case, but I feel as if I didn't get the whole story."

She suddenly wondered what it was that Ripley had wanted to tell her the last time she'd been in her father's office. Had it been about the case? Had he remembered something that could help with the investigation?

"This case started up again when Nicole came back to Tempest Grove looking for her sister," Bridget said. "But

Natasha was the start of it. Her disappearance is the key."

"Okay, then see what you can set up with this Ripley guy," Charlie said. "And see if I can sit in."

* * *

Ripley was already sitting in the lobby of Bishop & Company Investigations when Bridget and Charlie walked in, but he didn't look particularly happy to see them.

The investigator had agreed to meet after she'd called her father in an effort to track Ripley down.

Based on the scowl he was now wearing, she suspected he was only there because he'd been reluctant to turn down the request Bob had passed on.

The agency was closed on Saturdays, so the desk Paloma usually sat at was empty, however, Bob was sitting at his desk with his office door open.

"Don't mind me," Bob called out. "I'm just catching up on some paperwork from the week. Pretend I'm not here."

Crossing the room, Bridget closed his office door and turned back to Ripley.

"Thanks for meeting us," Bridget said with a smile that wasn't returned. "I know this is supposed to be your day off."

"That's okay, I would have just been sitting at home watching bad reruns anyway," Ripley said.

Getting to his feet, he smoothed back the white hair from his high, tan forehead and turned to Charlie.

"This is Special Agent Charlie Day," Bridget said. "She's

with the FBI's Washington field office. She's running the investigation into Nicole Webster's murder as well as Natasha Prescott's abduction and murder."

"I don't envy your task," Ripley said as he shook Charlie's offered hand. "And I'm not sure what I can do to help you. I wasn't able to solve Natasha's abduction the first time around, so I'd think you'd want to look for fresh leads."

Charlie smiled but Bridget saw her back stiffen.

Before she could respond, Bridget spoke up.

"If you don't mind, I'd like to have Argus Murphy join in remotely. He's also an analyst with the BAU, and he's been working with me to come up with a profile."

Pulling out her phone, Bridget tapped on Argus' name in her recent call list. Seconds later Argus was visible via FaceTime, his carrot-hued hair slightly mussed as he spoke from what appeared to be his dining room table.

After introductions were made, Bridget asked Ripley to walk the group through the original investigation again.

When he had finished his account of the events leading up to Natasha's disappearance and the ensuing investigation, Bridget was disappointed to realize he'd shared nothing new.

She wondered again what he'd been meaning to tell her.

"Thank you, Mr. Ripley," Argus said. "It's helpful to have the full background of the case. And what you've told me just solidifies the theory that I've come up with."

Bridget propped the phone on the desk in front of Ripley, and they all sat down facing the little screen.

"I believe someone close to Natasha developed a fixation on her," Argus said. "Perhaps someone with ties to the circle or with Wicca. Someone who knew that her mother had been involved with the group. Someone who had the patience to wait for the first of May to lure her out of her house."

Bridget nodded her agreement.

"We believe the date is significant," she added. "It suggests that her abductor knew it was Beltane, which is a Wiccan festival day. And since Natasha's remains were found by the Witch's Tree, rather than near Hammerling House, it's likely he wasn't taking part in the Circle's celebration."

A frown of confusion creased Ripley's face.

"What we're saying is that the killer wasn't an open member of the coven, but was aware of their rituals and movements," Bridget explained. "He used what he knew and waited for the opportunity to act. And we believe that after that first time, he likely never stopped killing."

"So, when Nicole showed up in Tempest Grove asking questions, he must have panicked," Charlie said. "The secret he'd kept for decades was at risk of being exposed."

The tiny head on the FaceTime screen nodded.

"That's right, and key data from the case files tells us with some certainty that the killer still lives in Tempest Grove, and that he's closely connected with one or more of three central points of interest."

Reaching into her bag, Bridget pulled out a folder and opened it on the desk. The printout inside showed a high-level map of Tempest Grove.

Three red dots had been used to label the Tempest Grove Baptist Church, Hammerling House, and Tempest Grove High School.

Lines had been inserted to connect each of the dots.

"What is that?" Ripley asked.

The investigator leaned forward as if intrigued with the map and theory despite himself.

"It's the result of my geolocation analysis," Argus explained. "It tells us that the man we're looking for is somehow involved with these three locations. The area enclosed by the lines is sort of like a devil's triangle. That's where you'll find your killer."

CHAPTER TWENTY-SEVEN

Bob opened his office door and stuck his head out into the lobby. He'd heard most of the group's conversation and knew that Charlie had stepped outside to make a phone call to Hale. She planned to ask him if he'd go with her to the Tempest Grove Baptist Church.

In fact, based on the theory Argus had put forward, Bob knew that Charlie would be arranging for agents to visit all three locations on the map, which was still lying on the desk.

From what he'd overheard, Charlie just needed to find task force members willing to go to Hammerling House, since Bridget had already volunteered herself and Santino to go over to the high school.

Bob opened his mouth to ask Bridget if she wanted to meet him later for lunch, then closed it again as she asked Ripley a question.

"Did you ever remember what it was you wanted to tell me the last time I was here?" Bridget asked. "I thought maybe it was about the investigation, but then...well, you didn't seem to bring up anything new."

Ripley glanced over at Bob standing in the doorway and shook his head.

"It'll wait," Ripley said. "This case you're working on now is more important. Besides, I might have had it wrong."

Bob frowned at the grim expression on the investigator's face. Ripley looked as if he was about to face a firing squad.

"What's this you wanted to tell her?" Bob asked, stepping out of his office and moving toward the desk.

"Like I said, it's nothing."

Ripley looked down at his hands and Bob could see they were shaky. Something was definitely bothering the man.

"It's obviously *something* or you wouldn't have mentioned it," Bob said. "And you look as pale as a ghost, so tell us what it is. What did you want to say?"

Resignation settled over Ripley's weathered face.

"Okay, fine," he said. "I should have told you long before now anyway. But I never knew how to bring it up. I tried to just forget all about it."

He exhaled wearily.

"But then Bridget started working on the case in Tempest Grove, and it all started coming back," he said. "I figured she had a right to know. Edith was her mother after all."

Bob froze in place at the sound of his wife's name.

"What does this have to do with Edith?" he asked.

Hearing the pain in her father's voice, Bridget held up a hand as if to stop Ripley's words.

"No, I want to hear this," Bob insisted. "What is it you

were going to tell my daughter about her mother? What do you know about my wife?"

"I saw Edith in Tempest Grove the day she died," Ripley blurted out. "Before she had her accident."

Feeling his knees give out, Bob sank into a chair, no longer sure he wanted to hear what Ripley was about to say.

But now Ripley was speaking quickly, with an intensity that suggested he'd been waiting a long time to get the information off his chest.

"Edith was sitting in her car outside the police station," Ripley said. "Of course, I didn't know her well, but I recognized her as the therapist who'd been helping Nikki Prescott cope after her sister's abduction."

He clenched both his fists on the desk in front of him.

"She was leaning her head against the window and when I stopped to speak to her...well, her voice was slurred."

Ripley couldn't meet Bob's eyes.

"I asked if she was okay, and she mumbled something about having a drink. I thought she was drunk."

He swallowed hard.

"I didn't want to make a fuss, since I knew she'd been helping Nikki's parents free of charge," he said. "I advised her not to drive and she said something about calling her husband, so I figured she'd be okay."

Lifting his eyes to Bob, he continued in a tortured voice.

"But *she wasn't*," he said. "The next time I saw her was later that evening when I responded to the scene of a crash. I saw that she was the sole occupant, and..."

He struggled to find the words to explain why he hadn't

said anything then. Why he hadn't admitted what he'd seen.

"When I found out she was dead, and I met you at the scene, I couldn't tell you. I knew you would blame me because I blamed myself for not getting her out of that car."

"I didn't tell anyone. I just tried to block the whole thing from my mind, but every time I passed the street where it had happened I remembered. So when I got an offer from the Richmond PD, I accepted."

"When I retired and moved back home, it felt as if my life was over, but then you offered me this job, and...well, I didn't want to risk it by admitting what had happened."

He looked over at Bridget.

"But when I met your daughter...it all came rushing back."

Rage and pain washed through Bob as he realized what Ripley was telling him.

"You knew Edith was in no shape to drive, but you left her in that car?" he said, bringing his fist down hard on the desk. "Then when you saw me at the scene...you said nothing? All these years I had to wonder *why*?"

Bob felt tears of rage prick the backs of his eyes.

"All those years I spent wondering *why me*? Why did my daughter have to lose her mother? Why did the woman I love have to die? And yet, you had the answer all along!"

He looked to Bridget, who wore a shell-shocked expression that broke his heart all over again.

"All those years I blamed myself for not being there...when I should have blamed *you* for not stopping her!"

Knowing even in his grief that his words were irrational, Bob crossed to the door and threw it open.

"Get out!" he boomed. "Get out of my office!"

Ripley stood and crossed to the door.

"I'm sorry," he said as she stepped out on the porch.

Without another word, Bob slammed the door behind him.

"Are you okay, Dad?"

Bridget stood behind him, her face pale, but her eyes dry.

He nodded stiffly, trying to hold back the flood of memories that were washing over him.

His mind had acted like a dam for so long, blocking any emotions that might interfere with his stressful job at the Wisteria Falls PD, or with raising Bridget on his own. But now that internal barrier was crumbling, letting the pain and hurt carry his thoughts to a place they'd never gone.

Now, for the first time, he questioned the car crash, and the events leading up to it. For the first time, he allowed himself to wonder. Had Edith's death really been an accident?

Before he could voice his doubts to Bridget, her phone buzzed in her pocket.

"It's Faye," she said. "I'll let it go to voicemail."

"No, answer it."

Remembering that the therapist had just suffered her own double tragedy, Bob listened as Bridget answered the call and activated the speaker.

"Faye, how are you? I'm here with my father and..."

"I'm not good," Faye said. "And neither is Joelle. She's been listening to the radio all morning, even though I told her not to listen to that idiot Spike Oswald."

The therapist's normally calm voice was practically vibrating with anxiety.

"She just took off from here like a bat out of hell, and I don't know where she might go or what she might do."

CHAPTER TWENTY-EIGHT

Joelle pushed her foot down hard on the gas pedal of the classic, baby-blue Camaro Rowan had bought for her on her fiftieth birthday. She'd had the car for almost a decade now, but it still felt like a treat to take it for a drive along the twisting country roads that wound between the hills and valleys around Moonstone Cavern.

When she'd stomped out of the house on Forester Way, she hadn't been sure where she was going. All she knew was that she was sad and mad and going crazy.

She needed to clear her head.

The open road had called to her, and Shackleton Highway seemed as good a road as any.

Leaving the windows open, she allowed the wind to tangle her long, snow-white strands of hair that had once been a dark, mysterious red.

The fiery color had drained away over time until all traces had vanished as if it had never been there at all.

But that wasn't why she was mad. Was it?

Right now she wasn't sure who or what had earned the anger and rage that weighed so heavily in her heart and caused her foot to rest so heavily on the pedal.

Of course, she had plenty of reasons.

Her daughters were both dead and waiting to be buried.

And the police had arrested an innocent man, likely sending him to an early grave, and had yet to find the man who had taken her daughters' lives.

Oh, and her husband couldn't see sense when it was staring him in the face.

Does Rowan actually think I'm going to let Pastor Parnell stand over my girls' coffins before we put them in the ground?

She didn't trust Parnell or the congregants at his church.

They spouted off about grace and love in public but spread lies, gossip, and hate behind closed doors.

But they weren't the ones driving her toward the border.

I only have myself to blame. I couldn't save my girls any more than the police or Rowan could. I let them both get stolen away.

Her foot eased off the gas as she rounded a wide bend and approached the turn-off to Moonstone Cavern.

If I'm mad at myself, then running away, or driving away, won't do a bit of good. It won't bring back my girls.

Slowing as she saw the historical marker, she found herself bumping the Camaro's wide wheels onto the shoulder of the road, right next to the metal sign with black lettering.

Die Hexenbaum
(The Witch's Tree)
1769

A flutter of yellow crime scene tape had twisted around the base of the marker but there was no other sign the FBI, local police, or crime scene investigators had ever been there.

Joelle opened the Camaro's door and climbed out onto the grass, wishing she'd stopped to put on something other than flip-flops before she'd run out of the house.

Stretching her legs, she stood by the marker and studied the words with angry eyes.

Hundreds of years ago another witch had stood in this place, facing a crowd of ignorant, angry settlers.

They'd strung up some poor old woman whose only likely sin had been a bold tongue and a curious nature.

Joelle wondered if Brunhilde Kistler's spirit still haunted the woods were she'd been left hanging. Or had she followed those who'd murdered her onward to their final destination?

Looking to the forest, she realized that Nicole might have walked through this same grass.

And maybe Natasha, too.

She took a tentative step forward, and then another, and then she was running through the grass toward the tree line.

When she saw the sycamore she came to a sudden stop.

"Die Hexenbaum."

The words escaped as an anguished whisper as her eyes lifted to the tree, looking for scars on the branches that would prove her daughter had been there.

Soon she was walking again, heading this time in the direction of Moonstone Cavern.

Ducking under tree branches and stepping over roots,

she wove her way through the forest until she stood beside a deep, jagged trench in the ground.

The steep incline into the shadowy trench was covered with brambles and bushes, and Joelle dropped her head into her hands, unable to suppress a sob as she imagined Natasha's small body lying in the dark, rocky ground year after year until she'd been nothing but bones.

Her head snapped back up as a rock went skittering down the side of the ravine.

Was that movement she'd seen in the woods?

She inched closer, straining to see, then stopped still.

Yes, someone was definitely moving through the trees.

"Hello?"

The sound of her own voice startled her, and she jumped slightly as a bird flew up and out of a nearby tree.

Taking off at a fast walk, she sensed the figure shadowing her, matching her step for step as it dodged between trees, weaving in and out of sight.

Heart pounding, she decided to lose her shadow and broke into a slow run, heading again for Moonstone Cavern.

As she came to a sudden break in the trees, she saw the opening to the cavern ahead.

A *Cavern Temporarily Closed* sign hung on a rope stretched from one side of the opening to the other.

Sucking in deep, calming breaths she walked forward to look around, noticing that the small parking lot in front of the cavern had been blocked off to prevent cars going along the road to pull in. The place was pretty much deserted.

Her pulse had just settled back to a normal rhythm when

she heard footsteps pounding in her direction.

Was it the figure that had been shadowing her in the woods? Looking around, Joelle impulsively ducked under the rope and crossed to the cavern entrance.

Slipping inside, she strained to see into the darkness, then fumbled for her phone. As she turned on the phone's flashlight, a voice spoke behind her.

"I thought that was you, Ginerva. How did you know I would be here? Did you follow me to the Witch's Tree?"

Recognition registered in Joelle's brain just as something thick and hard connected with her head.

Her legs gave way beneath her, and she fell to the ground, dropping her phone, and cutting off the only source of light.

"Did Nikki tell you it was me? That I took Natasha?"

Joelle tried to focus on the face above her, but it was too dark to see.

"Or maybe you really are a witch," the voice mocked. "Maybe you looked into your *crystal ball*."

The words were followed by a hollow laugh.

"But what you probably didn't know, is that I come from a long line of witches, as well as witch *hunters*."

She squinted up, holding her head in pain, as the man standing over her shone a bright light into her eyes.

"I don't follow the *do no harm* rule the Circle teaches its pathetic members. I follow my own rules. My own will is stronger than any magic you or the Circle can conjure."

Fear gripped her as she saw the rope coiled in his hand.

"Your daughters tried to cast their spells on me, but they

failed," he sneered. "As have you."

CHAPTER TWENTY-NINE

Bridget studied the passing street signs as Santino's red Chevy sped down Shackleton Highway, then checked her watch. Tempest Grove High School was closed on Saturdays, but according to the school's website, an all-county track meet had been scheduled for that morning, and she was hoping the expected crowds would still be there.

"There's Fairview Avenue," she called, prompting Santino to make a sharp turn. "The school should be just up ahead."

Sitting forward in her seat, she watched as the big school came into view, then slumped back as she saw a stream of cars waiting to pull out of the lot.

"Looks like the track meet is over," she said. "But there are bound to be people in the ticket office."

As Santino parked the Chevy by the curb outside the tiny ticket office, Bridget jumped out and hurried over to look past the counter. The small wooden building was empty.

"Who exactly are you hoping to find?" Santino asked as he surveyed the departing crowd.

"Anyone who worked here back when Natasha and Nicole

attended," Bridget said, heading toward the snack bar. "We need to find out if anyone was paying the girls too much attention, or if they'd had conflict with..."

Her voice trailed away as she spotted Merry Corwin, the secretary she'd met at the Baptist church.

"Mrs. Corwin?"

The woman turned with a ready smile.

"Yes?"

"I'm Special Agent Bishop with the FBI," Bridget said. "I came by the church to speak to Pastor Parnell the other day?"

The woman's smile hardened.

"Of course, how nice to see you, dear."

She looked around the crowd as if hoping to be rescued.

"My husband and I are volunteers here and we were just helping to clean up after the track meet," she said. "You know how messy teenagers can be."

"It's nice of you to volunteer," Bridget said. "Do you still have children in the school?"

"Good Lord, no," Merry said, adding a high-pitched laugh. "My husband used to be the principal here."

She lowered her voice and adopted a confidential tone.

"Brian still feels the need to volunteer here, although, with the paltry pension they gave him, I'm not sure why."

It suddenly dawned on Bridget that the woman's husband was Brian Corwin, the former high school principal who was one of the suspects on Argus' list.

Merry waved to a tall, distinguished-looking man who was carrying a garbage bag from table to table, picking up trash.

"Is that Brian?" Bridget asked hopefully. "I was hoping to ask him some questions about his time at the school."

The proud look on Merry's face melted into concern.

"What *about* his time at the school?" she said. "That was a long time ago. No one cares about that now."

"No one cares about what, Merry?"

Brian Corwin was now standing behind them.

He frowned at his wife as he tied the garbage bag closed and threw it in the already overflowing bin beside them.

"I'm Special Agent Bishop with the FBI," Bridget said. "I was just telling your wife that I wanted to ask you some questions about your time at the school."

"And I was telling her that I thought-"

Brain Corwin held up a hand.

"I can handle this, Merry," he said. "Now, why don't you go get me a cup of coffee while they still have some left at the snack bar? I'll deal with this."

He waited until his wife had reluctantly walked away, then turned back to Bridget.

"I'm assuming this is about Natasha Prescott's body being found," he said. "I was happy to hear that her parents will be able to bring her home. It will surely bring them peace. But there's nothing I can share that I didn't already tell the police back when Natasha went missing."

Turning impatiently as Merry raced back to deliver what appeared to be a lukewarm cup of coffee, Brian took the paper cup and drained it of its contents, then threw it into the bin.

"Now, the whole school went through a lot back then. We were all devastated," he said. "I had a child of my own at the time, so I knew how Joelle and Rowan must be feeling."

Bridget doubted he knew any such thing.

"I lost my passion for work after that," he said. "Sure, I went on until I could retire. I made sure I earned my pension, but it never was the same. I was relieved to pass on the torch to Joshua when the time came. And I've been enjoying retirement ever since."

"Where were you on Sunday night?" Bridget said.

Brian's voice grew icy.

"I was home with my wife, as usual."

Turning to Merry, Bridget raised an eyebrow.

"And he was with you the whole night, Mrs. Corwin?"

The woman quickly nodded.

"And did you ever have a theory about who abducted Natasha?" Bridget asked, returning her gaze to Brian.

"I went through all this with the police back when Natasha went missing," he said dismissively.

"According to the files I've seen, at the time you insisted she had probably just run away," Bridget reminded him. "But now it turns out Natasha Prescott was dead all this time. So, who do you think killed her and dumped her body in that ravine?"

Merry gasped and raised a hand to cover her mouth.

"I have no idea," Brian said, looking around as if hoping for an intervention from one of the other volunteers.

Lowering her hand, Merry leaned forward.

"Some people have suggested Pastor Parnell may have–"

"Pastor Parnell is a good man," Brian cut in sharply, glaring at his wife. "He was a youth pastor for all the kids around here. Back then, I trusted him with my son's salvation, and I trust him still."

Bridget looked past him to his wife.

"Mrs. Corwin, do you happen to know where Pastor Parnell was last Monday night?"

The woman hesitated then shook her head.

"No, I don't," she admitted. "I don't want to lose Pastor Parnell's trust or my job, but..."

"Anything you tell us will be held in confidence," Bridget assured her. "We're just gathering information. No one's accusing the pastor of anything."

Swallowing hard, the secretary sighed.

"Well, the pastor did leave fairly quickly after the Sunday night bible study group," she said. "And he came in late on Monday morning. He said he'd been up late. It seems ungenerous to say, but he looked disheveled."

She ignored her husband's tightening grip on her arm.

"His shoes were muddy, and he seemed flustered. Especially when we heard on the radio that the police were out by the caverns. I have to admit he was acting strangely."

Brian cleared his throat loudly.

"That's enough, Merry," he said. "I'm sure Pastor Parnell wouldn't appreciate you talking about him like that. Remember Proverbs 11:13. A gossip betrays a confidence, but a trustworthy person keeps a secret."

Bridget cleared her throat.

"Reporting suspicious activity in the course of a homicide investigation isn't exactly gossip, Mr. Corwin," Bridget said. "And keeping secrets can be considered obstruction of justice during a homicide investigation."

Bridget took out a card and handed it to Merry.

"If you think of anything else," she said, directing her words at Merry. "Please call me."

She watched as Brian Corwin pulled his wife toward the parking lot, then turned back to Santino.

"Brian Corwin works at the school and attends the church regularly," she said. "And his wife is his only alibi for the night of Nicole Webster's murder. So, I'd say he's still a suspect."

"But, he clearly has nothing to do with Hammerling House or the Circle," Santino pointed out. "I doubt he's ever stepped foot inside the place."

Bridget shrugged.

"Based on our current lack of viable suspects, two out of three isn't bad."

She took out her phone and pointed toward the trash bin, snapping several photos of the coffee cup lying on top before handing the phone to Santino.

"Record me collecting this cup," she said. "Now that Brian Corwin has disposed of it in a public place, it's fair game. We can test it for his DNA and find out once and for all if we can take him off Argus' suspect list."

CHAPTER THIRTY

Charlie followed Hale into the Tempest Grove Coffee Shop, ordered a chocolate croissant and a latte from the barista, then made a beeline for an open booth by the window. Realizing she hadn't had anything to eat since the night before, she took a big bite of the warm croissant and followed it up with a long, satisfying sip of the latte.

She was chewing another bite of the pastry when Bridget and Santino pushed through the door.

"They sell coffee here, you know," Charlie said, catching sight of the clear evidence collection bag in Bridget's hand.

"Very funny," Bridget replied, holding up the bag. "This cup was disposed of in public, and it may have Brian Corwin's DNA on it. I'm bringing it to the lab for testing."

Hale frowned.

"Who's Brian Corwin?"

"He was the principal at Tempest Grove High School when Natasha and Nicole Prescott were students," Bridget said. "He was a person of interest at the time. And I have to say that he seemed pretty flustered by our questions today."

She nodded toward the evidence bag.

"I figured we can test this to see if he can be eliminated."

Charlie nodded, thinking of a recent case she'd worked on.

"I worked a homicide recently where we sent the DNA results to a forensic genealogist," she said. "The woman built a family tree looking for suspects with the right DNA profile. She identified a fourth cousin of our perp, then followed the family line back to the present generation."

"That sounds like it would take ages," Hale said as he eyed the remains of Charlie's croissant.

Pushing her plate toward him, she shrugged.

"It's taken twenty-seven years to find out what happened to Natasha Prescott and prove a murder even occurred," she reminded him. "It may take a few more days or weeks for us to figure out who's responsible."

"A lot of cold cases are solved with forensic genealogy," Santino said. "Maybe you guys can figure out a way to get a disposed DNA sample from Pastor Parnell when you go by the church."

Hale stuck the last bite of the pastry into his mouth and stood up. Running an impatient hand through his dark hair, he gestured toward Charlie.

"I guess that's our cue to go," he said. "See you two later."

As they walked out to Charlie's Expedition, Hale sighed.

"Actually, I'm not sure I will see them later. If I want to take Calloway up on his offer, I'll have to start preparing this week. No more brainstorming over lattes for me."

He flashed her a teasing smile, but Charlie could tell that

the decision was weighing on him.

They drove toward Tempest Grove Baptist Church in silence, both lost in their thoughts, perhaps sensing they didn't have much time left.

Turning onto Liberty Parkway, Charlie caught sight of a tall spire ahead and followed the winding road to the church.

She was surprised to find the parking lot full.

As they walked up to the sanctuary and opened the door, Charlie realized too late that a wedding was in progress.

Hale took her hand and led her to an empty pew at the rear of the sanctuary, sliding silently onto the cushioned bench.

Once they were seated, he held onto her hand as the couple standing at the altar took their vows.

"Do you take this woman for better or worse, for richer or poorer, until death do you part?"

Hale leaned over to whisper in Charlie's ear.

"I do."

Charlie turned to meet his eyes.

"I do, too."

The whispered words slipped out before she could stop them, and she realized with painful certainty that she meant them. She did want to be with the man beside her until the end came for one of them. Whenever that may be.

"And now, by the powers vested in me by the State of West Virginia, I pronounce you husband and wife."

As the church organist started pounding out Mendelssohn's Wedding March, the entire congregation stood and turned to watch the happy couple exit the church.

Still holding Charlie's hand, Hale pulled her after him to the left side of the pew and started up the outer aisle, hoping to catch Pastor Parnell on the altar.

But as they reached the front of the sanctuary, they saw Parnell making his way down the steps, following the groomsmen down the aisle and out the front doors.

"So much for interrogating the pastor," Hale said. "But I have to say, it was the best wedding I've ever been to."

Charlie's heart quickened at the words, which were followed by a harsh buzzing in her pocket.

Quickly pulling out her phone, she looked down to see a text from Bridget.

Don't forget the pastor's DNA!

She showed the text to Hale, who rolled his eyes.

"So much for romance," he said wryly as he led her out the back of the church and pointed to the dumpster.

"You're kidding, right?" she asked.

Hale shook his head.

"Where else do you think we're gonna find a pastor's disposed DNA?"

When she still didn't look convinced, he shrugged and slipped off his jacket, then handed it to her.

"The things I do for love..."

Hoisting himself up and over the side of the dumpster, he disappeared inside with only a slight *thump* and some rustling of plastic and paper.

"You know, the pastor should learn how to recycle," Hale called out as his head reappeared over the side. "Take this."

He handed over a paper coffee cup with the name *Pastor P* written on the outside in black marker. Charlie took it from him using a clean tissue from her pocket.

With a loud grunt, Hale hoisted himself back up and over the side, landing smoothly on his feet beside Charlie.

As they made their way back to the Expedition and pulled back onto Liberty Parkway, Charlie saw that the sun was starting to set in the west.

Her good mood began to fade along with it.

They had agreed to make a decision tonight, and night was starting to fall. They couldn't avoid the subject much longer.

Sucking in a deep breath, she turned to him, ready to tell him what she was thinking, then hesitated.

"What's that sound?"

Looking around, she saw that a large crowd of people had gathered on a wide expanse of land that served as a town square. The gathering appeared to be some sort of rally.

A stocky man with a white crewcut stood on a makeshift stage that had been constructed at one end of the field.

Spike Oswald held a bullhorn in one hand as a man in a WARP 102.5 FM hoodie circulated through the crowd holding a *Burn, Witch, Burn* sign.

Rolling down her window, Charlie could make out the chanting coming from the crowd.

Close the Circle! Close the Circle! Close the Circle!

Spike Oswald's deep voice rose over the crowd, amplified by the bullhorn.

"We can't let these devil worshippers take over our

town!" Spike roared. "We need to shut the Circle down!"

Taking out her phone, Charlie tapped on Matthew Landon's number, hoping the Tempest Grove detective might be able to stop the rally from escalating.

When Landon answered his phone, he seemed confused.

"There's no law against free speech in this town," he said, then hesitated, sounding unsure. "Although I guess chanting about burning people could be considered hate speech."

"Just forget it," Charlie said. "I'll take care of it myself."

She pulled up to the curb and unfastened her seatbelt.

"What are you planning to do?" Hale asked.

Charlie opened the door.

"Don't do anything foolish," Hale said. "There are a lot of angry people over there."

Stepping out of the car, she walked toward the stage, pulling out her credentials.

"I need to talk to you, Mr. Oswald," she yelled, holding them up in one hand.

He looked down at her with a confused frown.

"What?"

"I need to speak to you," she repeated. "You can't be out here threatening to burn people and run them out of town."

Spike held the bullhorn to his mouth and pointed it in Charlie's direction.

"Now, the Circle is sending FBI agents to silence us!" he yelled. "What are you, some kind of devil-worshipper?"

Before she knew it, a circle of angry protestors had formed around her, chanting loudly. As Charlie tried to back away, she felt a hand grab her arm.

Hale was there, pulling her back toward the Expedition as Spike Oswald screamed after her.

"Burn the witch, burn the witch, burn the witch!"

CHAPTER THIRTY-ONE

Terrance Gage shifted on the hard wooden bench beside Russell as the boy talked to his mother, telling her about his week at school and the new friend he'd made in his science class. As he glanced at the clock on the wall, Gage felt Estelle's eyes on him. She was angry, that much was clear, and he was pretty sure he knew why.

"Can I speak to my child alone?" Estelle asked when there were no more than five minutes left before Sunday visiting hours would end. "I'd appreciate a few minutes of privacy."

He was tempted to refuse her request, but then he saw Russell tense up beside him.

There was no need to put the boy through a scene. How much harm could the woman do in five minutes?

Getting to his feet, Gage crossed to the door and told the guard he needed to use the restroom.

By the time he emerged from the men's room, visiting hours were over and Russell was waving goodbye to his mother and heading toward the exit.

As Gage looked back, he saw Estelle's hard eyes following

after him, an expression akin to hate on her face.

She'd never forgiven him for turning her into the police when he discovered that she was the one who'd run over Russell's father, knocking him to the ground and killing him while her son had been watching from the upstairs window.

Perhaps she thought I wouldn't seek justice for my best friend. But Kenny was a good man. He didn't deserve to die.

Gage also knew she resented the fact that he and Kyla were caring for her son, despite the fact that the boy was thriving.

At least, he had been, until Estelle started filling his head with foolish ideas about what his father would want.

Kenny would want Russell to be happy, healthy, and safe, just like every other good father out there. He wouldn't want the boy to grow up without a loving family around him.

As they drove away from the detention center, Gage looked over at his foster son with worried eyes.

In the past, he'd always allowed the boy to spend time alone with Estelle during visiting hours.

But based on what he'd overheard during Russell's conversation with Bridget on Friday night, he'd decided to sit in and hear what it was she had to say.

Besides, he'd wanted to ask about the parole hearing.

"I'll be out of here before you know it," she'd said, keeping her eyes trained on Gage. "They're going to release me early for good behavior."

Now riding toward home, Russell sat in silence.

"What did your mom want to speak to you about that she didn't want me to hear?" he finally asked. "If she's told you something you're worried about, you can let me know."

Russell didn't respond as he stared out the window.

Anger and frustration bubbled up inside Gage. How could he solve whatever problem was bothering Russell if he didn't know for sure what it was?

"If you won't talk to me, then I'll schedule a session for you with a therapist," he said, thinking of Faye Thackery.

Shrugging his thin shoulders, Russell pulled his phone out of his pocket and began scrolling.

"I've got a phone, too," Gage said heatedly.

He tapped on Faye's number, determined to set up an appointment for Russell, even if his foster son might not be living with him anymore when the time came.

"Gage? Are you calling about Joelle?"

Faye sounded frantic.

"What about Joelle?" he asked, instantly worried.

"She's missing," Faye said. "And her car's been found abandoned near Moonstone Cavern, by the Witch's Tree."

Assuring Faye that he was on his way, Gage quickly switched lanes, preparing to merge onto the highway heading north toward the West Virginia border and the woods around Moonstone Cavern."

"Where are we going?" Russell asked, suddenly looking around with interest. "I thought we were going home.

"The therapist I called is a friend of mine," Gage said. "She can't find her sister-in-law and she's worried, so we're going to try to help her."

Russell frowned.

"What's the Witch's Tree?"

They spent the next forty-five minutes having a lively discussion about the Witch's Tree, Brunhilde Kistler, and the persecution of witches over the centuries.

When Gage finally pulled past the historical marker, Russell stared at it with wide eyes.

Parking the Navigator behind a black Dodge Charger, Gage told Russell to stay in the car, then stepped out to see Detective Kirby standing beside a distraught Faye.

"I think she might have done something stupid," Faye was saying. "She might even try to harm herself."

She turned to Gage as he approached.

"Joelle's been through so much," she said. "Maybe it's finally gotten to be too much for her to bear."

Before Gage could respond, the phone in Faye's hand began to chime. She looked down with wide eyes.

"Oh, good, that's Bridget returning my call," she said.

Tapping on the display, she held the phone to her ear.

Gage could see that her hand was shaking.

"Bridget?" Faye said, her voice cracking on the word. "Joelle's gone missing. I need your help."

CHAPTER THIRTY-TWO

The sun was starting to set by the time Bridget pulled up to the historic marker for the Witch's Tree in her white Ford Explorer. Santino and Decker had already arrived and were waiting by the red Chevy pick-up. Bailey was standing with Ludwig, ready for the search to begin.

Looking around for Faye, Bridget's eyes fell on a baby-blue Camaro with West Virginia plates.

It was the same car she'd seen in the Prescotts' driveway the day she'd told them Nicole's body had been found.

"Thanks for calling in the cavalry."

Bridget turned around to see Faye.

The therapist's eyes were puffy and red-rimmed.

"Joelle got mad and stormed out yesterday," she said. "I've been staying with Rowan and Joelle. They were arguing and she just up and left. I thought maybe she just needed space and was blowing off steam."

Faye dabbed at her eyes with a soggy tissue she had wadded in her fist.

"I guess part of me thought maybe she'd been staying over at Hammerling House, but I called Gerard Ernst and he said he hasn't seen her and that nobody on the Circle's message board has heard from her this weekend."

"Then, when she didn't come home in time for our appointment with the funeral home to make the final arrangements, I knew something had to be terribly wrong."

"That's when I got the call from Detective Kirby saying that a patrol had seen a car parked out here. When they ran the plates, they saw it was registered to Joelle, but she was nowhere to be found."

"We've been keeping a pretty close eye on the area in the last week," Kirby said. "But it's pretty rough terrain around here. If your sister-in-law is out there, we're gonna need some help finding her."

Faye turned hopeful eyes to the German Shepherd standing next to Bailey.

"Is that why he's here? To help look for my sister?"

Bailey nodded without hesitation.

"Ludwig is trained for search and rescue operations," she confirmed. "If you let him smell an item of clothing, he'll search for the last person who wore it."

Bridget jumped in to assure Faye that the dog could search the same area as a dozen people could but in half the time.

She didn't add that the dog could find people who were living or dead, as well as body parts or clothing that had been left behind. She didn't want to bring unpleasant images to Faye's already troubled mind.

"Why don't you look in the Camaro for an item of Joelle's clothing?" Bailey suggested. "That'll help Ludwig focus on the scent we want him to find."

Within minutes Faye had retrieved a jacket from the car and returned to where Bailey stood.

"Okay, Ludwig," Bailey said, holding the jacket under the German Shepherd's nose. "Find it!"

Ludwig sniffed the material thoroughly, then lifted his nose into the dusky air.

At first, Bridget didn't think he was going to be able to pick up on the scent, and then he was off and running, heading toward the Witch's Tree.

Sprinting off behind the search and rescue dog, Bailey headed up the chase with Santino and Decker close behind, and Bridget bringing up the rear.

They followed Ludwig past the sycamore and on toward the ravine, following a similar path to what he'd taken the day he'd found Natasha's remains.

Worried that he was scenting on the same remains they'd found before, Bridget was relieved when the German Shepherd veered away from the ravine, heading directly toward Moonstone Cavern.

Suddenly they came to a break in the trees and burst out into a clearing beside the cavern's entrance.

A rope had been stretched from one side of the cavern opening to the other and a *Cavern Temporarily Closed* sign had been affixed to it.

Ludwig darted under the rope and dashed into the yawning cavern without hesitation. Seconds later sharp barks echoed from the dark opening.

"I've got a flashlight in my holster," Decker called to Bailey, who was already following the dog into the cavern.

Jogging up next to her, he switched on the flashlight.

He aimed the beam down toward the ground in front of him as they stepped inside, then jerked to a stop.

"There's blood on the ground," he called back to Santino and Bridget. "But...I don't see a body."

Suddenly Ludwig turned and made his way out of the cave, sniffing the ground as he went.

Once he was out of the cave, he lifted his nose into the air, his dark eyes blinking up at the waning light of the day.

Hesitating, he again lowered his nose to the ground and then began to move forward toward the parking area.

When he got to the road, the German Shepherd circled again, then looked back at Bailey with anxious eyes.

"He's lost the scent," Bailey said.

She crouched beside the dog and stroked his fur.

"Are those footprints?" she asked.

Bridget joined her in staring down at the road where a faint set of footprints could be seen in the dirt.

"And those are tire marks," Decker said, pointing to the shoulder of the road where a car had obviously been parked.

"Joelle's gone," Bridget said. "Someone's taken her."

* * *

Bridget hurried back to the parking lot, tasked with telling Faye what they'd found while the others stayed to cordon off the area.

As she'd left, Santino had been calling in an APB, describing Joelle as a missing person in imminent danger.

Unfortunately, he had no description of the car or the abductor to give.

When Bridget emerged from the trees, Faye turned to her with scared, hopeful eyes.

"Ludwig followed Joelle's scent to Moonstone Cavern," Bridget said. "The cavern was empty, but we found blood on the ground and footprints leading out to the road."

"What are you saying?" Faye asked.

Bridget exchanged a quick glance with Gage, suspecting he could read the bad news in her eyes.

"From the look of it, I believe Joelle may have been confronted in the cave and abducted. She's gone."

Faye shook her head in disbelief, then slumped against the nearest vehicle, which was Gage's Navigator.

Bridget put a supporting arm around the therapist as Bailey and Ludwig emerged from the woods and came jogging toward them.

As they approached the Navigator, Russell's eyes widened, and his hand moved instinctively to his jacket pocket.

It looked to Bridget as if the boy was terrified.

But once the agent and dog had run past, heading for Bailey's vehicle, Russell relaxed back into his seat.

Wondering what had spooked the teen, Bridget started toward the Navigator with a curious frown.

She was halfway across the lot when Bob's silver sedan pulled in. Bob climbed out from behind the wheel.

"Faye called you?" Bridget asked.

"Actually, I called her to check in," he admitted. "I heard

Joelle had stormed off in her Camaro yesterday."

He lowered his voice.

"Any sign of her?"

Shaking her head, Bridget sighed.

"We had a search and rescue dog follow her scent over to Moonstone Cavern. We found blood and footprints, but no Joelle. Looks as if she's been abducted."

Her father's face went pale.

"Have you put out an APB yet?" he asked.

Bailey spoke up from beside Ludwig, who was lapping water from a portable container.

"Deputy Santino just called it in," she confirmed. "He and Decker are having another look around the area to make sure we haven't missed anything."

As Gage tried to comfort Faye, Bridget looked in at Russell again, wondering what had gotten him so worked up when he'd seen Bailey and Ludwig running toward the vehicle.

It was almost as if he thought they were coming for him.

She noticed that once again his hand was shielding whatever was in his pocket.

The boy was definitely hiding something, and she wanted to find out what it was.

But first, they needed to find Joelle Prescott.

CHAPTER THIRTY-THREE

Raven looked into the backseat, wanting to reassure himself that Joelle Prescott was still unconscious and hadn't broken free of the ropes he'd used to bind her hands and feet. She was a seasoned witch after all, and would likely try to put some sort of spell or curse on him if he gave her the chance.

He'd known for many years that the woman had chosen Ginerva as her craft name.

And while she rarely divulged the name to anyone outside her inner circle of friends in the coven, it was a name he'd heard often growing up.

A name he associated with betrayal and malice.

If Ginerva's will had been done, I wouldn't exist.

It was true the woman had never done anything to show her hand or reveal her true intentions toward him.

The dark magic she used had always been closely guarded and kept out of sight behind closed doors.

But he'd been forewarned against her, and he'd always known the day would come when he would finally get his chance to destroy her and remove the threat she posed once and for all.

Of course, when her daughter had tried to bewitch him, he'd had a close call. The enchantment Natasha had cast over him had almost been his undoing.

But Raven knew that he'd inherited a talent for magic from his father and a ruthless iron will from his mother.

It was a powerful combination. One that had served him well over the years. And in the end, he'd managed to take the little witch's life and that of her sister.

Now her mother was at his mercy.

Too bad I have none.

Bringing the vehicle to a stop, Raven opened the door and climbed out into the woods.

He scanned the area and, satisfied there were enough fallen branches under the trees to serve his purpose, he began collecting the wood and loading it into the back, piling it as high as he could manage.

As he worked, an image of smoke and flames grew in his mind, sending a shiver of anticipation down his spine.

All his studying of witchcraft and witch-hunting over the years had taught him that to ensure a witch would never return in person or in spirit to haunt their executioners, they had to be burned to ashes.

His fiery plan would ensure that Ginerva and her progeny never came back to haunt him. Soon, he would be free from the curse that had hung over him since birth.

Returning to the vehicle, he looked into the back, once again making sure Ginerva was tightly bound, then climbed into the driver's seat.

He pulled back onto Shackleton Highway and headed for

Tempest Grove, knowing he didn't have much time.

He still needed to get the stake in place at the altar.

Then, once night had fallen and the full moon had risen, the fire could be set, and the flames could work their magic.

Once the fire had burned itself out, the three fire witches would all be dead and gone.

CHAPTER THIRTY-FOUR

Charlie had just opened the door to her office when the APB bulletin came in about Joelle Prescott's abduction. It was the first time she'd had a chance to stop by the Washington field office for several days, and her plan had been to check her interoffice mailbox and pick up a few files before heading home.

Instead, she found herself racing back into the hall.

Surprised to see Calloway in his office, she attempted to sneak past his open door without success.

"Agent Day? Can I have a word?"

She stopped outside his doorway.

"Actually, another woman's gone missing over in Tempest Grove," she said. "I've got to go."

"You can give me two minutes," Calloway said, sounding irritable. "Come in and close the door. I need to talk to you about Agent Hale."

Charlie's back stiffened at the words, but she stepped inside the office and pulled the door closed behind her.

"Okay, what is it you wanted to say about Agent Hale?"

"Oh, I think you know what it is. And I think you know what you're doing," Calloway said. "You're stopping a talented undercover agent from taking on a very important assignment."

He knotted his forehead in disapproval.

"We've not got enough seasoned, qualified agents as it is," Calloway complained. "The operation won't be quick or easy, and many other agents, the ones with spouses and kids, they won't take on this one. Not when we have no idea how long it will take. No idea how long the team will be under."

"The team?"

Calloway held up a hand.

"I've said more than I should have," he said. "Let me just end this conversation by saying that Hale will be deep undercover. And there will be serious risks involved as always, but he won't be alone. That should comfort you."

Narrowing her eyes, Charlie held the man's stony gaze.

"You think knowing he's in danger and not being there to back him up will bring me *comfort*?" she said.

She forced herself to stay calm as she stepped to the door.

"Thanks for the pep talk," she said, making no effort to keep the sarcasm out of her voice. "It really cheered me up."

Her hand was already on the door knob when Calloway spoke again.

"There is another option," he said. "If you're serious."

Charlie spun around to face him.

"Serious about what?"

"Serious about being there to back Hale up," Calloway

said. "We're still finalizing the team. You could be on it."

* * *

As Charlie drove east toward Tempest Grove, she ordered Siri to call Santino, who was still out in the backwoods around Moonstone Cavern searching for Joelle.

Her call went unanswered.

Next, she tried Bailey Flynn, but the call rolled straight to voicemail.

She was just about to try Bridget's number when a text message came in from Vivian Burke.

The DNA results are back from the bloody pitchfork.

The forensics examiner answered her call on the first ring.

"We were able to extract DNA from the blood on the pitchfork handle," she said. "And it matched the DNA from the tissue found under Calvin Hirsch's fingernails."

"So, you confirmed that the same man killed both Hirsch and Elora?" Charlie said. "Why don't you sound happy?"

"Well, it's Sunday afternoon and I've been working all weekend for one thing," Vivian snapped. "And for another, there was no match in CODIS."

Charlie's heart fell.

"So that means Abner and Vern are in the clear," she said, talking mainly to herself. "Who does that leave us?"

"Well, we also tested the disposed DNA you collected from Andrew Parnell and Brian Corwin," she said. "Both the pastor and the ex-principal are in the clear. Neither of the men is a match."

The results had left them with no viable suspects, four dead bodies, and a woman who'd been abducted.

As Charlie sped down Shackleton Highway, she slowed as she neared the historic marker for the Witch's Tree.

Pulling off onto the gravelly shoulder of the road, she saw several members of the Operation Hexenbaum task force huddled together, including Cecil, Kirby, and Argus.

As she stepped out of the Expedition, Argus hurried over.

"You just missed Gage," he said. "He went to take Russell home. And Bridget went to find Rowan Prescott. No one's heard from him since his wife went missing."

Charlie nodded.

"Well, you should know you're going to have to update your suspect list," she said. "It looks as if Pastor Parnell and Principal Corwin are in the clear. As are Abner and Vern Chumbley."

She couldn't keep the frustration out of her voice.

"Looks as if we're back to square one."

"Maybe not," Argus said, looking slightly pleased with himself. "Bridget told me that you guys were thinking to use forensic genealogy to try to get some traction with the DNA."

Remembering the discussion they'd had the day before, Charlie nodded without much enthusiasm.

"I know it's been used to solve some very old, very cold case," she said. "And we were hoping to find a genealogist to work with the data we got back from the genealogy sites. But I haven't had a chance to call around."

Argus cleared his throat.

"Actually, I've been dipping into genetic and forensic genealogy in my spare time," he said. "It's all the stuff I love. Compiling, collecting, and sorting data into charts."

He pulled his phone from his pocket.

"I've been working on a family tree for the man we're looking for," he said. "I used the DNA profile the FBI lab provided from the tissue found under Hirsch's nails."

A kernel of hope lit up in Charlie's chest.

"By entering the DNA profile of the evidence collected from the crime scenes into a publicly accessible genealogy database, I was able to identify a genetically related female living in Philadelphia," he said. "She's a fourth cousin to the person who left their DNA profile under Hirsch's nails."

He turned the phone to show Charlie a miniature image of a complex family tree.

"I've already mapped out a detailed family tree for this woman, working backward in time," he explained. "After building the tree all the way back to her great-great-grandparents, I'm now working my way forward in time, following each branch of the tree, making a list of all viable suspects with a matching DNA profile."

"How can you do that?"

"Using data records, like birth and marriage records and census records," Argus said. "I've been focusing on the data sources with a geographic link to the area in and around Tempest Grove."

His voice revealed his excitement as he continued.

"I couldn't believe it when I realized who was on one of

the branches in the family tree."

He paused for effect, then blurted out the answer.

"Helga Hammerling, the wife of Evander Hammerling," he said. "You know, the man who founded the Tempest Grove Eternal Circle of Life back in 1969."

Charlie nodded as if she knew who he was talking about.

"Based on our victims' connection to the Circle, and to Hammerling House, I've been trying to follow that branch, to see if Helga had any children still living in the area, but the city's vital records have yet to be digitized."

"Of course, I can go down to the courthouse in person to see what I can find out, but it's Sunday, and–"

"And I'm sure Detective Landon can get you in there," Charlie finished for him. "Have you seen him tonight?"

Argus shook his head.

"Well, I'll hunt him down," she said. "And if I can't find Landon, I'll go straight to Chief Aguilar. I'll let him know that we need access to the records in that building and that Joelle Prescott's life might depend on it."

CHAPTER THIRTY-FIVE

The sun had just touched the horizon in the west when Bridget turned onto Forester Way. She'd come to find Rowan Prescott. She needed to let him know that his wife wasn't holed up at Hammerling House or spending a few nights with Faye. Joelle wasn't just trying to cool off from their argument as she'd done in the past. She was missing and, if Bridget was honest with herself, feared dead.

But Rowan's truck wasn't in the driveway, and when she knocked on the front door there was no answer.

She looked up and down the street as if hoping to see him coming toward her, but the street was dark and empty.

Maybe he's already heard the news. Maybe he's already out there looking for his wife on his own.

Getting back into the Explorer, she thought for a minute, trying to decide where to check next, then started the engine.

Before she could back out of the driveway, she heard a loud voice fill the car. Spike Oswald was at it again.

Does the man never sleep?

Bridget reached to turn off the unwelcome voice when

she realized who Spike was interviewing on his show.

"Okay, loyal listeners out there, thanks to all of you who joined me at the WARP 102.5 FM rally this afternoon," Spike rasped. "And now we've got a very special guest with us in the studio. I'm sure you've all been following the tragic events surrounding the death of Nicole and Natasha Prescott in the news, and tonight I'm talking to their father, Rowan Prescott."

Staring toward the radio in surprise, Bridget turned up the volume, then winced as she heard Rowan's voice.

"Thanks for having me on, Spike," he said, sounding hesitant. "I just wanted to ask anyone with information on my daughters' murders to please call the Tempest Grove Police Department or the FBI tipline."

"The police haven't been much help so far, folks," Spike burst in. "So, let's give those boys in blue a hand and call in some tips for my man Rowan here. We're going to open the phone lines for any of our listeners who may have some information to share."

Bridget suddenly realized that the show must be live.

It's happening now. Rowan must be at the radio station.

She put the Explorer into reverse and started to back down the driveway, hoping to catch him before he left the station.

"Okay, we have our first caller of the evening," Spike said as Bridget's phone buzzed on the dashboard.

As Argus's name appeared on the display, she headed the Explorer toward downtown, then tapped to answer.

"What's up, Argus?" she asked. "Any luck at City Hall?"

"I'm inside now," he said. "Charlie pulled some strings with Chief Aguilar. I'm going through the microfiche now."

He sighed dramatically.

"I tell you, this town really needs to digitize their records," he complained. "My head and my back are-"

"Listen, Argus, I'm trying to find Rowan and I don't have much time. Have you found anything helpful yet?"

Argus' petulant tone was suddenly gone.

"Actually, yes," he said. "I looked up the Hammerling family tree. It looks as if Helga and Evander Hammerling produced only one living child."

Bridget raised an eyebrow.

"Okay, who's the child?"

"Well, she's not a child anymore," Argus said. "Her name is Meredith Hammerling, and she's well into her sixties now. Looks as if she grew up in Tempest Grove and, according to marriage records, she married a man named Brian Corwin. Property records show that they jointly own a house on Gooseberry Road."

He paused to take a breath and Bridget jumped in.

"Merry Corwin, the secretary at the Baptist church is a Hammerling?" she asked, trying to make sense of the news. "But, how can that be? She acts as if she hates the Circle and anything to do with Wicca or witchcraft."

"Her parents died years ago," Argus said. "But according to the probate records, they left their only daughter out of their will. That might mean there was an estrangement."

Bridget tried to think.

"So, who owns Hammerling House now?"

283

"They bequeathed Hammerling House to a trust that had been established for the benefit of their only grandson, Joshua Corwin," Argus explained. "The Hammerling Trust leases the building to the Circle of Eternal Light Foundation, which is registered as a non-profit."

Bridget frowned as she pictured the clean-cut man who'd stopped by the Prescott house to offer his condolences. The high-school principal had come wearing a suit and bearing a homemade casserole.

"So, the Hammerling branch of the tree ends with Joshua Corwin? Does that mean he's our prime suspect?"

"He would be," Argus agreed. "Except we already tested his father's DNA against the DNA we collected at the scene. It wasn't a match or even a partial match to the DNA under Hirsch's nails. Besides, Joshua was still a teenager back then. Only a year or two older than Natasha and Nicole."

"So, you're saying you've reached a dead-end?"

"It looks that way," Argus said.

He sounded deflated.

"As far as I can tell, the Hammerling line ends with Joshua Corwin and he's not a DNA match for our killer."

As the traffic light ahead turned red, Bridget stepped harder than necessary on the brake, bringing the Explorer to a jerking halt.

"You're trying to tell me that the killer's genetic link to the Hammerling family is just some sort of cosmic coincidence?" she asked. "I'm sorry, but I just don't buy it."

Her words were met with a startled silence.

"Well, I have doublechecked my findings," Argus finally said, sounding slightly offended. "And the data doesn't lie."

"No, but sometimes people do," Bridget replied, not yet ready to admit defeat. "Sometimes they lie, or they lose things, or they make a mistake."

"What are you saying?" Argus asked. "You think the data set I'm using is unreliable?"

Bridget exhaled in frustration.

"I think that data can sometimes be misleading," she clarified. "I'm saying that records can be filed improperly, or data can be entered incorrectly, or even falsified. Whatever the case may be, something isn't adding up."

When the light ahead turned green, she glanced in her rearview mirror and prepared to switch lanes.

"There's only one sure way to find out. I've got to go straight to the source. I've got to speak to Merry Corwin."

* * *

Traffic on Liberty Parkway was light as Bridget drove toward Tempest Grove Baptist Church.

The tall spire on the building's roof was illuminated, making it the only visible object in the night sky ahead other than the full moon hanging over it.

As she turned the Explorer into the parking lot, she saw that the sanctuary was dark, but that lights were on in the church office and a car was parked in the lot next to one of the church vans.

Checking her watch, she wondered if perhaps Merry and

Parnell were still inside counting up the day's offerings.

Bridget hesitated before she got out of the car.

She was alone and it was after dark.

Although Parnell's DNA had cleared him of killing Hirsch and Elora, Bridget couldn't know for sure he wasn't involved in some way.

Experience having taught her that it was better to be safe than sorry, she checked the Glock in her purse, slipped the small gun Santino had given her into an ankle holster under her right pantleg, and stepped out of the SUV.

She approached the church office and found the door unlocked and Pastor Parnell sitting at Merry's desk sifting through a stack of paper.

He looked up as Bridget stepped into the room, then did a doubletake, followed by a scowl.

"Oh, I thought you were Merry," he said.

Bridget smiled politely despite the chilly reception.

"Actually, Merry is the one I'm here to see."

The pastor studied her with narrow eyes, obviously wondering what she wanted with the secretary.

"She's gone to drop the offerings into the night depository box at the bank," he said. "I'm not sure how long it'll take."

He was clearly hoping she'd say she'd come back later, but Bridget stepped forward, unable to resist asking a few questions while she had the opportunity.

"I was wondering...does Merry have only one son?"

Parnell nodded.

"Yes, I believe so."

"So, Joshua doesn't have any siblings...or half-siblings?"

The pastor frowned.

"Why are you asking all these questions? What does the FBI want with a good man like Joshua Corwin and a god-fearing woman like his mother?"

Bridget heard a voice in the doorway behind her.

She turned around to see Merry Corwin.

"Yes, Agent Bishop, I'd also like to know. What do you want with me and my son?"

Bridget took a quick step back when she saw the small Ruger in the woman's hand.

"What in the world are you doing, Merry?" Parnell asked, his eyes wide behind his glasses. "You put that gun down right now before someone gets hurt."

He stood and started toward the older woman with a determined, angry stride.

A gunshot exploded through the little room. Bridget jumped back as a red hole appeared in the pastor's forehead.

Parnell's body jerked to a halt, then dropped to the ground with a heavy thud.

"I'm sorry I had to do that," Merry said in a brusque voice that contradicted her words. "Pastor Parnell was a righteous man. But he'd already heard and seen too much."

Her hand was steady as she kept her eyes and the gun trained on Bridget.

"Now, drop your purse on the floor," she said, stepping closer. "And don't talk yourself into doing anything foolish. I won't hesitate to lay you out there beside the good pastor if you give me any trouble."

Reluctantly, Bridget lowered her bag to the ground, knowing that Merry wasn't bluffing and that the woman was sure to get off a shot if she tried to go for her Glock now.

Merry waved the gun toward the door.

"Come on, move!" she ordered.

"Where are we going?" Bridget asked.

"You wanted to know about my son," Merry said. "Well, you're in luck. Because we're going to go find him."

CHAPTER THIRTY-SIX

Bridget watched as Merry Corwin took one last look at Andrew Parnell's dead body on the floor. The secretary gave a disapproving shake of her head as she saw the blood pooling on the freshly cleaned carpet.

"What a shame it had to come to this," she said. "I just hope someone comes by soon to clean up the mess. Of course, there will always be a stain."

Sticking the Ruger into Bridget's back, she forced the FBI agent to walk to the Explorer.

"Get in the driver's seat," Merry said. "I'll be sitting in the backseat holding this gun to the back of your head."

Bridget slowly lowered herself into the car, careful not to make any sudden moves that would give Merry the excuse to shoot her. She was just thinking of reaching down for the little gun in the ankle holster when Merry spoke again.

"Keep both hands on the wheel," she snapped. "Now, take me to Hammerling House. You said you want to know about my son, so I suggest you don't try any funny business on the way there...if you want to live long enough to meet him."

"Yes, I do want to know about your son," Bridget said,

trying to keep her voice steady. "And I want to know about you. I was surprised to learn your parents were the ones who founded the Circle of Eternal Light."

"Well, it's not something I advertise," Merry said, resting the gun on the seatback as if it was getting heavy. "And it's certainly not something I'm proud of. Now get going. We don't have all night."

Glancing in the rear-view mirror, Bridget felt a stab of fear as she met Merry's cold, crazed eyes.

She had to find a way to get the gun before anyone else was killed. And she needed to stall for time.

"I bet it was hard growing up in Hammerling House," Bridget said. "Kids can be cruel if they sense you're different, or if you follow a different religion."

"You're right about that. I was only twelve when my folks bought the house and started up the Circle," Merry said. "What girl of that age wouldn't be embarrassed by parents who set themselves up as the high priest and priestess of a coven? They wanted to get me involved, too, but I refused."

The disdain in her voice was palpable.

"I refused to take a craft name or go through an initiation," she said with an indignant huff. "When I met Brian in high school, I jumped at the chance to get away from that place. We got married at Tempest Grove Baptist Church the day I turned eighteen."

Pride filled her voice and Bridget glanced again in the rear-view mirror, hoping the storytelling would lull the woman into letting her guard down or lowering the gun.

But Merry's hard eyes and her gun were still trained directly on Bridget as the Explorer pulled out of the lot.

"After I left home I cleansed my life of near about everything in my past. I cut all ties with my parents and the Circle. I didn't want children of mine to go through that."

For the first time, at the mention of children, Merry's voice softened.

"Brian and I were so eager to start a family. We decorated a nursery and I learned how to knit baby blankets and booties," she said in a wistful tone. "But that nursery sat empty year after year."

The softness in her voice fell away.

"Pretty soon I realized what was going on. Someone had put a curse on me. That's why I was barren. They were trying to punish me for leaving."

Merry fell silent as if lost in memory.

"What did you do about it?" Bridget asked, coming to a stop at a redlight on Liberty Parkway.

"Why, I went back to Hammering House, of course," she said. "I told my mother she had better remove the curse or I'd burn the whole place down. But she denied it."

She emitted a bitter laugh.

"Mother told me that no one at the Circle wished me any harm. That she asked the Old Ones to protect me every day."

Her face creased into a sneer.

"*You must trust that the Goddess will bless you with a child if it is meant to be,*" she mimicked her mother in a mocking voice. "She actually expected me to believe that."

"But you have Joshua," Bridget said, trying to diffuse the woman's growing anger. "So, she lifted the curse, right?"

"Oh, no, I had to do that myself," Merry said. "With a little help from Joshua's father."

Bridget raised an eyebrow.

"Brian knows how to break a curse?" she asked. "He practices magic?"

"Not Brian," Merry said dismissively. "His seed was too weak to get past the curse. I needed a man with strong magic. Someone who could fight fire with fire and curse with curse."

She cleared her throat.

"When I left my mother that day, I saw Cypher listening by the door," she said. "He offered to break the curse."

"Who's Cypher?" Bridget asked.

She was driving slowly, hoping for a chance to disarm Merry before she could use the Ruger again.

"Cypher is just a craft name," Merry said. "His real name is Gerard Ernst. He's the high priest now at the Circle. That was his ambition all the while, I guess."

"So, Ernst is Joshua's father?" Bridget asked as the answers began to fall into place.

Merry nodded matter-of-factly.

"He brought me to the high altar. Said the only sure way to remove the curse was to reenact the joining of the God and Goddess. The reward would surely be a child."

She nudged the side of Bridget's head with the gun.

"Go faster," she said. "It'll be too late if we don't hurry."

"Too late for what?" Bridget asked, suddenly scared of

what they might find ahead. "What has Joshua done? Where has he taken Joelle?"

Merry scoffed.

"Joelle?" she said. "Her craft name is *Ginerva*. And it's her dark magic, and that of her daughters, that's caused all this to begin with. Joshua's only protecting himself."

"What do you mean?" Bridget asked. "What could Joelle and her daughters have done? Are you saying they threatened Joshua in some way?"

The questions seemed to infuriate the woman.

"Ginerva tried to stop my son from *ever being born*," she spit out. "She saw Ernst taking me to the high altar and told him he was making a mistake. She warned that he would call down a curse upon himself and his descendants if he lay with me and gave me a child. Her words cursed me and my son that night. The darkness inside my boy is her fault alone."

Jabbing the gun into Bridget's back, she pointed ahead to the gate outside Hammerling House.

"Park along the curb and get out."

Bridget hesitated, then did as she was instructed.

If she took the gun from Merry now, she may get shot or she may get away. But either way, she wouldn't find out where Joshua Corwin had taken Joelle. She would have to bide her time before making a move.

Once they were standing in front of the gate, Merry punched a code into the metal box beside it.

"I know Raven's passcode," she said smugly. "He always uses the same one."

"Raven?" Bridget asked, watching the gate swing open.

Merry ignored the question and waved the gun, gesturing for Bridget to walk through. Soon they were standing at the front door, which swung open to reveal Gerard Ernst's tall, stooped figure.

"Merry?"

His voice was a surprised croak.

"What are you doing here?"

Merry prodded Bridget inside and stepped in after her. She kicked the door closed with her foot and sighed.

"I'm here to save our son," she said. "And I've already had to kill poor Pastor Parnell."

Ernst stared at her in disbelief.

"You...*killed* the pastor?"

"Don't bother with the crocodile tears," Merry said. "You got what you wanted. You never liked Parnell."

The old man shook his head in denial.

"I never had anything against that man or that church. All I ever asked was for them to leave me in peace."

"Do you hear him?" Merry asked scornfully, glancing at Bridget. "Cypher wants to be left in peace."

She lifted the gun and aimed it at his head.

"I'll leave you in peace," she said. "But I have to make sure you won't go anywhere in the meantime. There's something I need to do. Something I should have done decades ago."

Forcing Ernest and Bridget back to the kitchen, she opened the door to the walk-in pantry.

"Get in," she said. "I've got to go find my boy and save

him from that *witch*."

She shoved the Ruger in Ernst's face, and he stumbled toward the pantry.

"What are you talking about, Merry?" he called. "What's gotten into you? You aren't thinking straight."

Merry ignored his plea as she turned the gun on Bridget.

"You, too," she said. "I can't have you following me and ruining everything, can I?"

"Where are you going, Merry?" Ernst called out as she slammed the pantry door and bolted it shut.

The woman's ominous reply sounded through the door.

"Where evil was started, there it must end."

CHAPTER THIRTY-SEVEN

The full moon hung high in the sky as Joshua Corwin carried Joelle toward the High Hollow, moving slowly and steadily along the path toward the high altar. Her fate had been sealed from the moment she'd cursed his very existence, and the inexorable march toward this night had begun twenty-seven years earlier when he'd taken Natasha Prescott's life.

As he tied Joelle's limp body to the thick wooden stake, using the same coil of rope he'd used to hang her daughter the week before, he mused over the course of events that had led them to this reckoning.

Joshua had still been a child when he realized he was different from the others around him. According to his mother, the darkness inside him was ancient and timeless, afflicted on him by the curse of a witch named Ginerva.

But it wasn't until he'd been enchanted by Natasha Prescott that he'd become aware of the Circle of Eternal Light. He had followed the girl there one day and met Cypher, who told him who his mother really was.

He hadn't known that Merry was the daughter of the high priest, Evander Hammerling, who had started the coven.

Cypher had introduced the boy to his grandfather, who'd been nearing his eighty-first birthday, and had offered to teach him the Craft so long as he didn't tell his mother what he was up to.

After helping his son pick out the craft name Raven, Cypher had taught him the basic beliefs of the Wiccan tradition and instructed him in magic.

Then on Beltane in 1996, Joshua's mother had discovered he'd been visiting Hammerling House to study the Craft with Gerard Ernst, who was now the high priest of the Circle.

She'd flown into a rage that night, and Joshua had learned the truth about his birth and about his fate.

Revealing that Ernst was his true father, Merry Corwin had forbidden her son from returning to Hammerling House or seeing his mentor again.

Joshua had driven off in his father's van, furious that he'd been betrayed by his own mother and banished from his own birthright.

He'd seen Natasha running toward the High Hollow, heading toward the Beltane festival celebration, and he'd lured her into the van, saying he would take her to the Witch's Tree where they would celebrate the festival with the spirit of Brunhilde Kistler.

But when he tried to kiss Natasha, she'd pushed him away, and he'd tripped over a root of the Witch's Tree and fallen.

Natasha had laughed, triggering the darkness inside him

and he had strangled her with his bare hands until the darkness had faded.

When he'd gone back to the van in search of a rope, thinking to make it look as if someone had reenacted the hanging at the Witch's Tree, he'd wrenched open the door to find Natasha's twin sister, cowering in the back.

He'd stood in shock for a long beat, stupidly giving the teenager a chance to bolt past him.

Then he had raced after her, almost catching her several times as they crashed through the woods.

But Nikki and her sister had both been on the track team, and she had proven too fast for him in the end.

She'd burst out of the woods into the path of Abner Chumbley's produce truck, and crashed onto the pavement, hitting her head.

After that, Joshua had run back to Natasha's body and carried her further into the woods. When he'd come to the ravine, he'd thrown her body in, then returned to the van.

Jumping inside, he sped home, arriving to find his mother in his room waiting for him.

"I have to leave," he'd said. "They'll be coming for me."

He'd told his mother everything, and they had both expected the police to knock on their door any minute, but she'd convinced him to stay.

When they heard that Nikki had been taken to the hospital with a head injury, and had lost her memory, they thought all would be well.

But the darkness had lived on in Joshua, driving him to kill again and again. And when Nikki had returned to

Tempest Grove, he'd known it was time to end the curse once and for all, which meant he'd had to destroy the witch who'd cast the curse, along with all her descendants.

And now the time had come.

He would close the circle upon the high altar and take his third victim from the same bloodline of witches, increasing his power threefold.

Joshua methodically stacked the branches he'd collected around the base of the wooden stake, preparing to turn the high altar into a pyre.

Once he was satisfied everything was ready, he called out to the dark spirits, summoning the power of ancient deities most witches were too timid to invoke.

As he watched with bright eyes, the flames began to dance under the wide eye of the full moon.

CHAPTER THIRTY-EIGHT

Bridget pounded on the heavy oak door of the pantry, yelling loudly for help as Gerard Ernst simply sat on the floor and waited. She looked frantically around the pantry for a tool to break the lock but saw nothing that looked strong enough to compete with the thick metal.

As she pulled once again on the latch, she sniffed and paused. Was that smoke?

Moving closer to the door, she sniffed again.

"There's a fire out there," Bridget said, her heart starting to race. "I can smell the smoke."

"Well, Merry always threatened to set this place on fire," Ernst said wearily. "But I never thought she'd actually do it with me inside."

Bridget stared down at the man in horrified disbelief, then bent to her ankle holster. Shooting off the latch might be the only way to escape the pantry alive.

And it was certainly the only way to escape in time to follow Merry and find out where Joshua had taken Joelle.

More smoke began to seep in through the crack under the door, causing Ernst to cough.

Finally prodded into action, the old man stood and began

to ram the solid door with his thin shoulder.

"Move back," she yelled at him as she lifted the small gun and took aim at the latch.

Steeling herself for the blast, she tightened her finger on the trigger, then hesitated.

A voice had sounded on the other side of the door.

"Help us!" Bridget yelled.

Suddenly, the door swung open, letting in a billowing gush of smoke.

Vern Chumbley stood in the kitchen.

"I saw your window smoking," he said. "I thought you might need some help."

"Thank you, Vern," Bridget said, coughing on the smoke that now filled the room. "Dial 911 and tell them there's a fire. And help Ernst to get outside."

Vern nodded and put a big arm around Ernst.

"You should get out, too," Vern said. "That fire looks hot."

"I will, Vern," Bridget promised "But I need to know where Merry went. Did you see her leave?"

He pointed toward the back of the house.

"I think he took her to High Hollow."

* * *

Bridget still held the little gun in her hand as she ran in the direction Vern had pointed. Thinking of her phone, lying in the bottom of her bag at the church, she knew she would have to find the woman on her own.

Luckily there was a full moon out to light her way, and Merry Corwin was unlikely to move very fast.

Of course, Merry had grown up in Hammerling House, so she would know her way around the woods.

Bridget hadn't gotten very far when she began to smell smoke again. At first, she thought the smoke from the house must have gotten in her hair and nose.

Then she saw a soft glow on the horizon and knew with certainty that there was a fire up ahead and that Joshua Corwin had set it.

She ran forward, following the flickering light and the acrid scent of smoke up the hill until she burst through the trees into a clearing.

Joelle Prescott was tied to a wooden stake, her head slumped and her white hair falling over one shoulder.

Flames flickered in the wood that had been piled around her, moving ever closer to her feet.

Hearing raised voices, Bridget looked past the burning altar and saw that Merry Corwin had reached the High Hollow first.

She was standing beside her son, pulling on the sleeve of his black ceremonial robe. As Bridget watched, the hood of the robe fell back, revealing Joshua Corwin's short hair and dark eyes that reflected the light of the flames.

"You've done what you came to do," Merry screamed at him. "Now let's get out of here while we still can."

Quickly circling the altar, Bridget crept up behind the mother and son, knowing she would have to act fast if she hoped to disarm Merry and take down Joshua in time to save Joelle from the flames.

She bent down and slipped her little gun back into her ankle holster, sucked in a deep breath, then charged forward, tackling Merry around the knees.

As Bridget had hoped, the gun flew from the older woman's hand, disappearing into the darkness beyond the trees, as Merry fell to the ground.

In one swift move, Bridget rolled to the side, pulled the gun back out of its holster, and jumped to her feet.

"Get down on your knees," she yelled to Joshua, holding the gun out in front of her. "You're under arrest."

Joshua stared at her for a long beat, then began to back away, his eyes trained on the gun.

"Don't do it," Merry called to him. "She'll shoot you!"

But her son just shook his head and kept moving back.

"There's no darkness in you," he said derisively, lifting his chin in defiance.

Staring at Bridget with dark, soulless eyes, Joshua slowly lifted a gun that he'd hidden in the wide pocket of his robe.

"You won't shoot me. Not if I shoot you-"

He jerked to a stop, his words abruptly ending as blood bubbled from his mouth and a dark stain began to spread over his chest.

Stumbling forward, he toppled face-first into the flames as Merry began to shriek in rage behind him.

Bridget grabbed the distraught woman and held her back just before she could go into the flames after him.

Suddenly, several figures emerged from the shadows.

Charlie was there, cuffing Merry and leading her away.

And Santino and Decker were using their jackets to beat a path through the flames.

Bridget watched as they cut Joelle down from the stake and carried her to safety. She exhaled in relief as she saw Joelle's eyes begin to flutter open, and then she coughed as the wind changed and a puff of smoke blew into her face.

Turning away from the fire, she saw Vern Chumbley standing by the tree line.

He waved when he saw her and called out.

"I dialed 911 just like you told me!" he said with a wide smile. "The firetrucks are on their way!"

She waved back, then looked up at the full moon as the sirens began to wail.

CHAPTER THIRTY-NINE

Faye Thackery was waiting in her yard when the big gray Navigator pulled into the driveway. She waved as Terrance Gage brought the big vehicle to a stop, then waited as he and a tall, thin teenager with a dark fade and a red sports jersey stepped out into the spring sunshine.

Leading them to the side entrance, the therapist ushered them into her small home office, offering Gage a cup of tea and Russell a glass of lemonade.

"Thanks for seeing us on such short notice," Gage said. "I know you must be busy with the funeral being held tomorrow, so I really appreciate it."

"I owe you and the rest of the task force a great deal of thanks for saving Joelle and finding out what happened to my nieces," she said. "It's the least I can do."

Russell sipped at his lemonade, then cocked his head.

"What did happen to your nieces?" he asked.

Gage made a motion for the boy to be quiet, but Faye waved him off.

"It's okay to ask questions," she said. "And sometimes we have to talk about difficult things."

She smiled at Russell.

"We need to teach your Uncle Gage that just because we don't talk about sad or upsetting things, that doesn't mean they go away. And sometimes, when we do talk about them, it can make us feel better."

Russell looked doubtful but he nodded along with Faye.

"I had two nieces," Faye said. "Nikki and Natasha. They both died, which makes me very sad."

"My father died," Russell said, staring down into his lemonade. "It makes me sad, too."

Studying the boy's tense features, Faye could see he was struggling to hold back his emotions.

"There's something else making you sad though, isn't there, Russell?" she asked.

He nodded.

"Can you tell me about it?"

This time he shook his head.

"Why not?" she asked. "What's stopping you?"

"My mom told me not to," he said quietly.

Faye saw the boy's inner struggle playing out on his face. There was obviously something terribly wrong, and he'd been trying to deal with it on his own.

"I think, if she knew how much it was bothering you to keep it a secret, she'd understand," Faye said.

Russell looked over at Gage.

"You promise not to be mad?" he asked.

The question earned a relieved look from Gage.

"Yes, whatever you tell me, I won't be mad."

Inhaling deeply, Russell looked down at his shoes.

"Mom's been giving me money to buy pills," he said. "She has me bring them to her when we visit. That's why she didn't want you there."

He swallowed hard and looked up at Gage.

"Are you going to arrest me?" he asked.

"No," Gage said, managing to keep his temper in spite of the furious gleam in his eyes. "And I'm not even going to ground you. This isn't your fault. And you have nothing to be ashamed of."

Russell nodded glumly, but Faye thought she saw a relaxing to his face and shoulders.

He'd set down a load or had at least passed it on to his foster father, and she could tell he already felt lighter.

Later, as she walked Gage and Russell to the Navigator, she put a hand on Gage's arm.

"I hope you'll make it to the funeral tomorrow," she said. "I'd really like for you to be there. And please, bring your family, too."

* * *

Faye stood under the big oak tree and watched as the twin coffins were lowered into the ground side by side.

The service had been emotional, and the soggy tissue in her hand had been well used, but she was comforted by the fact that Nikki and Natasha were both home now and that they were together again after so many years apart.

"It's a lovely tree. I think the girls would like it."

Faye looked over to Joelle, who still had a bandage on her

head but looked otherwise well.

Rowan stood beside his wife, wearing a dark suit and a solemn expression. But the anger she'd seen destroying him from the inside appeared to be gone.

The realization of how close he'd come to losing his wife had shaken him, perhaps bringing him back to his senses, and Faye had been relieved to hear that he'd sworn off listening to WARP 102.5 FM after watching the online video replay of Spike Oswald's recent rally.

As the mourners began to file past the graves, dropping in roses and flowers as they paid their respects, Faye was happy to see that Gage had made it after all.

He paused beside the grave with Russell on one side and an attractive woman on the other. Faye assumed she must be Kyla.

She smiled as Gage met her eyes, and he motioned for his family to wait for him as he made his way over.

"Thanks for the session yesterday," Gage said. "Both Russell and I are feeling a lot better about everything. And now that I know what's wrong, I can deal with it. I think we're going to be alright."

He cocked his head and searched her eyes.

"How about you?" he asked. "Are you going to be okay?"

"Yeah, I think I am. Or at least I will be," she said, managing a smile. "Maybe now that Joshua Corwin is gone, and Natasha has been found, we can all finally rest in peace."

CHAPTER FORTY

Bridget looked up at the Tempest Grove Women's Detention Center with solemn eyes. She wasn't sure why she had agreed to come speak to Merry Corwin. After all, the woman was facing charges of murder, arson, attempted murder, and obstructing the course of justice, as well as a slew of other charges. And Bridget had been named in documents as one of her intended victims.

But Merry had expressly asked to speak to her and had made the strange request to speak to her father, as well.

So, curiosity had gotten the better of Bridget, and she had agreed to bring her father and meet the woman during Sunday's visiting hours.

"She didn't tell you what she wanted?" Bob asked as they made their way through the security line. "And you're sure she wanted me to come, too?"

"That's what her lawyer said," Bridget confirmed. "And she's added us both to her list of approved visitors. I already checked before we drove over here."

As they waited in the holding area to be admitted, Bridget updated her father on the latest developments in the case.

"The DNA tests on Joshua Corwin's remains came back,"

she said. "It's been confirmed that he was Gerard Ernst's biological son. Last I heard, Brian Corwin filed for divorce."

"So, you don't think the guy knew anything about any of this?" Bob asked. "He didn't know that his wife and son were both psychopaths?"

Bridget shrugged.

"Maybe he spent so much time at work and then on the golf course that he could allow himself not to see it," she said. "Or maybe they were just very good at hiding it."

Suddenly the metal doors opened, and a flood of visitors flowed into the large visiting room.

Merry Corwin sat at a long wooden table wearing an orange jumpsuit and white slippers. Her face was make-up-free, and her white bob was tucked neatly behind her ears.

"I'm sure you are wondering why I invited you here," she said as if she had invited them over for tea.

She looked at Bob and cocked her head.

"As a parent, I thought you'd be able to understand," she added. "Of course, what I have to say does impact you, too."

Meeting her father's eyes over Merry's head, Bridget saw that her father was just as confused as she was.

"Let me start by saying that I never intended to hurt anyone. I just wanted my child to be happy," she insisted. "Everything I did was for my son. You must believe that."

"Just what is it you're admitting you've done?" Bob asked.

Merry's mouth pursed into a pout, and she glanced pointedly at the clock on the wall.

"I will get to that in just a minute," she said. "I don't care to be rushed. Now, as I was saying, I just wanted my child to be happy. But I realized early on that Joshua wasn't like other children. There was a darkness in him. After a while, I realized he was cursed."

"A curse?" Bob asked. "Are you serious?"

He frowned over at her as if he suspected a prank.

"Absolutely," Merry said. "My poor boy was living under a shadow. And the doctors we took him to couldn't help. So, when Joshua told me he had killed Natasha, that darkness had taken over him and made him do it, I did what I had to do to protect him."

"And what exactly did you do?" Bridget asked.

She was starting to think the trip had been a huge waste of time. The woman was delusional at best and a manipulative psychopath at worst.

"Well, I tried to point the police in another direction," she admitted. "I thought if they suspected someone else, they would leave my boy alone. So I spread a little harmless gossip about Coach Hirsh and made a few anonymous calls to Spike Oswald at WARP 102.5 FM."

"Harmless?" Bridget said, feeling her anger rise. "You ruined the man's whole life. How is that harmless?"

Merry ignored the question.

"After everyone started thinking Coach Hirsch was responsible, I tried to tell myself everything would be okay, but then I overheard a conversation that got me worried."

She glanced at Bob.

"Your wife had started counseling Nikki Prescott after

her sister's abduction," she said. "It was very sweet of her. But I heard her telling Nikki's Aunt Faye that she was getting ready to make a breakthrough. She said that Nikki had remembered seeing a van. She'd been planning to go to the police and let them know."

Merry shook her head at the memory.

"Well, I couldn't let that happen, could I?"

The older woman shifted on the bench.

"So, I asked your mother to have a cup of tea with me," Merry said, meeting and holding Bridget's eyes. "I told her I had some concerns about my interaction with Nikki at the church. As we were talking I happened to spill my drink."

Her eyes had grown bright and hard.

"Your kind mother was good enough to go get me some napkins. That gave me a chance to slip my little concoction in her drink. You see, my mother had a *Book of Shadows* with a special tea recipe. She called it Tattletale Tea. It was supposed to stop gossips and whiners. But if you substitute the chamomile for hemlock, well, it can be deadly."

Bridget stared at the woman across from her in shock, then looked at her father, who was wearing an identical expression.

"You're telling us that you poisoned Edith's drink?" Bob asked in a numb voice. "You're saying that's why she died and not because of the car crash?"

A smug smile crossed Merry's face and then was gone.

"I just thought you'd like to know," she said. "I know when my son died, it was such a comfort to be there to see how he passed. I thought it was a shame you didn't get that opportunity with your wife and mother."

Signaling to the guards that she was ready to leave, Merry pulled herself to her full height and strode from the room.

"Do you believe her?" Bridget asked after a full minute of silence. "Or do you think she's delusional?"

Bob shook his head, then rose slowly, as if in shock.

"I think she's telling the truth," he said. "All these years I've been wondering what happened. Wondering why me? Even after Ripley told me what he saw, I couldn't get my head around it. And now, as horrible as it is, at least we know."

Bridget wasn't sure she understood.

"We know what?"

"We know why Edith died," he said softly. "We know she was out there trying to help children. Trying to make a difference. And we know it wasn't some just cosmic bad luck that chose her to die. It was an evil, spiteful woman acting out of self-interest and perhaps even mental illness."

He held Bridget's eyes.

"I know I'm in shock now, and I may change my mind. But right now, I'm glad I finally know the truth."

Following her father out of the detention center, Bridget wasn't so sure she felt the same relief. She had a feeling there would be many hours in the future spent with Faye.

And Merry Corwin will likely be the main subject.

But as she climbed back into the passenger seat of Bob's silver sedan, a small voice spoke in her head.

It was a voice she recognized and had lately missed.

It doesn't matter how I died, Bridget...only how I lived.

* * *

Bridget was still feeling slightly stunned by the recent revelation when her father dropped her off at home.

He turned down the invitation to come inside, explaining that Paloma would be waiting for him at home, although she thought the sight of the black Expedition in her driveway might have something to do with his refusal.

"And I need to give Ripley a call," he said. "I owe him an apology. Besides, Daphne's been missing her partner."

The words earned him a smile.

As Bridget walked into the house, Hank ran up to greet her, excited to have her home at a decent hour, and Santino was in the kitchen dishing out pizza from a box.

"You made it," Bridget said, as Charlie took a bite of cheesy pizza. "I wasn't sure you would."

"Well, Hale is home packing a few things now," she said. "And then we'll both be heading out. I can't say where, but I can say I've packed more than one swimsuit. And I'm excited. I know it's supposed to be work, but right now, I feel as if I'm getting ready for my honeymoon."

Once Charlie had gone, Bridget and Santino took their pizza and wine out onto the back porch.

She decided she'd wait to tell Santino about Merry's revelation until later. She needed time for it to sink in.

Taking a sip of wine, she caught sight of the cardinal

hopping along a branch. It looked as if the little red bird had found a new home, at least for now.

"What do you think about Chalie and Hale going off on an adventure like that?" Bridget asked. "Are you jealous?"

Santino shook his head.

"I'm perfectly content right here," he said, smiling over at her. "I have no interest in being anywhere else."

Suddenly he stood and fumbled in his pocket, then sank onto one knee in front of her, holding out a ring.

"In fact, I'm hoping you'll tell me I never have to leave."

THE END

ACKNOWLEDGEMENTS

THIS BOOK IS DEDICATED TO the much-loved memory of my mother, Linda Jean, and my sister, Melanie. During its writing, I was lucky enough to have the unfailing love and support of my amazing husband, Giles, and my five adored children, Michael, Joey, Linda, Owen, and Juliet.

I am also extremely grateful for the love and encouragement of my extended family, including Melissa Romero, Leopoldo Romero, David Woodhall, and Tessa Woodhall.

ABOUT THE AUTHOR

Melinda Woodhall is the author of heart-pounding, emotional thrillers with a twist, including the *Mercy Harbor Thriller Series*, the *Veronica Lee Thriller Series*, the *Detective Nessa Ainsley Novella Series*, and the new *Bridget Bishop FBI Mystery Thriller Series*.

When she's not writing, Melinda can be found reading, gardening, and playing in the back garden with her tortoise. Melinda is a native Floridian and the proud mother of five children. She lives with her family in Orlando.

Visit Melinda's website at www.melindawoodhall.com

Other Books by Melinda Woodhall

Her Last Summer	*Steal Her Breath*
Her Final Fall	*Take Her Life*
Her Winter of Darkness	*Make Her Pay*
Her Silent Spring	*Break Her Heart*
Her Day to Die	*Lessons in Evil*
Her Darkest Night	*Taken By Evil*
Her Fatal Hour	*Where Evil Hides*
Her Bitter End	*Road to Evil*
The River Girls	*When Evil Calls*
Girl Eight	*Valley of Evil*
Catch the Girl	*Save Her from Evil*
Girls Who Lie	*His Soul to Keep*

Made in the USA
Monee, IL
14 September 2025

25673986R00185